the summer we made promises

THE DESTIN DIARIES 

HOPE HOLLOWAY
AND
CECELIA SCOTT

The Summer We Made Promises

The Destin Diaries – Book 3

Hope Holloway & Cecelia Scott

The Destin Diaries

The Summer We Met – Book 1
The Summer We Danced – Book 2
The Summer We Made Promises – Book 3
The Summer We Kept Secrets – Book 4
The Summer We Let Go – Book 5
The Summer We Celebrated – Book 6
The Summer We Sailed Away – Book 7

June 1, 1991

We're back in Destin!!! I'm writing in my brand new blue fake suede notebook that Mom let me buy at Borders when we went to the mall. (That's this super cool new bookstore with a café where I got a raspberry Italian soda because I am fancy now.) Anyway, I had to ditch the Lisa Frank unicorns because hello, I am FOURTEEN!! (I still love Lisa Frank, but do not tell Eli because his mockery of me never ends.)

So, last night we rolled in and the Wylies were already here, which is THE BEST. We were starving (the Ritz crackers and Dr Pepper from the gas station did not count as a meal), so the dads ran to Publix and then Mom and Aunt Jo Ellen made dinner. And it was perfect. We ate what Dad calls al fresco—which I think just means outside. But of course, Uncle Artie had to say, "I know Al Fresco! Italian guy!" like it was the funniest joke of all time. (It wasn't but he's so nice and goofy.) The grown-ups all poured more wine and laughed a lot.

The first night in Destin is always the best. It's like something changes, like a light switch goes on and the fun starts.

And, honestly, it starts with Mom, which is bizarre to realize. I mean, she's still Mom—she will absolutely give you the Maggie Lawson Death

Stare™ if you step out of line—but she doesn't seem as uptight here. I think it's Aunt Jo Ellen. They were sorority sisters, and every summer, it's like Mom gets all college-y again. (Not too much, obviously. She still made Crista go to bed at 9:30, even though us older kids stayed up.)

We ate at the big wooden picnic table under those twinkle lights that the people who own this house always hang up before summer. You can see the ocean over the dunes, and the air smells like Destin—I can't even describe it. Like sunscreen and salt and watermelon Bubblicious and <u>pure happiness</u>.

And the BEST part: my closest friends in the universe are here—Tessa and Kate! The twins turned fourteen too, and somehow Tessa looks even older and has all these cute outfits, while Kate is still basically the same (meaning: obsessed with books, always looking for her glasses). But I love them both SO much. Of course, we had to sing our summer song (Walkin' on Sunshine, natch) at full volume while twirling around the deck. (Dad said we sounded like "dying cats," but he was just mad because we interrupted his Beach Boys cassette that he plays all the time. Little Deuce Coop (sp?) whatever that means. We got it, Dad.)

Oh, and a shock to no one—Peter McCarthy is still cute. 🩶 Eli brought him along (again), because apparently, seventeen-year-old boys have to travel in pairs. They act like they're soooo much older than us just because they're going to be seniors.

After we ate, we started making summer promises—things we had to do before August.

Tessa announced she'd slalom on one waterski because she's fearless like that. Naturally, Eli instantly volunteered to drive the boat. (Shocking.)

I promised Kate I'd read one of her Vampire Diaries books, even though I already know it's gonna be super weird. (She swears it's amazing, but we shall see.) Mom and Aunt Jo Ellen promised to learn how to make pizza from scratch—apparently, their friends the Cavallaris are going to teach them.

Uncle Artie said if he dies from eating their pizza (ha ha), we have to scatter his ashes in the Gulf of Mexico from the boat. Like, actual ashes, floating in the water. (!!!) We all cracked up, but he was like, "No, seriously! You have to promise! It's where I want my final resting place!" So now it's officially on the list, but only if Uncle Artie dies from the Mom Pizza, which we're pretty sure he won't.

Anyway, it's SUMMER. It's DESTIN. And there will be no RESTING. Just fun!

Let the best three months of the year

begin!!!

Love,

Vivien Lawson, AKA the one who secretly promised not to let Peter McCarthy know that I still have an ungodly crush on him and wish he'd notice me. (Maybe this will be the summer, diary. Maybe!!!!)

Chapter One
Vivien

Present Day

Vivien slid the blue notebook back in the plastic Caboodle she kept under her bed, unable to wipe the smile from her face. Every once in a while, she picked up one of the diaries she'd kept all those decades ago, seeing those years through an adult's eyes. And, she thought as she pushed up looked out at the morning sunrise, it was added fun to be in Destin once again.

In some ways, everything had changed—the beach cottage was now a six-bedroom event and the teenagers were all in their fifties. In other ways, nothing had changed. They were still the Lawsons and the Wylies doing Destin together.

Last night, many of those same faces were around an outdoor table, dining al fresco again. The "dads" were gone, sadly. The "moms" certainly weren't sorority sister besties. But the heart of these two families was still connected and, Vivien hoped, getting stronger every day.

She stole a glance at her daughter, who slept contentedly in the huge California king bed they'd been sharing for a few months.

With Vivien attempting to rebuild her life after a divorce, and twenty-four-year-old Lacey just figuring hers out, they somehow had turned this whole unexpected adventure into amazing mother-daughter time.

This wouldn't last, Vivien knew. Like the seasons she read about in those old diaries, this one would change. Lacey would meet someone special and Vivien would rightly become number two in her life.

That was the way of things, but wow, she was enjoying these halcyon days in Destin.

She headed into the bathroom for a hot shower, then to the closet, choosing linen pants and a light top that would easily handle the warmth of May for a busy day.

By the time she was dressed and stepped back into the room, the rising sun streamed bright through the gauzy white curtains.

"Morning."

She turned at the sound of Lacey's raspy greeting, seeing her sitting up, balancing a laptop on the comforter, her fingers poised over the keyboard but not typing.

"Oh, you're awake," Vivien said. "And working already?"

"Yeah...sort of." She lowered the screen, looking distracted. Or maybe she was over this "season" of sharing a room with her mother. It might be dreamy and fun to Vivien, but Lacey was a young woman and probably would love some privacy. The setup wasn't ideal, but every time they turned around, the Summer House had more guests.

The two most recent still shocking Vivien when she thought about it.

"Crista's going home today," she reminded Lacey. "I'm sure you'd love that room—"

"I'm fine, Mom. Let Jo Ellen have it. She's seventy-eight and shouldn't sleep two floors down all alone."

"That's sweet, honey," Vivien said. "Unless Jo Ellen refuses to sleep on the same level as Maggie, despite this alleged 'ceasefire' between them."

"Based on the chill at dinner?" Lacey lifted her brows. "I hope nobody has a gun in this house, ceasefire or not."

"Peter will have one," she said on a laugh. "And he's on his way over right now."

"Oh?" Lacey looked at Vivien. "Are you two having breakfast dates now?"

"This isn't a date," Vivien said. "I actually asked for more advice for Maggie and Jo Ellen. I mean, they're staying here with the sole purpose of unraveling the history of how my father ended up in prison. Peter has access to law enforcement files from the past. If Artie had a role in my father's arrest..."

Her voice trailed off as she thought about the situation. Had Jo Ellen's late—and quite great—husband been the one to put Roger Lawson behind bars? And if so, did that mean the rift between Jo Ellen and Maggie would never be healed?

Vivien knew one thing about her mother: Maggie

Lawson could hold a grudge like a Rottweiler with a bone.

"No *if*, since they both think Artie did turn him in," Lacey said. "I'm not sure I understand what else they want to know."

"They want to know why," Vivien told her. "*Why* would Arthur Wylie turn his close friend in to the police?"

"Um, because his close friend—rest my grandfather's soul—was committing fraud, money-laundering, and tax evasion, and Artie was a *law ethics* professor?" Lacey snorted. "It's not complicated."

But it was.

Vivien nodded, all too familiar with Roger's white-collar crimes. "If Artie was the anonymous tipster who turned my father in, like they seem to think, then it not only affects the past—it impacts our future. You work for Tessa now, and Eli is crazy about Kate. Those relationships are at risk. Understanding Artie's motivation might help all of us heal from the past."

Or set us back thirty years, she thought, but chose to be optimistic and not add that.

Lacey sighed and shut her laptop. "So Peter thinks he can find out more from old police files?"

"Maybe. After all, he's a detective with the Pensacola PD. He has more access than those two do. They are clueless as to where to start and he's..." She smiled. "Smart, handsome, and capable."

"Careful, Mommy, your heart-eyes are showing."

She laughed. "I do like him," she said and thought of

how many pages in her teenage diary mentioned Peter McCarthy—usually with exclamation points and hearts galore. "Maybe not in the way I did as a teenager, but…" She touched her face with a self-deprecating laugh. "I ain't a teenager anymore."

"You're beautiful," Lacey said softly, true love in her sleepy gaze. "And you're officially divorced. That means you are free to have breakfast, lunch, or dinner with your handsome, capable detective."

The bell chimed at the front door. Vivien exhaled, smoothing her top. "And there he is."

She blew a kiss and stepped into the hall, pausing at the open door to the last bedroom where Crista, Vivien's younger sister, was chatting and laughing with her seven-year-old daughter.

"We're packing to go home, Aunt Vivien," Nolie announced. "I'm really sad!"

"We are all sad, honey," Vivien said, bending over to kiss her little head. On the way up, she gave a hard look to her sister. "And how are you feeling, Mama?"

Crista flushed and touched her stomach, glancing at Nolie, who still didn't know she was going to be a big sister. "This morning? Quite good. Hope it lasts for the five-hour drive home."

"I hope so, too." The doorbell rang again and she gave a wave and trotted down the stairs.

At the bottom, she paused and looked around the main floor, which was nearly finished, at least from a décor standpoint.

She'd nailed this living and gathering space, and the

gorgeous kitchen, she thought with pride. The only thing missing was the perfect light fixture to hang at the top of the vaulted ceiling, but the one she wanted cost an arm and *two* legs.

If they ended up keeping the Summer House, like she hoped, she could put a far less expensive chandelier in that spot. A slight disappointment, but—

This time, he knocked.

"Someone wants to get in the front door," her mother's voice came from the deck, slightly harsh and demanding. Well, it was Maggie. Vivien didn't expect sweet and gentle from that woman.

"I've got it," she called back.

When she opened the front door, she greeted Peter with the same smile she wore every time she saw the man. He was so...Peter.

Strong, steady, good-looking, and now he had that glimmer in his brown eyes when he gazed at her. He liked her and she liked...the idea of him liking her.

Was that the same as just plain liking him? Oh, too much thinking for pre-coffee.

"Morning, Detective."

He smiled at the title she always used, pulling his hands out of the pockets of his khaki pants, reaching to give her a light hug. "Morning, Viv. I was beginning to think I had the wrong beachfront mansion."

She laughed and stepped back, letting him in. "I was upstairs. Are you ready for your next case?"

He huffed a laugh. "Since the one that brought me here is nothing but dead ends, sure. Bring it."

She led him through the house and they stopped in the kitchen for coffee. As they did, Jo Ellen came up from the ground floor, looking wearier than when she went to bed.

Vivien slipped an arm around her. "We'll get Crista's room ready for you tonight," she promised.

"I'm fine. I'd like to stay where I am."

"Then I'm ordering some legitimate furniture for that room," Vivien said. "Do you have a few minutes to talk to Peter?"

Jo Ellen gave him a strange look, a mix of fear and hope and even a little tenderness. "How funny to see you after all these years, Peter," she said. "You really still look like a teenage boy to me."

"Better upgrade your glasses, Aunt Jo," he joked. "When I look at you, I think of mint chocolate chip ice cream. You were the one who always remembered to get me the flavor none of the other kids liked."

She chuckled and pointed at him. "Yes, I remember that. I'll be sure to get you some while I'm here, Peter."

He gave her a warm smile. "Let's see if I can really help you first, then you can reward me."

"Well, I'm not very hopeful, but...it's important to Mags. And all I really want is to be her friend again."

"Oh, Jo Ellen." Vivien put a hand on the older woman's narrow shoulder, touched by the admission. "We're going to help you. We're going to find out the truth of what happened, I promise."

As they walked out to join Maggie, Vivien remembered those two forty-something moms laughing, cooking, and spending summers here thirty years ago. She really hoped she could keep that promise and heal this once-lovely friendship.

No surprise to Vivien, Maggie insisted they sit at the outdoor dining table and turn the whole conversation into something formal.

Destin hadn't yet worked its old magic on Vivien's mother. She hadn't relaxed at all in the days since she'd blown in unannounced, uninvited, and ready to boot them all to the curb for the sin of "fraternizing" with the Wylies—apparently breaking a promise she'd made to Vivien's dad before he died.

"It's really not like us to bring in outsiders on the subject," Maggie said to start things off as she put her little Yorkie on the ground and Pittypat scampered inside. "In other words, everything we discuss is private."

Peter just smiled and slid a look to Vivien. "Considering I spent all seven summers with you right here on this property, Mrs. L, I don't think I qualify as an outsider. My last name might not be Wylie or Lawson, but I'm a brother to your children and a cousin to yours." He nodded to Jo Ellen. "Maybe not by blood. You can trust me. I assure you."

Apparently believing him, Maggie nodded. "Good," she said simply. "But can you help us?"

"I can try. I know that putting together pieces of the past can be daunting when you're dealing with the police and ancient, closed cases. As I understand it, you want to know if Artie was the anonymous tipster who launched the investigation into your husband's crimes."

"I *know* he is," Maggie said.

"We don't know that for an absolute fact," Jo Ellen countered. "Artie never went into detail—"

"Because he was ashamed of what he did!" Maggie spat back.

"He never did anything shameful in his life, and you know it."

"Do I?" Maggie underscored that with one of her many withering glares. "He stabbed his best friend in the back. Roger told me—"

Peter held up two hands with the flair of a referee. "Ladies, ladies. Please. Let's stay focused."

Amen to that, Vivien thought as she looked at the two women and considered how far they'd come from the old days. This wasn't going to be a peaceful summer if it took too long to get the answers they wanted. This needed to move and get resolved—fast.

"What we really want to know," Jo Ellen said softly, "is why both of our husbands made us promise—separately—not to ever speak to each other again. At least, that's what I want to know."

Maggie just flicked her brow in silent agreement. They needed to know why—and if they should keep that promise. After all, the men who'd forced them to make it were both gone.

"While I begin to do more research," Peter said, "you two can do a lot, too."

"Like what?" Maggie asked.

"How about a conversation with the attorney who helped you put this property in a trust?" he suggested.

"That attorney, John Waverly, died several years ago," Maggie said flatly. "His son, also an attorney, Justin, took over the work of managing the property and handling any legal issues. He was the one who helped me discover a loophole that said I could give the house to Roger's children because he died in prison. But Justin has nothing to do with this. He was a kid when all this happened."

Peter shrugged. "He should have the files from when the house was purchased and Roger was arrested. Something in there could be a clue."

"That's a waste of time," Maggie said.

"Maggie!" Jo Ellen leaned over the table, her frustration visible. "You can't shoot everything down."

"I can shoot *that* down. Artie didn't even know we bought the house, so—"

"Yes, he did," Jo Ellen said.

"He...did?" Maggie's eyes widened. "Roger told me he didn't tell a soul he'd put the house in my name. He wanted me to keep it and didn't want anyone to know I had it."

Jo Ellen shrugged and gave a "you don't know everything" look that had Vivien bracing. No one gave that look to Maggie Lawson and lived.

"When I was going through Artie's things, I found an envelope," Jo Ellen explained. "Roger's obit was in it, from the Atlanta newspaper, along with a picture of the cottage after the hurricane hit in 1995. It wasn't completely destroyed, but wrecked."

"That doesn't mean anything," Maggie said. "He spent seven summers in the house. He probably saw it in the newspapers after the storm—"

"On the back off that picture was one of those yellow sticky notes with Roger's handwriting," Jo Ellen continued, undaunted. "It said something like, 'I should have waited and gotten it for half as much. Thanks, pal.'"

Vivien sucked in a breath at this revelation. Artie had known her father bought this property? That was news.

Maggie looked just as shocked. "You're lying," she announced, pushing up like she wanted to stand up and run.

But Jo Ellen reached across the space and put a hand on her arm.

"Maggie." She angled her head and sighed. "You know me better than that."

Maggie shook her head. "No. It's impossible. Hurricane Opal hit *after* he was arrested. He would never have sent a picture of the house to the man who turned him in. You've got your facts mixed up, Jo."

Jo Ellen inched back, creases deepening on her forehead. "Maybe I'm remembering it wrong, but I could have Kate find the note and take a picture. We should leave no stone unturned if we're going to solve this mystery."

"You're right about that," Peter said. "Have Kate look. And please contact the lawyer to get the oldest files out of storage. I'll have another conversation with my contact at the Atlanta PD, too, and report back."

Maggie just took a deep breath, silenced.

Jo Ellen smiled at him. "And I'll be sure there's mint chocolate chip for you, Peter," she said sweetly.

He thanked her with a warm smile, and stood when it was clear Maggie was completely done with this meeting.

Vivien walked him to the door in silence, but as they stepped outside into the morning sun, he put his arm around her and pulled her close.

"I've been in prison interrogation rooms with more love," he whispered.

"Right?" she scoffed. "Can I borrow a bulletproof vest for the next few weeks?"

"You may need it, sadly."

"It is sad," she said. "They used to be such good friends, remember?"

"I do," he said. "Thick as thieves, always joking and cooking and doing some secret sorority handshake. It's a shame to see them like this."

She rubbed her arms despite the heat. "With Eli gone and Crista leaving, I'm the only Lawson child to bear the brunt of Maggie's wrath."

"I think Jo Ellen's bearing most of it, but you always have a shoulder to fall on." He got a little closer to her ear. "Mine."

She smiled up at him and put a hand on that shoulder, which was broad and strong. "I'll take you up on that, Detective."

"Can you sneak out for that dinner this week?" he

asked. "Another trip to the rooftop in town or somewhere else?"

"I'd love that," she said. "Assuming you don't have anything come up with your case."

He grunted in frustration, his usual reaction when he talked about the missing person case that had brought him to Destin in the first place.

"Dead ends daily," he told her. "I've been looking for one clue for this guy for, what? A month? But someone claimed to have seen him over in Seaside, which means he could still be around. In the meantime, I gotta eat dinner and I really gotta eat dinner with you." He gave a wry grin. "You'll need the escape."

"Will I ever," she said. "I do have a new client starting up this week, but nothing that will stop me from seeing you."

"You do?" His face lit up, obviously happy for her. "I know you went back to Fiona the Fearsome. Did she send you someone else?"

"Fiona's far less fearsome brother. Remember the guy we thought was conning her but turned out to be her brother? You looked him up and found out he is a hedge fund manager, not a hapless handyman."

"Oh, I remember." He gave a smirk. "I saw him tailing you every time you moved at that fashion show."

She inched back, not sure what part of that to react to. That Danny was tailing her—or Peter was...jealous?

"He was trying to get me to reconcile with his sister," she told him. "And remodel some rooms in his Destin house."

He gave her a "get real" look. "Yeah, I'm sure that's it, Viv. Come on. The dude could barely wipe his drool around you."

Peter *was* jealous. She gave him a purposely coy smile, unnaturally tickled by the reaction.

"You have nothing to worry about," she said, keeping a tease in her voice because it was fun. Come on—Peter McCarthy *jealous?*

Take that, fourteen-year-old Vivien.

"I'm not worried," he said with the same cool confidence he'd exhibited with the feuding mothers on the deck. "But that guy's slick. I'd get paid up front if I were you."

Danny Sullivan wasn't slick. He was good-looking, loaded, and charming, yes. Was that *slick?* Maybe to Peter.

She gave his arm a playful jab. "I will. And I'll take *you* out to dinner with my first client fee just to prove it."

"Can't wait." He stole the lightest, fastest kiss and headed down the stairs to his car, leaving her standing in the hot Destin sun thinking about him...and Danny.

Well, it was going to be an *interesting* summer.

Chapter Two
Maggie

aggie Lawson sat stiffly at the outdoor dining table after Peter left. But the echo of their conversation hung in the air, as thick as the Florida humidity with the sickening smell of a broken friendship.

For the past two days, Maggie and Jo Ellen managed to either avoid each other or be surrounded by their kids and family. But this conversation had to happen if they were to achieve their goal of finding the missing pieces of the Roger and Artie puzzle.

Still, it was shocking to realize that, all these years later, they had plummeted to this level after being the best of best friends. Well, Artie did it, of course. If he'd have kept his big *ethical* mouth shut...

Maggie tamped down the thought, far too intelligent to think that Artie was alone in carrying the blame. Obviously, Roger had a part, too. He'd committed the criminal acts and, more importantly, had ordered Maggie to never speak to a Wylie again.

She shifted uncomfortably in her chair and finally looked across the table at a woman she'd once called a soul-sister, and not just because they'd lived in a house together with the same Greek letters on the door.

Jo and *Mags* were the proverbial peas in a sorority pod.

And then they'd met their husbands at the University of Georgia. First, Roger, a frat boy who'd come to a Tri-Delt party and swept Maggie right off her feet. Then, a few months later, Jo Ellen met Artie, the senior nerd who'd tutored her when she was struggling with a political science class.

The four of them were close right up until they graduated and married. But Jo Ellen longed for her cold and miserable Ithaca, so Artie applied to Cornell Law School.

Even a thousand miles apart, expensive phone calls, handwritten letters, and Christmas cards kept Maggie and Jo Ellen connected. When they were both pregnant at the same time with Vivien and Jo's twins, they shared the experience. All along they exchanged baby stories, recipes, life updates, and grade school pictures as their families grew up.

Then one winter, Maggie heard about a beachfront cottage that they could rent for a whole summer and she had a wild idea for the Wylies to squeeze in that house with them.

Roger had to go back and forth from Atlanta during the week, but Artie was a professor with the summers off. They all came from Ithaca for one whole summer, which turned into seven summers and the best memories with two families joined like one.

Once. Long ago.

Pushing the memories away, Maggie lifted her gaze to meet Jo Ellen's soft brown eyes, rimmed with sadness. Grief? Probably. Artie had died less than a year ago. But that sadness was surely because of what had become of their once great and mighty friendship.

Jo looked downright weary, though she'd aged pretty well. Some deep lines, some soft jowls, but still that sweet, pretty Yankee girl who showed up in Maggie's dorm room in the fall of 1965, carrying a suitcase full of optimism and kindness.

Right now, she was composed, with her delicate fingers curled around the handle of her coffee cup. She stared back, not with anger, but with something far worse —pity.

Maggie bristled at it.

"I don't know why I thought this would go any differently," Maggie muttered, keeping her voice low. "You defend him like it's your personal crusade."

Jo Ellen sighed, shaking her head. "Because it is both —a crusade *and* personal. Good heavens, he was my husband. I loved him, and I can't believe he ever did anything to hurt anyone."

Maggie felt her lips press into a taut line before she leaned forward. "Then what do you call turning in a man he swore was his best friend? He knew what would happen to Roger. He had to. And he still did it."

"Artie was a man of integrity," Jo Ellen said. "He believed it was the right thing to do when he learned Roger broke the law. He was laundering money and defrauding investors. You didn't know, Maggie. But Artie did. And he couldn't just... let it slide."

Maggie scoffed. "Ah, the great, noble whistleblower. Or could it have been he was just jealous because he was a college professor and Roger owned a thriving architectural firm?"

Jo Ellen gave a soft laugh. "As if Artie cared about money. He loved his job, his family, and any time he got to fish. But you have to know that Artie loved Roger, too. That's why I want to understand what changed, and why he did this. I want to figure out why they both ordered us to stop being friends. And, for heaven's sake, I want you to stop demonizing my perfect husband."

"A perfect husband?" Maggie gave a wry smile. "I believe they call that a unicorn."

Jo Ellen started to laugh, then stopped, as if she realized they weren't supposed to laugh together anymore.

As if any kind of lightheartedness fell under that umbrella order each of their husbands had delivered: *Don't talk to each other ever again.*

"Okay, not perfect," Jo Ellen conceded. "He snored. And had a weakness for donuts and dumb jokes. Oh, and toward the end, all he ever did was watch the news and that got annoying."

Maggie shot her a look. "That's the worst thing he did?" She wished she could say that about her husband who...well, yes, willingly broke the law. "At least you had him twenty-nine years longer than I had Roger."

Jo Ellen exhaled, quiet as if Maggie had effectively put her in her place. Finally, she lifted her coffee, but plunked it back down as if she knew it would be cold and bitter.

"Can I ask you a question, Mags?"

Maggie braced for something harsh and personal and annoying.

"Why are we really here?"

"I thought we agreed that together we had a better chance of finding out the whole story."

"But who are we doing it for?" Jo Ellen leaned closer. "For us? Please—we're both seventy-eight. Our days are dwindling, our lives are lived. Our families are what matter now."

"I just enjoyed a month in Europe," Maggie replied. "My days are certainly not *dwindling*."

"But we're here for them." Jo Ellen pointed to the house. "For our kids and grandkids."

"I gave mine a multimillion-dollar house to keep or sell," Maggie said dryly. "I've done enough for my kids."

"Well, I haven't," Jo Ellen said. "And the reason I'm here is because my Katie's eyes sparkle when she talks about Eli."

Oh, this again. "She's had a crush on Eli since she was twelve, Jo. That's no reason—"

"This is different," Jo Ellen said. "This is adult and real and I want her to be happy. And Eli can't stop smiling when she's in the room. Did you notice before they left?"

"Yes." She looked skyward. "Kind of hard not to."

Jo Ellen chuckled. "You don't have to make that face

that looks like you sucked on a lemon. We used to joke about our kids getting married."

"*Tessa* and Eli," Maggie reminded her, losing the fight not to smile. "But Kate? No, I didn't see that coming."

Jo Ellen reached out her hand across the table again, her touch feather-light—but it still burned. "That's why I'm doing this. One of the reasons, anyway."

Maggie eyed her. "What are the other reasons?"

"Well, I want his name cleared. You want to be angry at me forever? Fine. But Artie deserved better than to have you hate him in death for something he might not have even done the way you think he did."

Maggie swallowed, her throat tight, but before she could respond, Jo Ellen added pressure and continued in a whisper, "And I would like the break in these two families to heal. Wouldn't you?"

Maggie looked down at Jo Ellen's hand, counting a few age spots, seeing the older woman's slightly protruding knuckles tighten over hers.

Something slipped in her heart. A feeling she didn't know or like or even remember. That longing for...more. More laughter, more wine, more adventures, more gossip, more secrets and confidences and ways to figure out life.

More...*friendship*.

But Roger had forbidden this friendship, and she couldn't break her promise to him.

She slowly pulled her hand out from under Jo Ellen's. "I want to talk to Crista before she leaves," she said.

Jo Ellen smiled up at her. "Okay. But I'm not going anywhere, Mags."

"Don't I know it," Maggie quipped, purposely making her voice light as she walked into the house, searching for her dog. "Pitty, darling? Where are you?"

The tiny Yorkie answered with a bark from upstairs but didn't come running like she normally did when Maggie called her.

Had she lost Aunt Pittypat, too? On a sigh, she trudged up the stairs.

There, she found Pittypat tucked into Nolie's cross-legged lap, being adored by her "other" mistress.

"Grandma," Nolie said, her bright, seven-year-old eyes lifting at Maggie's approach. "Pittypat's upset."

"Suitcases do that to her." She stepped into the room and gestured toward the open one on the bed. "She thinks you're going to leave her."

Nolie stuck her bottom lip out. "I am."

"How did the meeting with Peter go, Mama?" Crista asked as she folded a top and placed it in the suitcase.

"Pffft." Maggie waved her hand and sat on a chair by the window. "Do you want to take Pittypat home, Nolie?"

Her brown eyes widened. "Could I, Grandma? She's your dog and Mommy says you're staying here."

"I am and she is, but right this minute—" She lifted a brow and smiled at Pittypat, who was currently on her back, four paws in the air, enjoying a never-ending belly rub from Nolie. "I feel like there's yet another traitor in our midst."

"Mama!"

"Grandma, I'm not...whatever that is!"

"Of course you're not, honey." Maggie reached both arms out, touched when Nolie abandoned the dog and ran to her. "I'm just tired and old and bitter. I love you, Nolie, and I actually think taking Pittypat home with you is a good idea. I've got my hands full at this house and if she wants to go out in the middle of the night, I'd probably fall down the stairs."

"Oh!" Nolie squeezed tighter as if the very idea was unthinkable.

She sighed and put a hand on Nolie's cheek. "Will you walk her in the rose garden every day?"

Nolie grinned. "So she fertilizes," she whispered, sharing their little inside joke.

Maggie leaned forward and kissed her granddaughter, nothing but love in her heart. "And come back here soon. Because I will miss you and Pitty terribly."

The little dog came trotting over, wanting to get in the middle of the love.

"Will you do me a favor and take her out now?" Maggie asked.

"Yes, of course! Am I done packing, Mommy?"

"You are," Crista said. "Take one more beach walk with Aunt Pittypat and hurry back. We'll eat and hit the road. Do not go far, Nolie. Just to the bottom of the boardwalk."

"Okay! C'mon, Pitty!"

The two of them darted out and Crista watched them go, sighing as she faced Maggie.

"Now you can tell me," Crista said. "How did it go with Peter?"

"Oh, fine, I suppose. I just want to get to the bottom of it and..." She shook her head. "Listen, I have a favor. There's a box in the attic loft that has some of your father's things in it. A metal strongbox, rather sizeable. I need it."

"Can I ship it?"

And risk losing whatever might be in it? Maggie shook her head. "Just bring it next time you come down, or give it to Eli if he makes the trip."

"Sure," she agreed, perching on the edge of the bed, a little paler than usual.

Maggie leaned forward, still not used to the shocking news that forty-three-year-old Crista was pregnant with her second child. "How are you feeling?"

Crista hesitated before answering. "Exhausted. Nauseous. Emotional, apparently. I've had, you know, crying spells."

Maggie snorted. "You? Tears?"

Crista huffed a weak laugh. "I had been doing better at controlling my emotions, then along came a hormone overload and..." She shrugged. "I'm crying a lot. I certainly cried when I lied to you. I'm still very sorry, Mama."

Maggie didn't respond immediately. She *had* been wounded by the lie when Crista told her she was in Atlanta but was really here—with Tessa Wylie tutoring Nolie.

But, since then, she'd seen a marked change in her

dyslexic granddaughter. She begrudgingly approved of Crista's decision to get help from an unconventional source. Because of Tessa, who was dyslexic herself, Nolie would surely pass the exam she needed to move up to third grade.

"I understand why you did what you did, Crista," she finally said.

Crista sighed, clearly repentant for her lie. But there was more to that sigh...because they had to talk about the obvious change a baby meant.

Never one to beat around a bush, Maggie started the conversation. "You'll need my bedroom," she said.

A look of something like fear and surprise flashed in her eyes. "Oh, Mama. Not for a while. We'll put the baby in our room for the first six months, then he or she can share with Nolie. Then we can do something with Anthony's office..." Her voice faded, along with her insistence and enthusiasm. "It will be different," she added softly. "And...and..."

"And crowded," Maggie finished for her. "I don't want to be an intrusion, Crista. I have never wanted that."

"I know! You aren't!"

"You and Anthony have been very generous, letting me live with you these past few years." Maggie smoothed her linen slacks, not meeting Crista's gaze. "But the baby might mean...we live differently."

Crista frowned, her silence proof that Maggie's suspicions were accurate. Crista and Anthony had talked about this.

"You deserve this time alone as a family," Maggie said.

For a long moment, Crista just stared at her, and try as she might to hide it, Maggie could see relief in her daughter's eyes.

"After all this is over..." Maggie waved in the general direction of the house and beach. "I'll figure something out."

"I love having you live with us and we'll need help, believe me. But if you..."

Maggie held up her hand. "I'm fine. You just grow your little baby, because nothing makes me happier than a grandchild."

Crista reached out to hug Maggie. "Oh, Mama. I feel bad. I feel like I'm letting you down. I hate that."

"Not at all," she said, sounding far more certain of her future than she felt. "You finish packing now. I'm going to say goodbye to Pittypat."

"Are you sure you want us to take her back, Mama? That dog gives you such joy."

"She gives Nolie joy, too." She put her hands on the armrests and pushed up. "I have enough on my plate while I'm here."

"Thank you," Crista whispered as she stood. "I appreciate..."

Maggie just smiled as she walked to the door, then glanced over her shoulder. "See? I'm not the ogre you all make me out to be."

She didn't wait for Crista's heartfelt denial, but headed downstairs. A few minutes later, she walked down the long boardwalk that crossed the dunes and led to the beach. May was a gorgeous month here, she thought, turning her face to the sun.

She didn't care about an age spot or two now, letting the sunlight warm her and the faint salt-scented breeze lift her heart. She caught sight of Nolie and Pittypat right at the end of the boardwalk, playing in the sand.

For a moment, she was taken back decades in time. She could see Crista, her baby, playing in the sunshine. The teenagers would have been out on their boogie boards, with Tessa's infernal boombox screaming about walking on sunshine.

The memories were shockingly clear, as though they happened yesterday.

Roger and Artie would be out fishing on the boat and Jo inside, planning what they would make for dinner.

Easy days. Lazy nights. True friendship...until a traitor ruined it all.

Would having the answers to why Artie made that choice change anything? It wouldn't bring Roger back. Nor would it change his bad, bad choices. But maybe it would...heal people.

She'd never admit it but...wasn't that what she really wanted? For her poor children to be able to somehow let go of the anchor of shame that Roger hung around their necks?

And while that was happening, ...maybe she could stop being such a raging shrew. Maybe she could let go of the anger and resentment that she had toward Roger and Artie and the courts that took all they had.

Was she too old to change? She was here in Destin, where she'd once been a carefree young mother. Maybe the sunshine and air and waves could soften this bitter old crone one more time.

Nolie came tearing up the boardwalk toward her, arms out, with Pittypat keeping pace and kicking up sand.

Her heart shifted so much she could feel it in her chest. An ache, a pressure, a literal punch of love.

And a reminder that it wasn't the air or water or sun that changed a person in Destin. It was family and laughter and friends.

Could that happen again? She didn't know, but deep inside, she hoped so.

Chapter Three

Lacey

Guilt. That had to be what made Lacey almost hang up when the automated phone system at Holmes Regional Medical Center started to play annoying "hold" music.

And if she felt guilt for making this call—what would she feel if she got what she wanted and did something with the information? More guilt.

But also, a weird sense of rightness and peace.

Lacey sighed and leaned back, the phone pressed to her ear, since she didn't dare risk putting the call on speaker. She'd hidden herself in the small office on the main floor, tucked between the laundry room and Tessa's bedroom.

At the thought of Tessa, she shivered a bit, certain that her friend, boss, and mentor would not be happy if she knew what Lacey was doing.

With her laptop open to the website of a florist for the Bat Mitzvah she was currently planning for Tessa Wylie Events, Lacey glanced around the space that still felt like "Uncle Eli's office." He'd used the small Ikea desk for his own paperwork and put a drafting table under the window for his architecture business.

But he'd gone back to Atlanta, so Lacey and Tessa moved their budding event planning business from the dining room table to this more private space.

She sure hoped it was private because what she was doing was...top secret.

"We appreciate your patience," a recorded voice lilted in her ear. "Holmes Regional Medical Center has been Brevard County's largest..."

She inched the phone away so she didn't have to hear the hospital commercial and willed her call to go through to the medical records department.

She tapped her nails against the desk, eyes unfocused on the screen in front of her, listening to the promise that her call would be picked up by the first available operator.

Was this wrong? For some reason, she remembered Grandma Maggie talking to her about her conscience when she was about Nolie's age.

"When your conscience tells you it hurts, then you might be hurting someone else."

Was that her conscience speaking that made her chest hurt? Was she hurting Tessa by trying to find out... *something*? A name. A city. The identity of a baby who, twenty-five years ago, had been given up for adoption by Tessa Wylie.

Tessa had said she didn't want to intrude on this person's life, but Lacey had seen a longing in her friend's eyes and knew that she had to do...

This.

Lacey shifted on an uncomfortable faux leather office chair, blowing out a breath.

It started when Lacey had *guessed* that Tessa had had a baby, which didn't take any extraordinary powers of deduction or special mind-reading sorcery. They'd gotten very close in the last two months, and Lacey could see the way Tessa reacted anytime someone commented what a great mother she would have been.

She joked about ships that sailed, and flicked her fingers as if the very idea of motherhood was preposterous. But Lacey sensed she was hiding an old pain. Couldn't anyone else?

Apparently not, and Tessa had told her that no one knew except her late father. Not her mother, not her twin sister.

The secret had been burning a hole in Lacey ever since that late afternoon at the wine bar when, in a completely off-guard and candid moment, Tessa admitted that she'd had a baby. When she did, she told Lacey everything she knew about the child...

He was seven pounds and ten ounces, nineteen inches long, and born at seven sixteen p.m. on February 19, 2000, in Holmes Regional Medical Center in Melbourne, Florida.

For some reason, Lacey had committed the confession to memory.

Well, for *this* reason. So she could...pry.

No, no, *no*. She was *helping*, not prying. It was obvious Tessa would love to know her son, but she was terrified of ruining his life, not hers. If Lacey could just find out something about him, maybe the kid wouldn't care that he was the result of a fling when Tessa worked as a waitress on a Carnival Cruise ship.

He wouldn't care that his biological mother didn't get the father's last name, and hadn't realized she was pregnant until she was fairly far along. Would he care that she didn't tell anyone but her father, Artie, who had helped arrange the adoption?

Lacey didn't know. But Tessa had made Lacey promise to keep her secret. Well, to be technical and accurate, Lacey reminded her pesky conscience, she'd promised not to tell Vivien or Kate, specifically.

She hadn't promised she wouldn't look the boy up to find out who, where, and what he was now.

Which was all she was doing by hiding in this office making secret calls while Tessa took her morning run on the beach and showered.

Lacey swallowed hard as the hold music cut off with a faint click.

"Medical Records, this is Mrs. Carmichael."

Okay, here we go.

Lacey forced a bright, casual tone. "Hi, Mrs. Carmichael. Thanks for taking my call. I was hoping you could help me track down some birth records. It's for my brother—he's been trying to piece together some family medical history, and we only have a few details."

There was a pause on the other end, followed by a skeptical, "All right, but birth records are confidential and not given by phone. But I'll check and see what I can tell you."

"That would be awesome."

"Was he adopted?"

She swallowed. "Uh, yes, he was."

"Then you'd need to be able to match the records we have on file before I can tell you anything, and I can't tell you much, hon."

"What would I have to match?"

"His actual birthdate, time of birth, and some vital statistics. I'll need the patient's last four digits of her social security—that's the biological mother—but even then, I cannot tell you anything medical or share any personal information on file. I'm sorry, but that's the law."

"I understand." As her mind whirred, she touched the computer screen, remembering that Tessa had to use the last four digits of her social security number when she had Lacey apply for a business credit card.

She clicked a few buttons and found them in an instant. "I can provide everything you asked for," she said.

Mrs. Carmichael sighed. "All right, give me the details, and I'll see what I can find."

Lacey inhaled. "He was born on February 19, 2000, at seven-sixteen p.m., and was seven pounds and ten ounces, nineteen inches long. And the last four digits of the biological mother's social are..." She threw a look at the door she hadn't locked and prayed Tessa didn't walk in as she read the numbers to Mrs. Carmichael.

"All right, hon," she finally said. "You sit tight for a minute and let's do some looking."

"Thank you. Thank you so much." She tried not to

sound breathless but listened to the sound of clacking keys in the background. For...ever.

"Anything?" she asked.

"Well, that was a busy night at Holmes," the woman said on a chuckle. "But only one boy was born."

"Oh." Lacey's heart pounded. "Do you have a name?"

She heard another sigh on the other end. "Now, I can't give you adoptive parents' names. But that would be your family, I suppose, since it's your brother."

"Yes, yes. Can you confirm that? Just so I know you have the right child?"

"If I can find..." A pause. Then, almost as if speaking to herself, Mrs. Carmichael muttered, "Matteo..."

Did she say Matteo? Was that his first name or last?

"I can only tell you this, ma'am," Mrs. Carmichael said. "This baby was quite healthy. If you're looking for medical records, he had the proper shots, had a perfect Apgar score, and didn't have a single medical report filed while he was in Holmes. I can give you the delivery doctor's—no, no, I can't. He's retired. I have a pediatrician's name, but that's all. No guarantee she's still working twenty-five years later."

"That's fine, it will help."

"It's Dr. Martha Elias in Satellite Beach, Florida."

She scribbled furiously. "That's great, thank you. Anything else? Anything at all?"

"No, ma'am. That was a closed adoption and I can't even give you the agency that handled it."

"Of course not," Lacey said, her voice a little breath-less. "Thank you for your time."

She hung up and stared at the computer screen. Now what?

She stood, not surprised her legs were shaking, then opened the door and peeked into the hall. Tessa's bedroom door was closed, with the sound of the shower running audible from the en suite.

Tessa loved a long shower and she'd wash her hair after running, so...there was time.

Think, Lacey, think. Would the family still live in the same town as the pediatrician? Twenty-five years later? Probably not, but it was all she had.

Back at the laptop, she typed, *Matteo Satellite Beach.*

If this didn't work, she could cross-reference public records and—

Roman Matteo, Star Athlete from Satellite High, Signs Multimillion-Dollar Contract with Jacksonville Jaguars.

She stared at the headline at the top of the search results that popped up immediately, then scanned down. More about this football player named Roman Matteo from a small town on the east coast of Florida. Much more. Local news, sports news, national news.

She *had* said Matteo, right?

Lacey clicked on the first one and zeroed right in on the picture of one very happy young man holding up a football jersey with a number 14 on it, smiling and looking right into the camera with...the most distinct amber eyes.

Tessa's eyes.

"Holy jackpot, Batman. That was easy."

But was it *too* easy?

She clicked on another story and another, trying to find more pictures.

The "signed with Jags" news story was everywhere, but then she found a feature story in *Florida Today*, which must be the local newspaper, and scanned every word.

Faith and Bob Matteo call Roman the light of their life, the son...

All of the blood in her veins froze.

...the son they adopted.

Taking a steadying breath, she continued to read, seeing that he was twenty-two...three years ago. Which meant he was twenty-five now.

This *had* to be him.

A brief biography of twenty-five-year-old Roman Matteo quickly emerged from the local news stories, Facebook posts, and sports updates. Born in Melbourne, raised in Satellite Beach, played football at the University of Florida, and now, was a second-string receiver for the Jacksonville Jaguars.

Nice genes, Tessa.

And speaking of Tessa, she could walk in any second. So Lacey clicked out of the search and erased her browser history on the laptop. Then, she snagged her phone and tapped the Instagram app.

Please be public, please be public.

There were a few accounts with the same name, but

only one was verified with ninety-seven thousand followers and Jacksonville Jaguars in the bio.

She clicked on his profile and slid down to a rare closeup. Clicking it, she dropped back in her chair, exhaling shakily.

This is him.

Her fingers hovered over the message button. Should she or shouldn't she?

Was she throwing a monkey-wrench into happy lives...or inching two people who really should meet a little bit closer? Who deserved a son more than spectacular Tessa Wylie?

Or was Lacey just walking into something she should never start?

She took a deep breath and tapped the message square on his page.

Hey Roman,

This is a little out of the blue, but I promise I'm not some weird random fan. I know your biological birth mother. If you're open to learning more about her, I'd love to talk. No pressure—just wanted to reach out.

Was that too bold? Should she send—

"Lacey? Where are you?"

As the door popped open, her trembling finger accidently hit the screen and...*shoot*. It sent! Every drop of blood in Lacey's head drained into a hot pool around her heart.

What did she just do?

Tessa stood in the doorway, arms crossed, her hair damp and hanging over a beach coverup.

"Closed door?" she asked with a teasing raised brow. "You job hunting? 'Cause you look like you're about to commit a federal crime."

Lacey forced a laugh. "Not today. Just... researching."

"Researching what?"

She stared at her computer screen, as blank as her brain. What was her answer? What was she doing? Didn't she have an alibi at the ready?

"Dating apps." The explanation slipped out as she glanced at her phone. "And no, I don't want to talk about it."

A flicker of surprise flashed in eyes that were the precise color of the ones in the pictures she'd just seen.

"Good," Tessa said. "Remember, I'm the one who told you to find a cute guy."

Not *this* cute. Not *that* guy. But Lacey just shrugged. "It's weird, is all. Don't ask questions. I hate this part of the process."

"Who doesn't? Although, I've never done a dating app. Can I see your profile?"

"No."

She drew back. "Well, okay."

"I mean, it's all just so personal and demeaning."

"There is nothing demeaning about it," Tessa said, coming deeper into the office, glancing around. "I know we have to work on Bat Mitzvah stuff today."

That's what her excuse should have been. The Bat Mitzvah flowers. *Dating app?* What the heck was wrong with her?

"But can I postpone that?" Tessa asked, obviously unaware of Lacey's mental meltdown.

"Sure. What's up?"

She closed the door, surprising Lacey. "I want to spend some time with my mother," she said. "I have to use this unexpected chance to be with her."

Lacey nodded, then frowned at her choice of words. "Use it?"

"Yeah." She leaned against the desk, not noticing that Lacey very slowly and casually lowered her laptop screen. Nothing incriminating was on it...she hoped. "My mom and I aren't..." She huffed a laugh. "We're not close like you and Viv."

Lacey nodded, not really hearing a word. She'd sent that text! What if—

"I mean, there's no animosity," Tessa continued. "But she and Kate have always been so much more...sympatico, you know? I was a Daddy's girl."

Lacey nodded, knowing how much Tessa adored her late father.

"And she's here, and really struggling more than she's letting on."

"Because of Maggie?" Lacey guessed, forcing herself to pay attention to the conversation.

"Because of Maggie's coldness, yes. And grief. The same heavy burden I'm carrying. I think she and I need some alone time to just talk about Dad and help each other heal."

"Of course you do, Tess." Lacey reached for her hand. "I think that's a great idea."

"Whoa, must have been a winner on that dating app." She lifted Lacey's hand. "Your palms are sweaty."

"Are they?" She pulled her hand away and swiped it on her jean skirt. "I'm just hot in here and nervous about...the Bat Mitzvah."

"Don't be, but I do think it's a good opportunity for you to have more ownership of a project. I'm here, of course, and I'll do client interface. Also, I have a couple of new business prospects. But can you do the heavy lifting on this party? I made that list—"

"Yes, of course I can, Tessa!" She might have been a little too enthusiastic—guilt again? "I know exactly what needs to be ordered and arranged and I'd love to handle the catering meeting. You just go and have fun with your mother."

"Thanks, hon. I'm taking her on the boat for some sun and relaxation time." Tessa sighed, smiling at her and holding her gaze for several heartbeats. "You're an angel, you know that, Lace?"

Oh, heavens. She was *so not* an angel.

"I just adore you, and Vivien better watch out because I want you as my daughter."

Lacey tried to laugh, but more guilt crawled up her chest and nearly strangled her.

"Oh, Tess." She reached over to hug her, hoping she didn't get called out on the fact that her whole body was vibrating with nerves.

As she did, her phone buzzed. She jerked back to grab it and hide what it might say, knocking it to the floor.

"Whoops." Tessa instantly was down, beating her to

it. As she grabbed the phone, she glanced at the screen. "Oh, my, Roman Matteo? He's your app guy?"

Lacey actually couldn't see straight for a moment. "Do you...know him?"

"Why would I?"

Dizzy. She was downright dizzy and sweating. "Because he's...an NFL player."

"Really?" She squinted at the screen and Lacey thought she'd pass out. "Way to go, you."

"You've never heard of him?" Lacey tried to snag the phone, but Tessa swooped it away.

"Pfft. Please. I don't think I've watched a whole football game in my life. Come on, let me see him."

"No."

"Lacey! I have to have right of first approval." She clicked the notification button and Lacey was certain she'd pass out.

"Whoa." She dragged the word out. "He's a cutie. And look what he said." Tessa grinned and angled the screen so Lacey could read the message and take the phone.

"What?" she croaked.

"'Yes, let's talk.'"

"He wants to talk?" Her voice broke with nerves.

Laughing, Tessa pressed the phone into Lacey's hand. "Looks like you have a date on your calendar, Miss Lacey Knight."

"With...Roman Matteo." She searched Tessa's face. "You're sure you never heard of him?"

"Told you, no football for me. But I guess I'll hear of

him now, since just the mention of his name seems to *wreck* you." She laughed and pushed off the desk. "Have fun but be careful. He looks like a player. And I don't mean football."

She winked, pivoted, and disappeared out the door, leaving it open so Lacey could hear her footsteps disappear down the hall.

Only then did she collapse in horror and stare at the response from...*Tessa's son.*

What the heck had she gotten herself into?

Chapter Four
Tessa

Tessa and Jo Ellen crossed Gulf Shore Drive and walked the short distance to the entrance of the neighborhood marina. There, a twenty-nine-foot Sea Ray that Tessa had skillfully managed to negotiate as payment from a client waited in its slip.

Getting her client to agree to give her the beautiful cabin cruiser had been a massive coup on Tessa's part—a boat was a huge perk in a place surrounded by water. But the real benefit was the fact that this marina reminded her so much of her father.

The privately-owned warren of wharves with rental slips had been upgraded and rebuilt over the years, but it had the same understated vibe, appealing to the owners of small boats and the locals.

Artie and Roger had always worked a deal with the guy who ran the marina to rent a cheap fishing vessel for the months they'd spent here. Her father loved to take out whatever boat they had, throw down a line, and fish until he ran out of bait.

He and Tessa had some great talks on this small waterway that connected to Destin Harbor. Now, she just liked to sit on her boat and think about him.

As she and her mother walked across the wooden docks, chatting about how the marina had expanded over thirty years, Tessa knew the same memories were dancing in Jo Ellen's head.

As they made their way to her slip, they passed the marina office, a sun-washed wooden building with cheery blue trim. Before they reached it, the manager stepped out of a screen door and waved to them.

"Hey, Tessa," he called in greeting. "Good to see you again."

"Hey, Clay." Tessa slowed her step as they approached the young man, a really dedicated worker in his mid-thirties. "This is my mother, Jo Ellen Wylie. Mom, this is Clay Donahue."

Jo Ellen's eyes flickered with recognition at the name. "A Donahue still runs this place?"

Clay grinned. "Yes, ma'am. My family's been managing this marina since my grandfather's days. Not that he's given anything up," he added with a laugh. "Grandad Seamus comes here plenty, trying not to tell me how to do my job." He tipped his chin toward the door of the small building. "He's back there now, as a matter of fact."

Jo Ellen gasped. "Seamus Donahue is here?"

"Who's looking for me?" The screen door swung again, and out stepped a tall, white-haired man in a faded Guy Harvey T-shirt. Well into his seventies, he had the leathery sun-weathered look of someone who'd spent a lifetime on the water. His hair still held a bit of a curl, and his sea-blue eyes scanned them with curiosity. "Need some fishing tips, ladies?"

"Seamus!" Jo Ellen stepped forward, lifting the brim of her sunhat and then taking it off as though she needed to get a better look. "I can't believe it! It's Jo Ellen, Artie Wylie's wife."

"What in the heck?" He reached out and wrapped her in a hug, practically scooping her out of her sandals. "Artie Wylie?" He eased her back and looked around. "Where is that SOB? He still owes me a beer for that forty-five-pound snapper I helped him haul in."

Tessa's heart dropped and so did her mother's expression. Enough that Tessa was certain she saw Jo Ellen's eyes fill, so she stepped up to answer the question.

"Hi, Seamus," she said. "I'm Tessa, Artie and Jo Ellen's daughter."

"Course you are! I'd know your daddy's eyes anywhere. And just as pretty as you were when you were a young thing and could tangle up a line faster than a cat in a crab trap. Hello there, little lady."

He gave her a hug, too, and looked around expectantly for a second before leveling his gaze on her.

"He's gone, isn't he?" he asked, the simple, sad question telling her that she wouldn't have to say a word. No doubt her expression said it all.

"About seven months ago," Tessa said softly, easily recalling the man with the Irish name and the Alabama accent who had been friends with her father. How had she never seen him here in the past month or so? "But he sure loved fishing with you, Seamus. It was one of the great joys of his life."

"Aw, shucks." He shook his head and took a minute to let an emotion hit, then turned to Jo Ellen. "I'm sorry for your loss. I buried Suzanne a few years back and, good Lord, it ain't easy."

She only answered with a tight smile, so Tessa put a hand on his arm. "Thank you, Seamus. And we're sorry for your loss, too."

He nodded. "Must be thirty years, then, since y'all never came back after Opal hit."

"Not until this year," Tessa confirmed.

"Bet you're shocked at the changes." He gestured around them. "That hurricane was the beginning of... well, not the end. Just the *new* Destin. After the storm, the real money poured in here, nothin' but new builds and tourists. Got so expensive not even the spring break kids could afford a trip here anymore. Not many of us left who really remember this town before Opal."

"I can't believe how different it is," Jo Ellen agreed. "The house we rented is gone now, but the Lawsons built a mansion on it."

"The..." He inched back. "Roger and, uh, Maggie, was it? They live here now?"

"Oh, no," Tessa said. "Roger passed away many, many years ago. Maggie lives in Atlanta, but she owned the property and rebuilt on it this year."

"Huh. Well, that's just a nice blast from the past." He turned to Tessa. "You need to rent a boat or fishing equipment?"

She laughed. "We're not fishing. I have the Sea Ray in slip fifteen-A."

"I thought that went with the big rental some corporation owned," he said, thumbing in the general direction of her former client's house.

"It's mine now," she said, smiling up at him. "And I wanted to take my mom for a ride. I don't fish anymore."

"Well, ain't nobody quite as good as your daddy. And he could fix up a broken rod and reel like no one I ever met." He chuckled and shook his head. "When he'd come down here in the summers, I'd just drop a pile of busted gear on his lap and he'd put some thick glasses on and pick up a screwdriver and start fiddlin'. Next thing you know, it was good as new and I could give it to the kids."

"Your kids?" Tessa asked.

"No, no. Me and Suzanne ran a ministry called The Abundant Catch that teaches some underprivileged kids how to fish and learn about Jesus. Artie used to say when he retired down here that all he'd do is fix up broken gear and teach those kids how to fish." His voice thickened. "Bet he's bringing in the big catch up in heaven now."

Tessa's own throat tightened as a lump formed. "I didn't know he planned to retire here," she said, turning to her mother with a question in her gaze.

"He had some pipe dreams, but it was always easier to stay in Ithaca," Jo Ellen said with a shrug. "But I know he's smiling down on you, Seamus. Every time we'd go out on Lake Cayuga, he'd talk about fishing with you."

"Nice to know he remembered me. And good to see you again, ladies. If you ever want to pick up where he left off, I got plenty of rods that need love." Seamus pointed to Tessa, a glint in his blue eyes. "You cast like you were swattin' flies, but you tried hard. Your daddy said that was what mattered."

Holding on to that sweet memory, Tessa said goodbye and they promised to stop by the office again.

A moment later, they reached the beautiful cruiser that she intended to rename *Good Time Girl* when she got around to having the boat name painted on the back.

"I just got the owner paperwork and insurance," she told her mother. "So you can be my first legal passenger, Mom. Welcome aboard!"

"Goodness, this is exciting."

Tessa helped her climb onto the deck, then showed her around, including the small cabin underneath with a single bunk, a bare-minimum kitchenette, and a head.

After she untied the lines, Tessa got behind the helm and started the engine, letting it rumble before she pulled out of the slip. As she was about to accelerate, she saw her mother, sitting on the bow bench, wipe a tear.

Oh. The grief would never stop, would it?

She blinked back a few of her own and took them out to the harbor for a slow ride around, thinking about Dad fixing rods and reels for poor little kids. How was it that she didn't know that about him?

And that just made her wonder...what else didn't she know about her father?

AN HOUR LATER, they had cold drinks open and sat in the beautiful sunshine, anchored with a perfect view of the shops and wharf of HarborWalk Village.

Jo Ellen sighed and leaned back on the cushions that made a comfy seating area in the back of the boat.

"I miss him so much," she confessed. "Out here? On the water? Oh, there was nothing he loved more."

"I know, Mom. It was bittersweet talking to Seamus. I don't meet many people who knew him."

"Not in Florida. The memories are everywhere up at home."

"You should stay here for a while," Tessa suggested. "It's good for you."

"If Maggie doesn't claw my eyes out, it is."

"You two will find your rhythm. You were so close. Always laughing and drinking wine and working on something in the kitchen. You should cook together while you're here." Tessa pushed up her sunglasses to underscore this great idea. "Not only do we need it since Jonah went to California, but you and Maggie could get close again. God knows we'd all be happier and healthier for it."

Her mother considered that, and nodded. "Maybe. We did like cooking up concoctions together." She was quiet for a long moment, staring out again. "Sometimes it feels like yesterday. Sometimes it feels like another lifetime."

"Dad or cooking with Maggie?"

"Both," she said with a smile. "But I was thinking about Artie."

Tessa took a slow sip. "I thought I'd get used to it. Not in a way that makes it easier, but just...accustomed to it. But it still catches me off-guard. Like, I'll reach for my phone to call him or think about something I need to tell him, and then..." She trailed off, fighting a lump in her throat. "Then I remember he's gone."

They sat silent for a while, only the sound of the water against the hull and a distant steel drum playing from a restaurant on the wharf.

"Tessa," Jo Ellen finally said, leaning forward. "I know you and I were never that close. That you were always closer to your father."

Tessa's chest tightened. She hadn't expected that. But then, wasn't that why she'd come out here today? "Mom—"

"No, let me say this." Jo Ellen stood and made her way to the center of the boat, slipping into the passenger seat next to Tessa. "You and Kate were always so different. She was an open book, and I think I clung to that. You were more private and independent. I should've tried harder to meet you where you were, instead of expecting you to be more like her. I'm sorry."

Tessa's chest ached at this apology. "Don't be. I was a Daddy's girl."

"I know," Jo Ellen said softly. "And I never resented that. But I do wish I'd been someone you felt like you could come to when you needed...a parent."

For a quick second, Tessa wondered if her father had shared her secret. Did her mother know she'd had a baby all those years ago?

No. He'd never betray her like that. He'd promised. Jo Ellen would have been so upset.

Then, anyway. Now? She doubted it would get the same reaction.

Maybe this was it. This was her chance to confide in her. After all, she'd told Lacey. Couldn't she tell her own mother about the son she'd given up all those years ago?

The words pressed at the back of her throat, but when she opened her mouth, all that came out was: "There are things I haven't told you. About my life."

Jo Ellen held her gaze, something flickering in her expression—understanding, maybe. Sadness.

"I'm sure there are."

Tessa blinked and kept her mouth closed. She couldn't do it. She just couldn't.

Shifting on her seat, she searched for a new subject. "How did I not know that Dad wanted to retire in Destin?" she asked, grabbing the first thing that occurred to her.

Jo Ellen sighed, her fingers sliding over the can of soda she held. "I don't know how serious he was. You know, we'd get home after a summer here and by February, he just didn't want to deal with the snow and ice. Of course, there was his job at Cornell with all the politics in the department. He loved the freedom of being in Destin."

A quiet moment settled between them, full of unspoken memories.

"I didn't know he fixed fishing gear, either. I mean, his own, yes. And the ones I ruined by getting the lines tangled like..." Tessa rolled her eyes. "A cat in a crab trap."

They both laughed.

"I wish I did know how to fix gear," she said after a moment. "I'd help old Seamus out just to honor Dad."

"He'd like that," her mother said. "And he'd like me to get his rods and reels down here to donate them. I think I'll try and figure that out."

"Awesome, Mom," she said. "Let's definitely make that happen."

"It's not enough," Jo Ellen said softly, looking off to the other side of the harbor. "Never enough."

"I know." Tessa took a sip of water and leaned back. "I mean, do you even remember his memorial service? It was a blur. I don't know who was there, let alone what we said."

Her mother sighed noisily. "I'm sure he was looking down and disappointed."

"Why?" Tessa asked.

"He used to ask that I would throw his ashes in the Gulf of Mexico." She gave a tight smile. "Obviously, I didn't."

Tessa sat up. "We can. Where are they?"

"In a box on my dresser in Ithaca."

"Mom." She leaned forward. "Let's honor his request, please. Let's do another memorial service that we'll actually see because we're not bawling our eyes out."

Jo Ellen just looked at her. "Another one? Wasn't one enough?"

"We'll call it a Celebration of Life," she said. "We'll get Kate and her kids down here. She can bring the ashes and the rods along with the files and paperwork you said Peter wanted."

"Oh, I don't know if I can handle...that."

"Mom! The man made you promise to put his ashes in the Gulf, right?"

"Yes."

"Well, we owe him this!" Tessa reached for her. "Please. I'll organize everything."

After a few seconds, she nodded. "I think it's a beautiful idea, Tessa. When we get back, we can call Kate."

Tessa smiled, beyond satisfied with that decision and this day. Yes, there were a few old memories that hurt, but all in all, this was exactly why she'd wanted this boat ride and this time with her mother.

Chapter Five
Vivien

V ivien pulled into the driveway of the stunning modern home overlooking Four Prong Lake in the heart of one of Destin's most upscale areas, and shook her head with a half-laugh. All she could see was sleek lines, soaring glass, and tropical landscaping that looked plucked from a resort catalog.

And not a broken sprinkler head in sight.

Had she really thought Danny Sullivan was a fake handyman? Well, he had doused her in water and had all the markings of a con artist. So, the mistake was understandable but, whoa, she'd been so wrong about him.

Now she knew that Danny was a successful independent hedge fund manager who had moved here to keep an eye on his prickly widowed sister, Fiona Buckman, who was Vivien's client. That meant he had both a soft heart and a thick skin. She also knew he'd lived here less than a year, had another place in New York, and that he looked awfully good without his shirt on.

Not that how he looked mattered. She was here to give him some professional help with "a big empty space"—at least that was how he'd described it when she'd seen him at Tessa's event a few days ago. Who cared that he was charming, handsome, and had that wry sense of humor that Vivien found so attractive in a man?

And Peter was jealous of... How did he put it? *The dude could barely wipe his drool around you.*

As if, Peter.

Anyway, the only thing that needed to be attractive for this job was his budget—based on the look of this place, she assumed it was—and her design work.

The oversized front door opened before she reached it.

Danny leaned against the frame, barefoot, wearing dark blue shorts and a short-sleeved button-down. But it was his relaxed and mildly amused expression on a very handsome face that got her attention.

"I turned the sprinkler system off to avoid another disaster."

She gave him a lighthearted thumbs-up. "And I purposely wore my lucky Belgian linen pants to assure you that you did no lasting damage with a wayward valve."

He let his gaze sweep over her with appreciation. "I'm so glad. They looked well and truly destroyed the last time I saw them. How did you manage it?"

"You met the lady who owns the bridal salon, right? She did me a solid."

"I hope you'll let me cover the cost," he said, gesturing for her to step inside.

She glanced around and let out a light and playful whistle at the blinding sunlight pouring over Travertine floors and a wide staircase with a wrought-iron railing. "Oh, you will, trust me."

He laughed. "You're a good sport after that spontaneous baptism. And you'd never forgive me if you could have seen me at war with the water valve. I was pressing buttons like it was a game-show buzzer. You were the unfortunate prize."

She smiled at his effortless charm. "Can you blame me for thinking you were scamming Fiona?"

"Because of my tragic lack of home improvement skills?"

"That, and the fact that you had...very un-handyman-like energy."

He regarded her, arms crossed. Eyes that fell somewhere between silver and blue studied her as a slow smile added subtle dimples to his features. "What kind of energy did I have?"

Vivien lifted her chin, amused enough to be honest and meet his banter with her own. "There was a reason I dubbed you The Hapless Handyman."

He threw his head back with a hearty laugh. "Tell me there's a T-shirt, please."

"Don't tempt me, Hapless."

He chuckled. "And then tell me I've lost that title."

"Yes," she assured him, hesitating when she thought about the new nickname Tessa had hung on him—the Hedge Fund Hunk.

Danny narrowed his eyes, teasing, "Don't think I didn't see that mental pause. That's the face of a woman sitting on something much worse."

"Now, you're just...Mr. Sullivan, my newest client."

"It's Danny." He gestured her through the entryway toward the stairs. "You want to see my blank canvas, Picasso? Or look around the rooms that are 'furnished,' and I do use that term with the lowest possible expectations. There's minimalist and then there's..." He pointed to a nearly empty open-concept space. "This."

She glanced around and took in what was visible—a cream leather sectional that she didn't love, but knew cost a fortune, an empty dining room, and a gourmet kitchen with a massive center island. It was all very livable, if not "decorated."

The floor plan spilled out to a pool deck that overlooked the twenty-five-acre lake surrounded by beautiful homes much like this one. The lots were tight and the houses close, but the water view made up for that. Like many of the homes, he had a dock, but no boat.

It was clear he'd put his time and money into the outside, with a large seating area, pool furniture, another kitchen, and more gorgeous plants and trees.

"I know, I know." He sounded apologetic. "It has Airbnb vibes and no...I don't know. What's missing besides...everything?"

"Style? Soul? Framed art?"

He cracked up, obviously enjoying the exchange. "You're ruthless and I love that, Vivien. In my own defense, I've lived here less than a year and am a certified workaholic. I spend most of my free time out back. I bought the place because of that whole resort vibe outside. All of my real furniture and, yes, art is in my condo in Tribeca."

"Do you ever go back there or are you pretty much here permanently?" she asked.

"I go back periodically, but...my sister." He rolled his eyes. "I know she can be difficult, but I do feel it's important to be nearby since her husband passed away."

Vivien nodded, knowing just how difficult Fiona could be. "Special place in heaven for you, sir."

"She's had some tough breaks and has always been very maternal to me, at ten years my senior. And when she bought that white elephant house in Indian Bayou and announced she wanted to keep running his business?" He shrugged. "I knew she'd need help and I was looking for a way out of the New York City grind. It worked."

"That's noble and brotherly of you."

"She would argue with that description."

Vivien raised a sardonic brow. "Your sister would argue with sunshine."

"True. But she is my only family. I came down here and this place was on the market, so...I bought it. I mean, I love the woman, but I don't want to live with her. I'm not *that* noble or brotherly."

"Are you staying long enough to really decorate or is this a temporary and quick fix?"

"Eh, not sure yet. But for now, I don't really want to spend much time or energy on this floor. There's this blank space upstairs, however..." He motioned to the stairs. "I know it can be something, but I can't figure out what. Take a look?"

"Absolutely."

She walked with him up the stairs, using the vantage point to see the whole of the first floor, which had tremendous potential.

"My office and bedroom are all first floor," he told her. "I never come up here. But the guest rooms are here, and I do get a decent amount of visits from business colleagues and friends from New York. I'd like a place to hang out that isn't all about water, swimming, or sunshine. Not that I mind any of that, I just want options."

They reached the top of the stairs, and he led her into a loft space that stretched across the back of the house. Sunlight flooded through more windows overlooking the lake, and an empty expanse of polished white oak floors offered endless possibilities.

"I work from home most of the year," Danny said. "Thought I'd turn this into something more usable. I don't have a TV downstairs and don't really want one, but I'd like a place to watch games and movies, entertain friends."

Vivien walked the perimeter, her designer's eye already clicking into gear. "Well, the bones are incredible. High ceilings, great light, and that view..." She turned back toward him. "Do you want a true sports bar vibe? Or something a little more polished?"

"Somewhere in the middle," he said, crossing his

arms and thinking. "Comfortable. Nothing too theme-y. And absolutely no neon beer signs."

She laughed. "Thank God."

"I'm nothing like my sister in the design area," he added.

She gave him a sidelong glance. "In terms of taste or... demands?"

"Both," he said quickly. "I'm wide open to your ideas and trust your taste to reflect mine. I'd like to keep it in line with my personality, but if I decide I want to sell, it should be neutral enough to do that."

Nodding, she narrowed her eyes and pictured what she could do. "Like a man cave, but not dark and depressing," she said. "A wet bar there, a TV on that wall. Comfortable seating, window darkening treatments for when you want to watch a movie."

"Yes and yes," he said.

They talked through ideas—stone backsplash, low-profile lighting, modular seating. He loved her idea for a pool table with black felt, so she sketched a few notes on her iPad, and took pictures and measurements.

All the while, she sensed him watching her—not in a way that made her self-conscious, but... aware.

"Would you mind taking a peek at my guest suites, too?" he asked as she closed up her tablet. "They are bare minimum now, and I wouldn't mind a refresh—art, décor. Maybe matching towels."

She smiled and followed him down the hall to two good-sized bedrooms that looked a lot like the ones in the Summer House that she'd yet to decorate.

"In fact," she murmured to herself, looking around. "I could replicate..."

"Pardon?"

"Just thinking. I'm doing several guest rooms in the Summer House and if you don't mind, I could simply use the same themes and colors. If I buy double the furniture, I'll get a discount."

"Sounds good. So you're doing your own house, too?"

"It's a family house," she said. "My brother is sort of the lead on it and I'm staging it for sale."

His brows rose. "You're selling that beautiful waterfront property? Why?"

She gave a soft laugh. "How much time do you have? It's a long story."

"I have time for a cup of coffee after this, if you'd like."

"I would, thank you." They finished touring the rooms, discussed some very simple ideas, and headed back downstairs.

A few minutes later, they sat outside at a table under an umbrella, sipping French press coffee with cream.

"This is definitely the best room in the house," she said, looking around at the potted palms and the sunshine glinting on the large, contemporary pool.

"I work out here a lot," he said. "Makes the poor schmucks on Wall Street jealous."

"What do you do, exactly?"

"Investments, mostly," he said. "I worked for a huge bank for decades, but was able to spin off my own fund a few years ago." He lifted his coffee cup and gave her a pointed look. "So how did you and your family come to own that house on Gulf Shore Drive?"

She opted for the short version of her long tale, leaving out the part about her father dying in prison while serving time for white-collar crimes. Instead, she explained that they all had homes in Atlanta, but years ago, they'd spent summers in a much smaller cottage on the same property.

"My mother held on to it as a rental until last year, when she decided to rebuild a much bigger house and give it to us."

"Now that's a good and generous parent."

Also demanding and difficult, but she kept Maggie's shortcomings to herself. "Yes, but we haven't decided if we're keeping it or selling."

"From an investment standpoint? Definitely keep it," he said. "I mean, if you can."

"That's my vote," she replied. "Now that I've lived there for two months, I'd like to stay here in Destin and build my design business."

"Nothing keeping you in Atlanta?" he asked. "Or...no one?"

She smiled at the sly question. "I'm recently divorced," she said softly. "Nothing really compelling to keep me there."

"How recent?" he asked.

"Well...the ink isn't quite dry."

"Oh." He leaned back and studied her, thinking. "How are you feeling, then?"

She appreciated the question. "I'm okay. It wasn't

really my doing," she added. "My husband had a classic mid-life crisis and woke up one morning wanting...more than I was apparently giving him."

He winced. "Oof. Sorry, Vivien."

"It was complicated, since I work for his home building company. Well, I did."

"Kids? Oh, wait. I met your daughter. Lacey?"

"That's her. My one and only, also my dearest friend. Currently sharing a room, that's how close we are."

He chuckled, but his smile faded. "I don't have kids," he said. "Huge miss in my life."

"Were you ever..."

"Married? Yes. Briefly in my thirties, to another investment banker. We were more married to our jobs than each other." He looked down at his coffee. "It ended before it got messy."

"That's probably rare."

"It felt like a relief," he said, meeting her gaze again. "Which told me everything I needed to know."

"It's never easy," she said. "And probably a blessing you didn't have kids."

"It doesn't feel that way now that my friends are all talking about being grandparents," he said, a surprisingly raw note in his voice.

"Well, I'm not there yet," she said, taking a sip.

They were quiet for a beat, letting the silence be filled with the splash of the pool waterfall and the hum of a motorboat on the lake.

"So, the ink's not dry yet, huh?" He lifted a brow. "Is it safe to guess you're not seeing anyone?"

She looked over the rim of her cup. "I...socialize."

"But do you date? Or is it too soon?"

"Whoa, pretty smooth transition, Danny," she teased, purposely not answering the question.

"I'm trying to keep the banter-to-flirting ratio respectable."

She studied him for just a moment, then chose her words carefully. "It's not too soon," she said slowly. "In fact, I've had a few dinners with a good friend who..." *Who might be more*, but she didn't say that out loud.

"Well, how about this? Next time you're back here measuring things or sketching layouts, I'd love to cook for you. Blackened grouper, pineapple salsa."

"Tempting."

"No pressure. Just an offer. When it feels right." He inched closer. "Honestly? I've been thinking about asking you that ever since I doused you in sprinkler water."

She gave him a side eye. "Really."

"I hope I didn't overstep the client bounds."

She considered that, holding his mesmerizing gaze, feeling a flutter in her belly that might actually qualify as...butterflies.

Had she ever felt that with Peter?

"Dang, she's thinking too hard."

"I'm just wondering if...that means I have your business."

"My business and my attention," he said. "Take the one you want. Or both."

"We'll start with...that sports bar upstairs. *Sans* neon." She pushed back her chair, bringing the chat to an end. "I'll send you some sketches, a proposal, and we'll schedule the next meeting very soon. Text me your email address and we'll get it started."

He stood, too, quiet as they went back into the house toward the front door. He opened it and stepped outside with her, pausing on the brick pavers.

"Thank you for coming over, Vivien. I look forward to working with you." He extended his hand, which she took, ready to shake it, but he clasped her fingers and drew her a smidge closer. "I'm not trying to make things complicated," he added softly. "I hope you know that."

Despite the sunshine, chills blossomed on her body and the butterflies took flight again.

She smiled up at him, hoping she wasn't flushed. "Too late."

That made him laugh and he reluctantly let go of her hand, staying right where he was, watching her with that amused smile as she drove off.

Complicated? Yeah. That was one way of putting it.

June 20, 1991

We went to Cavallaris this morning—me, Tessa, Dad, and Uncle Artie. It's the little Italian deli-shop that always smells like garlic and olives and fresh bread, all rolled into one big hug.

Even though Frank and Betty Cavallari are the owners, they're also our friends because they go out every week with our 'rents. Ever since we've been coming to Destin, the six of them take off to "dinner" and come back pretty, uh, happy. It's kind of cute and weird.

Anyhoo, Dad disappeared instantly into the back room with Frank to talk about who knows what. So Uncle Artie handled the shopping because Mom and Aunt Jo Ellen are making something that sounds disgusting...bologna-ayze? With spaghetti? No idea, but Betty has convinced them that they can be the next Julia Child, so whatever.

Betty was tossing ingredients to Uncle Artie like they were footballs—onions, "San Marzano" tomatoes (apparently better than regular tomatoes), pancetta. Tessa and I got out of the way pretty fast. Betty let us try a couple different olives. I like green—Tessa had black. Ugh. One of them was so salty I thought my mouth would fall off.

We got Cokes and sat at one of the tiny tables near the window and Betty gave us a couple of Italian wedding cookies wrapped in wax paper. Powdered sugar everywhere. Pretty sure I have some in my hair. Still worth it.

The radio was just far enough off the station that Michael Bolton sounded worse than usual. There was a really adorable little kid playing with the pay phone pretending to call Batman on it. Honestly, so precious.

We saw a couple of kids we know from the beach walk by, including Dustin Mathers who Tessa said was cute but made her mad. I know why—he never notices her and just treats her like every other girl. Anyway, that got us talking about Peter...who does the same thing to me.

It's nothing—going nowhere, never will, he's so much older than I am. He's seventeen! So I just admire from afar. But when he does talk to me, he doesn't make me too nervous anymore. He's nice (like, waaaay nicer than Eli) and very easy on the eyes, ha ha.

Anyway, Dad finally came out from the back with Frank, and Artie asked them why they looked like...something about a cat eating a canary. Gross. Anyway, it was fun but we went back to the beach which was way better than shopping in town.

Oh, Mom's calling. Time for bologna and spaghetti or whatever.

Love,

Viv

P.S. MUST ADD! It's called "Bolognese" and it was the absolute most delicious food I ever ate in my whole life with all this meat and red sauce and these long flat noodles that were a thousand times better than spaghetti, called tagliatelle. Aunt Jo Ellen gave me the recipe since I loved it so much. (She said someday I'll cook!) It's on the back of this page so I never lose it!

P.S#2. Mom is so different here! Why is that? When she cooks at home, it's a little scary. She has so many rules and things have to be done a certain way and it just isn't fun. But with Aunt Jo Ellen, all she does is laugh when they cook and do "back up support" which apparently means pouring wine. I wish she were more like she is here when we are at home. It's like having a different mom.

Chapter Six
Maggie

Maggie somehow managed not to gasp at what she just been told, but kept one hand clenched tightly around her phone while the other rested on her lap.

Disappeared?

She couldn't have heard that right.

"Justin, I'm sorry," she said to the attorney on the other end of the line. "Did you say...the case files disappeared?"

"I'm as baffled as you are, Mrs. Lawson." The man gave an awkward laugh, and she could picture him clearly. In his late forties, buttoned up, and quite capable. She'd been thrilled to learn he'd taken over his father's cases when old John Waverly passed away a few years back.

But she wasn't thrilled right now. Not with this news.

Over the years, she'd had no reason to discuss Roger's crimes with Justin—his father had handled the criminal case. In fact, John Waverly deserved the credit for negotiating a plea bargain deal that allowed Roger to serve seven years instead of twenty-five.

And it was John who'd created a trust that protected

this property from government seizure, placing it in Maggie's name. She'd never quite understood how he'd done that, but Roger had told her plainly and clearly: "Do not sell that property. Just let John Waverly rent it for you, save the money, and tell no one you own it until I'm out of jail."

Of course, he never got out of jail…only into an early grave. She'd been terrified to do anything at all with it lest some despicable human from the government announce they wanted the property.

But that never happened.

Then, one day two years ago, John's son, Justin, had contacted her out of the blue, telling her that he'd been reviewing some of his father's files and looked at the trust.

Thanks to a new law he'd learned of, she not only could sell the house, but any profit made from the sale of this house had to go to her children because their father had died while incarcerated. She'd never heard of anything like it, but for this wonderful gift, she had placed young Justin Waverly in the highest possible esteem.

But that esteem just plummeted to rock bottom.

The files were *gone?* She was certain somewhere in the mountains of paperwork, they'd discover why Artie had turned Roger in to the police.

"Have you searched all possible storage places, file basements…wherever you keep old documents?" she demanded.

"High and low, and I did so personally," he said. "Honestly, this makes no sense at all, Mrs. Lawson. Even though we are under no legal obligation to hold case files that long, it was my father's express orders that we never destroy files. But these...have disappeared."

"Could someone have taken them?" she asked as a whole new wave of worry took hold.

"Highly unlikely," he said. "Files that old are in a massive underground storage facility that only staff of this firm can access. The only other possibility is that my father had them sent to you."

"He most certainly did not," Maggie snapped. "I would have remembered."

"Well, I have the paperwork for the Lawson Trust and your personal legal documents, Mrs. Lawson, but nothing else."

Maggie squeezed her eyes shut in abject frustration.

"Were you looking for something in particular?" Justin asked. "Is there something I could find in court records?"

She sighed. She was looking for the proverbial needle in a haystack and the haystack was gone.

"Just...history. How the case started, who launched the investigation, that sort of thing."

He thought for a moment. "Have you tried the Atlanta police department?" he asked. "It's been a while, but they might have something."

"My son has a contact in law enforcement, but he advised us to see what your father had kept." She looked out at the soft dunes that gave way to the endless stretch of shimmering emerald waves.

Normally, that view alone would soothe her frayed

nerves but this blasted phone call had soured the air, making it feel heavy and thick despite the ocean breeze.

It didn't help that Jo Ellen sat five feet away playing some inane word game on a tablet computer that kept chirping incessantly.

"I'm sorry but we don't have a thing for you," he said again. "I don't know where else to try but I promise, if I think of anything, I'll let you know."

Maggie inhaled sharply. "Thank you. I'd appreciate a call the moment you find anything."

"Of course, Mrs. Lawson. I'm sorry."

She ended the call with a tap, missing the days when a receiver could be slammed good and hard to deliver a clear message.

Jo Ellen looked up from the screen. "No luck?"

"Bad luck, the only kind we have, it seems. How do files that have to be a foot thick just disappear?"

Jo Ellen lifted a glass of iced tea. "Now what?"

"Your files. When are you getting them?" Maggie asked.

"I haven't reached Kate yet," Jo Ellen said.

"You can't reach your own daughter?" Maggie asked, frustrated that Jo didn't sense the urgency.

"She's busy with end of the school year things for her kids and she works full-time," Jo Ellen said. "But Tessa and I made plans to talk to Kate tonight. We want to talk to her about...something."

At her obvious vague tone, Maggie eyed the other woman. "What...something?" she asked.

"Just..." She waved her hand. "Just a Wylie family thing. Nothing you need to know about."

Maggie bristled—she hated to be out of the loop on anything. But she let the comment go and looked out at the water again, sitting in tense silence with a woman who used to know her every thought and feeling.

In some ways, these past few days, Maggie sensed Jo still wanted that kind of relationship. But they'd both made promises to their husbands, whether they understood why or not.

Still, should a promise be kept if the reason for it was unknown, dead, and never to be discovered? Did talking to Jo Ellen now break that promise?

The thought made her heart—the one no one thought she had—hitch and hurt.

Before she could brood any further, Vivien stepped out onto the deck, her expression curious. She hesitated when she saw them sitting there, like she'd just interrupted a funeral.

"Everything okay out here?" Vivien asked, glancing between them.

Maggie straightened, forcing a composed expression. "We hit a dead end with the attorney. Roger's case files are missing. Can you believe that?"

Vivien's eyes widened. "Missing? All of them?"

"Yes," Maggie confirmed, her lips pressed into a thin line. "Gone without a trace."

"That seems bizarre," Vivien said. "But I guess the case is thirty years old. Surely a law firm doesn't keep everything forever."

"John Waverly did," Maggie said. "Anyway, we don't know what to do next to crack this case."

"Crack the case, Nancy Drew?" Jo Ellen teased. "We can call it *The Secret of Gulf Shore Drive*."

Maggie had to laugh at that, too, since they'd both been raised on the books and always connected over them. "Sadly, it's *The Case of the Brick Wall* we're facing," she said. "And no idea what clue to follow next."

Vivien pulled out a chair. "I have a thought."

They turned to her, both interested.

"What about the Cavallaris?"

"Frank and Betty?" Maggie blinked at her. "Surely they're dead by now."

"Oh, no." Jo Ellen finally put her tablet on the table. "Kate and Eli went to see them a while back."

Maggie launched a brow north. Good heavens, she hated to be in the dark. "And was anyone ever going to tell me this?"

"There was no reason, Mom," Vivien said softly. "They just found out that they lived not far from here and went to see how they were."

"And how are they?"

"Confused and might have dementia," Jo Ellen replied.

"Really?" Maggie blinked, her heart squeezing. "I liked Betty so much. I never really cared much for Frank. He had some very seedy acquaintances in town, but Betty taught us to cook so many things, Jo. Remember?"

"Like Bolognese," Vivien said.

"Yes!" Maggie and Jo Ellen exclaimed in unison.

"It was so good I wrote about it in my diary." Vivien laughed. "I even kept the recipe you gave me, Aunt Jo Ellen. It's funny, because I read that entry last night."

"Why do you think they have dementia?" Maggie asked, not interested in recipes right then.

"Eli and Kate said they were very muddled about the past," Jo Ellen said. "But they're living in Santa Rosa Beach, which is close. Do you want to go see them, Mags? I could get the address from Kate."

Did she? Not particularly, but maybe they remembered something. She and Roger had gone out with them one last time after the Wylies left in a hurry that last summer. But Roger wasn't himself that night, and she didn't learn why until he was arrested a month or so later.

If she saw Betty and Frank, she'd have to tell them all about Roger, and she hated that subject.

"I don't want to visit them, not if they were confused," Maggie said, searching for an out. "I mean, they could lead us down some completely wrong path."

"They very well might," Vivien agreed, getting their attention again. "They both remember things differently."

"How so?" Maggie asked.

Vivien sighed and made a face. "I'm not sure I should tell you."

Maggie leaned in and gave Vivien her most commanding expression. "You will tell me and you will tell me now."

The slightest smile crossed her daughter's face, as if her words had no impact, but then she tipped her head in concession. "Okay, but it's...kind of out there. Betty thought that maybe, um..." She flushed a little and laughed. "That you, Mom, and Uncle Artie might have been...you know."

"No, I do not."

"Having an affair."

For a moment, Maggie just stared at her, utterly dumbstruck. Then she started snickering and looked at Jo Ellen, who was visibly fighting the urge to do exactly the same thing.

"Me and...*Artie?*" She choked the words.

"That's not all," Vivien said, which was almost enough to make Maggie stop laughing. "At the same time, in a different room, Frank told Eli that Roger and...you..." She looked directly at Jo Ellen. "Were...involved."

Jo Ellen gasped noisily. "No!"

"Oh, my..." Maggie couldn't quite find the words. "That's...that's..."

"Preposterous!" Jo Ellen burst out. "Was Betty drunk?"

Maggie snorted. "Was Betty ever *not* drunk? The woman chugged chianti like it was afternoon tea."

Jo Ellen leaned in and made that face that Maggie knew oh so well. Whatever was about to come out of her mouth would be just a little...scandalous.

"Because," Jo Ellen stage-whispered, "unless she had some juice, she didn't...*you know.*"

Maggie bit her lip against another laugh and an age-old ache to sit in a corner with Jo and just...gossip. What a guilty pleasure. And yet another thing Roger had stolen when he forced her to make that promise.

"I don't know," she lied. "But that much booze probably went a long way to causing today's confusion. Artie and me? I mean, give me a break."

Jo Ellen gave a sad smile. "He was a wonderful man and incapable of infidelity and just let me tell you, Mags—your husband might have had his flaws, but he adored you. Worshipped the ground you walked on. He—"

Maggie held up a hand. "I know, Jo. I remember."

For a few seconds, they were both quiet, then Vivien cleared her throat to ask, "Do you want their address?"

Maggie and Jo Ellen shared a look, silent, then they both shook their heads, proving that they could still communicate without speaking.

"But I'll tell you what I do want, Vivien," Jo Ellen said.

"Anything," Vivien replied.

"That recipe. Do you still have it?"

"Yes. It's on the back of that diary entry, if you want to write it down."

"I do, and I want to take it to the store." She reached a hand over the table toward Maggie. "Because tonight, my old friend—not *old*-old, you know what I mean. Tonight, we are..."

"Making bolognese," Maggie finished, a smile pulling.

"I'll get the recipe," Vivien said, shooting up as if hesitation might break the moment.

"I'll get my handbag." Jo Ellen rose, too. "Can you still drive, Maggie?"

"Honey, please. I'm seventy-eight, not a hundred."

"She's a great driver," Vivien called as she went inside. "You guys can take my car."

They both left the deck, and Maggie stayed very still, staring back at the water, trying to process all her feelings. It wasn't easy.

From the disappointing news about the files, to the ridiculous rewriting of history by Frank and Betty, to the sweet release of endorphins from being with the woman who was once her best friend.

Not to mention that every time they spoke, she was breaking a promise to Roger.

Vivien breezed back, holding a colorful notebook. "Here you go. Let me take a picture of it for you and—"

"Just give me the recipe, Vivien," Maggie said as she stood. "I can't read tiny words on a screen."

"But I have writing on the other side and I don't want to tear it out."

"Vivien." She glowered at her daughter. "You can tape it back in and feel safe in the fact that I have no desire to read your childhood diary entries. Come on. I'm feeling benevolent toward Jo Ellen. Do you want to ruin that?"

She huffed a breath, opened the notebook on the table, and tore out the page, handing it to Maggie. "Benevolent is good. I hope that lasts."

Maggie gave a tight smile and took the paper, folding it neatly to slide it in her handbag.

Yes, she was breaking a promise, but right then, she didn't care.

NOTHING WAS LIKE THEY REMEMBERED. Traffic was insane, with at least five million cars on the road. Parking was impossible, requiring Maggie to swear not once but twice trying to get in a spot. Publix was ten times the size it used to be, the sun was hotter than the second level of hell, and the recipe was written by a fourteen-year-old in chicken scratch not made for seventy-eight-year-old eyes.

But Maggie simply couldn't recall feeling so...light.

Not since the last time she'd been in this very town with this very woman on a very similar shopping mission.

They were halfway through their grocery list— onions, celery, carrots, the good canned tomatoes—when they came to a stop in the spice aisle.

"Nutmeg," Maggie read aloud, squinting at the paper, then the shelf. "Just a pinch."

Jo Ellen turned a few bottles. "Do you see it?"

"I don't know what I see," Maggie said. "Why isn't it alphabetical? Basil's next to turmeric. That should be illegal."

"Well, you write your congressman, Maggie. In the meantime, find the nutmeg."

Maggie scanned the rows, then spotted a tiny glass jar wedged behind some coriander. "Wait—is that it?" She reached for it, knocking over a tower of garlic powder canisters. One hit the bottom shelf and rolled across the floor.

"Whoops." Jo Ellen snorted. "Clean up on aisle six. Geriatric Spice Girls have caused a mess."

"Speak for yourself," Maggie whispered, laughing. "But if we are, I'm Posh Spice."

"Nope. Scary Spice."

Maggie swooped the nutmeg into the cart and glared at her friend. "Well, you're not Baby Spice. More like... Seventy-something Spice?"

"I'll take it, but how did that happen, Mags?" Jo went to throw an arm around Maggie, and when she did, she knocked half a dozen bottles of dried rosemary, making them jump back and squeal a little.

"We are not to be trusted in a grocery store!" Maggie exclaimed as they both giggled like they were twenty-year-old Tri-Delts again, sharing cheap wine and late-night Taco Bell.

Jo Ellen wiped her eyes as they did a cursory cleanup and guiltily pushed the cart away from the scene and into the next aisle for more destruction.

"Nutmeg," Jo Ellen mused. "You know what that reminds me of? Remember that formal in '67? When that guy—what was his name? Todd something—thought you were *Swiss* because you said you liked nutmeg?"

"Sweater Vest Todd!" Maggie hooted. "He thought 'neutral' meant 'from a neutral country'!"

They both lost it again, and Jo Ellen had to hold onto the shelf to steady herself.

Maggie studied her friend, feeling breathless...then

swamped with guilt. What if Roger could look down from…from wherever he was…and see them?

What would he say? How could she justify standing in Publix laughing like loons thirty years after she'd given him her word she would have nothing to do with anyone named Wylie?

She didn't know. But she didn't have to, and this felt… good. Roger would want her to feel good, wouldn't he?

Jo Ellen's smile softened. "I miss us."

Maggie nodded, blinking a little too much as she let the doubt and unwelcome sensations spiral through her.

Should she be doing this? No. Could she stop? She had to.

Clearing her throat, she glanced around, hoping they weren't making a scene. "Okay, Jo. Go find the pancetta."

"Come with me." Jo grabbed her arm. "You know you can't trust me alone."

"I'll stay here," she said, forcing the smile off her face.

Jo Ellen instantly looked crestfallen. "It's okay to laugh," she said softly. "Artie used to say laughter was oxygen for the soul. And you, Mags? You're suffocating."

Maggie just nodded, unable to muster a response while Jo shrugged and walked away.

Tears, unwelcome and unwanted, stung her lids. Desperate for a distraction, she shoved her hand into her purse to double-check the list. There must be something she could go buy.

She tugged out the wrinkled page and opened it, squinting at Vivien's rather poor penmanship.

Oh, wrong side. This wasn't the recipe, it was—

P.S.#2. Mom is so different here!

She froze at the words written at the bottom of the page. Everything in her wanted to turn it over and look at the recipe, but she couldn't help herself and kept reading.

Why is that? When she cooks at home, it's a little scary. She has so many rules and things have to be done a certain way and it just isn't fun. But with Aunt Jo Ellen, all she does is laugh and do what she calls "back up support" which apparently means pouring wine. I wish she were more like she is here when we are at home. It's like having a different mom.

Maggie stood still, staring at the words. A lump formed in her throat before she even realized she'd stopped breathing.

Vivien had written that at fourteen, but somehow the feeling cut with more precision now—when there was so little left to do about it.

She folded the page carefully and slipped it back into her purse.

Was it...Jo Ellen? Did *she* make Maggie different or better? Yes, at least in fourteen-year-old Vivien's estimation.

"Guess what?" Jo Ellen called as she returned, lifting the pancetta like a trophy. "I charmed the butcher into slicing it paper-thin. Betty would be proud."

"She would," Maggie said, clearing her throat. Then added, quieter, "I think Vivien would be proud, too."

Jo Ellen gave her a confused look, but Maggie ushered her toward the front of the store.

As they unloaded the cart, Jo Ellen eyed Maggie and looked like she wanted to say something but just couldn't.

"Did we forget something?" Maggie asked.

"No, no. I just…I, um, want to tell you something."

"Please, Jo. I know I'm all uptight and no fun and not breathing your laughter or whatever. I made my husband a—"

"We're having a Celebration of Life event for Artie," she said quickly. "Tessa and I decided we'd like to honor the promise we made a long time ago to put his ashes in the Gulf. We thought we'd make a party out of it. I mean, a celebration. Not a wild party, but…you know. A thing. On her boat."

Maggie felt her fingers curl gently around the edges of the deli-wrapped pancetta. "All right."

"I'd like you to be there," Jo Ellen added softly.

"Is plastic okay, ma'am?" The question pulled Maggie and she turned, happy to look away.

"Yes, please. Thank you."

"Will you be there?" Jo Ellen pressed. "Could you…please?"

Silence stretched between them before Maggie shook her head. "I can't," she said.

"Can't or won't?"

Maggie hesitated. "I made a promise to my own dead husband, Jo. Going to Artie's memorial service would be…beyond the pale."

Jo Ellen exhaled, then nodded. "Okay."

They were silent as Maggie slid her card through the

machine and pushed the cart toward the exit, aching for air in lungs that were...yes, suffocating.

Chapter Seven

Lacey

Was Lacey breaking a promise? Smashing it with both hands? Risking the best job, greatest mentor, and coolest friend she'd ever had?

Maybe, but she might also be giving the most amazing gift to Tessa Wylie.

Lacey couldn't be sure until she met Roman Matteo in person. That was all she hoped to accomplish with this trip. It was a brief opportunity to meet the man Tessa had brought into the world—she couldn't deny she was beyond curious—and determine his feelings about his adoption and birth mother.

And, possibly, it could be a chance to help two people who really wanted to know about each other but didn't know exactly how to proceed. If they didn't want that, she would let the whole subject drop after this rendezvous at a diner in the famously adorable town of Rosemary Beach.

She drove nearly an hour along the highway that hugged the Gulf. Nerves made her stomach twist like a knot, and she couldn't help but glance at her phone on the passenger seat, half-expecting someone to call and catch her in a lie.

She'd told her mother and Tessa that she was meeting an old friend from college who was vacationing in Rosemary Beach. *Ugh.* Lacey hated lying, but what else could she do?

Guilt gnawed at her, but it wasn't enough to make her turn around. She *had* to do this. In her deepest soul, she knew this was the right thing to do. She knew Tessa well enough to believe she would embrace the chance to come face-to-face with her son.

And Roman had jumped at the opportunity to learn more about his birth mother. He'd agreed to drive to the Panhandle all the way from...Jacksonville? She didn't know where he lived, but that was the team he played for, so it was a reasonable guess. He *wanted* to come.

So maybe Lacey was actually facilitating a lifelong dream for them. And not betraying her "second mother."

Clinging to that hope, she navigated the wide, clean streets of a town so new, it hadn't existed back in the days when her parents came to Destin as kids. The buildings were blinding white, with sloped roofs, darling shops, and plenty of tourists taking it all in.

She glanced at her GPS to see how close she was to the restaurant and decided to pull into a lot rather than try to push her luck with street parking. After a quick check of the time and a deep breath, she climbed out and eyed the side street that led to a place called Gloria's Diner.

She had no idea how he'd picked the place, but he'd

messaged her to meet him here at one o'clock. The location was far enough from Destin to avoid running into anyone who might recognize her, but close enough to not feel like she was going on a cross-country mission.

Strolling the wide, covered sidewalk, she passed a women's clothing shop optimistically named Young at Heart. She barely noticed the cute clothes in the front window display, or the mannequin being styled in a springy floral dress by a woman about her age.

She pulled the diner door open and took a deep, steadying breath.

"Hello, there, welcome to Gloria's," a woman greeted her from the hostess stand. "Table for..."

Lacey swallowed and looked around, her gaze falling on a man sitting at a bench in the entryway. She recognized him instantly, and not just because of the expectant look on a face she'd already over-studied on Instagram.

Holy...wow. Better in person, if that was possible.

Roman Matteo rose slowly to what had to be a few inches over six feet, pinning her with that lion's gold gaze. "Lacey?"

She managed to nod, not yet trusting her voice.

He turned to the hostess and slayed her with a smile. "Now it's a table for two, Liz. Thanks."

Liz beamed at him, a soft flush in her cheeks as she gathered their menus. "Of course. Right this way."

A moment later, they were sitting across from each other in a booth by the window that looked out at the busy sidewalk and charming architecture.

After they took Liz up on her offer of coffee, they just

sat there for a long, slightly uncomfortable moment, neither uttering a word.

"So," Lacey finally said on a sigh. "Thanks for meeting me. It's a long way from..."

"From everywhere," he finished with an easy laugh. "What can I say? I love a good adventure and this sounded like one."

She couldn't help smiling. Makes friends easily, loves a good adventure?

So Tessa.

"'Cause I sure wasn't expecting this when I checked my DMs." Roman leaned back casually, one arm draped over the back of the booth. "But just to be clear—you said you knew this woman. You're not, like, my sister or something, are you?"

Lacey couldn't help but laugh, some of her nerves fading. "No, I'm not...we're not related."

"How do you know her?" His smile faded and he dropped his arm. "I guess you should start with her name."

"Her name is..." She stopped and swallowed. "I'm not sure if I should tell you."

His eyes flickered with surprise. "Wasn't that the point of this meeting?"

"It could be, but..." She took a sip of water when a server brought it along with the coffee, waiting until they were alone again to finish. "She has no idea I'm meeting you. No idea who you are, in fact."

Again, surprise lit his eyes. "Oh, I thought you were

like some kind of messenger or, I don't know, go-between."

"No, I'm some kind of..." She closed her eyes. "Meddler. I found you on my own and I thought that maybe you two would like to know each other."

"Oh." He nodded, taking a moment to process that. "Does she want to know me?"

"She's curious but that's all she's said. I assume she doesn't want to upset your life."

"Or maybe I'd upset hers." His amber eyes narrowed. "I wouldn't want to do that."

She shook her head. "I don't think so, but I don't know. The fact is, no one else knows she had a baby and gave it—you—up for adoption. Well, her father knew, but he died last year."

He regarded her for a long time, silent, thinking as he took a sip of black coffee. "I'm curious, too. Really curious. There's only one reason I haven't tried to find her—well, two. My mom and dad are the greatest, most supportive, most amazing humans who ever lived. I don't want them to ever feel like they're not enough."

She smiled at that, intrigued by the unexpected proclamation, so not what she would have predicted from a muscular, handsome football player who probably cultivated a deliberately tough image.

"I never wanted to hurt them," he continued. "They did tell me I was adopted—*chosen* is the word they use—at a very young age. They made it seem like the greatest privilege of all time, and I have to admit, it was. It *is*. Most of my life, we all just forgot I was adopted."

"But you're curious."

"Sometimes burning with it," he admitted on a laugh. "When you find out you climbed out of a totally different gene pool, you wonder, you know?"

She understood. Especially *that* gene pool.

"So, is she doing okay?" he asked, concern in his eyes. "Is she healthy? Happy? Having a good life with more kids and all? How old is she? What's she like?"

The questions poured out like they'd been pent up a long, long time.

Lacey considered her responses, wondering how to best describe an enigma like Tessa Wylie.

"Well, for starters, she's amazing," she said. "And she's one of the most unique women I've ever met."

"Tell me about her," he said, the tiny note of urgency in his voice making her heart shift in her chest.

Lacey finally poured some cream into her coffee, stirring as she gathered her thoughts.

"First of all, she's beautiful. Like...you-can't-look-away gorgeous. She's a bundle of energy and loves to dance and sing—off-key, but everything she does and says is hilarious. She tries to act like she's super cool, but has a heart made of pure mush."

She looked up from the coffee and sucked in a soft breath at the expression on his face and the glistening tears in his eyes.

Oof. That was more than...curiosity.

"Yeah," she said quickly, kind of unnerved by the sight of this athletic god looking like he might come apart at the seams. "She's great."

He took a deep inhale. "That's good," he said. "I'm glad...that's good."

After a beat, Lacey felt like she should address his more practical questions and not merely gush over Tessa.

"Let's see, she's about to turn fifty, has no kids and never married, and she's an event planner," she added. "Worked for the Ritz for years, but just started her own business and is, no surprise, very good at it."

He drank some coffee again, processing. "Never married?" he asked, as if that fact stuck with him. "Why not?"

"She claims no man has ever matched up to her father, who I never got to meet, so—"

"How did you meet her? When?" He frowned. "It seems like you've known her a long time."

"Only a few months," she admitted. "But my mother knew her as a kid. It's a long story, but the short version is that they vacationed in Destin together as kids. They reconnected after a long separation, and now my mom and I are living with Tessa in—"

"Tessa? That's her name?"

Dang it! She grunted at her mistake. "Yeah, Tessa. Short for Theresa." She closed her eyes. "Goodness, I hope I'm doing the right thing."

"You are," he said quickly. "For me, at least. What about my dad?"

Ouch. She just sighed and shook her head. "She, um, doesn't really know...him."

His eyes flickered, then softened. "Hey, we all make

mistakes. God knows I've had my share of dumb overnights."

She sighed with relief because he clearly wasn't going to hold Tessa's decisions against her.

"I mean, it would be cool to know him, but I've always felt more connected to her."

He'd always felt connected to her? Again, Lacey wondered if he'd given the whole thing a lot more thought than he'd admitted.

The server returned, giving Lacey a much-needed break from the conversation. They both ordered omelets and bacon, and just as they were alone again, a middle-aged man came up to the table.

"'Scuze me, but can you settle a bet?" he asked Roman. "My kid says you're Matteo, number 14? For the Jags?"

Roman's expression slid into a smile that Lacey bet had stopped a few hearts. Hers might have even fluttered a bit.

"Yeah, man. He's right." He leaned back and looked at a boy about ten years old, pointing right at the child. "Go, Jags, buddy."

"Can you..." The man made a gesture of writing.

"Sure, sure." He waved the kid over. "Come on."

Instantly, the boy was up, scrambling over with a pen and paper napkin. "Hi," he said shyly.

"What's your name, big guy?"

"Tyler."

"You play football, Tyler?"

He nodded. "Yeah, but I'm not very good."

"Neither am I or I'd be first string," he joked, taking the pen and scribbling his name and #14 next to it. "Don't give up," he added. "Some of us are just late bloomers."

"Thanks. Thank you." The boy beamed at the autograph. "Roman Matteo. Wow. This is so cool!"

His father nodded and backed away. "Thank you, Mr. Matteo. Sorry to bother you."

"Not at all." Roman gave an easy wave. "It's all good, man."

The other man slowed his step. "You should be first string."

Roman laughed, revealing a set of teeth that would make an orthodontist cry with envy. "Tell the coach."

Then he turned back to Lacey, the interaction leaving a spark in eyes so much like Tessa's, it took her breath away. "Sorry about that."

"No, no. You're so nice. That was really sweet of you."

He looked hard at her for a moment, the gaze intense enough for her to wonder just what he could be thinking.

"I want to meet her," he finally said.

She dropped back against the leather. "I don't know... I'd have to tell her or ask her and...I don't know."

"Well, what did you expect would happen when you contacted me?" The question sounded like a tease, but he had every right to ask that.

She shrugged. "Honestly, I wasn't sure. I wanted to know who you are and if you are happy and good and living a nice life. I wanted to know if...you're like her."

"Am I?"

"Carbon copy," she said. "Just the twenty-five-year-old male version."

He dropped his head back with a groan. "Now I *really* want to meet her. Can I?"

The food came and saved her from answering, but Lacey's mind spun out of control.

What would Tessa say? Would she be mad and betrayed? Or overjoyed and relieved? Would meeting him end Lacey's relationship with that amazing woman, or launch a new, even closer one?

"I took a risk," Lacey confessed as she picked up her fork but merely stared at the omelet. "I kind of moved on instinct and speed."

"That's the only way to live." He lifted a piece of bacon, pointing it toward her. "So, what's on the line? What did you risk, exactly?"

She set her fork down to explain. "Tessa has been like another mother to me," she said. "I was kind of lost professionally and from the moment we met, she took me under her wing and is teaching me her business. We've formed a great bond and she's always joking she wants to steal me from my mom. We're close and connected, and she trusted me with this very deep secret that no one else knows."

He took a bite of the bacon, thinking as he looked at her. "And that's why she told you? Your bond? Maybe she was throwing out a lifeline and hoping you'd do exactly what you've done—find me."

She considered that, and discarded the possibility. If

Tessa wanted to meet him, she could have figured out how. "Actually, she didn't tell me. I guessed it."

"How?"

"She has this expression she wears whenever someone tells her what a great mother she would have been," Lacey said, thinking about the many times she'd seen that look on Tessa's face. "It's like...regret and sadness and longing and disappointment and acceptance all rolled into one. One day, she said something—I don't remember what—and I saw that look and I blurted out the question, asking if she'd ever had a child."

He stared at her, silent.

"She admitted that she had, and recited the day and time and place you were born, with a birth weight, length, and just enough details to make it so, so real. I gave it a week or two, but couldn't stop thinking about it. About...you. So I decided to try and call the hospital and see if I could suss anything from their medical records. I got a chatty lady and—"

"They *told* you?" He seemed surprised—almost as if he'd done the same kind of search and didn't have any luck.

"The woman slipped up and said your last name and mentioned a pediatrician in Satellite Beach. I did some digging and it wasn't that hard to find you."

He exhaled. "Wow. Resourceful. But how did you know I was the right kid?"

"I looked you up, found a picture and..."

"Saw the resemblance?" he guessed.

She nodded. "It's strong. Your eyes, mostly. You just have an air about you that's like her."

He dropped his elbows on the table and looked at her. "Would she recognize me instantly?"

"If she knew who you were, yes."

"What if she didn't?" he asked.

"Then I don't think she'd see it. I mean, if she isn't looking for it, probably not. Honestly, I don't know."

"What if I could find some reason to go to Destin and kind of get to know her...without telling her the truth and breaking your promise to her?"

She pressed her hand on her chest. "I'm not sure I could handle that kind of subterfuge. I almost had a heart attack when she walked in and caught me looking you up on Instagram. I dropped my phone and she looked right at you."

"But no recognition?" he asked.

Shaking her head, she smiled. "No. But I had to lie and I hate that. I really, really hate lying."

"What did you tell her?"

She felt a flush rise as she recalled the exchange. "I said I was on a dating app and...you know."

"Oh?" He chuckled. "Way to think fast, Lacey. I like that."

"It was awful," she told him. "She stared at you and saw your name. Her own...son."

"What did she say?"

"That you're cute."

He smirked and pressed his finger into his cheek and

twisted an imaginary dimple. Then his smile faded. "Well, I guess we have a solution to the dilemma, then."

Her fork froze midway to her mouth. She was not following at all. "We do?"

"I can meet her as your new, uh, boyfriend. Or Tinder date. Or whatever you call it."

The blood whooshed out of her head, leaving her a little dizzy. "*Excuse me?*"

"Timing's perfect," he said as casually as if they were discussing the weather. "I'm free until training starts in Jacksonville. I'm just chilling in Satellite Beach with my parents for the off-season. Which is sad, I know, but they basically live in heaven and I love hanging with them. I can easily find a rental. And I can meet Tessa, get to know her, and—"

"No!"

He flinched at her vehement reaction. "Why not?"

"Because it's totally dishonest," she said. "I can't tell her or anyone that! And, please, who would believe that you, an autograph-giving celebrity athlete, would be on the apps and want *me?*"

Tipping his head, he looked dismayed. "Why not? You're a doll."

A *doll?* She wasn't sure how she should take that, but the butterflies in her stomach certainly liked it.

"I mean, I'd love to go out with you," he added. "Assuming you really are single."

"I am."

"So am I," he said, leaning in over the table. "Let's date."

She searched his face, speechless and lightheaded. "I can't lie like that. I've already broken a promise, but that would be a complete betrayal."

"Not if we're really dating." A half-smile lifted the corner of his lips. "We'll just make it real. Then you'll be telling the truth."

"You're crazy." She pointed at him. "Out of your ever-lovin' mind. Cuckoo for Cocoa Puffs. Completely—"

He put a hand over her pointed finger and lowered it to the table, his palm just rough enough to be incredibly masculine, his touch light enough to make her whole body react. But it was the look in his eyes that nearly did her in.

"I want to meet her," he said. "I don't want you to ruin your relationship with her, I don't want to totally upset her apple cart, and I don't want either of us to lie."

"Well, you'll..." She tried to think straight, but it was hard. Impossible, actually. "You'll have to think of some other ruse. I'm not going to be part of it."

"It's not a *ruse*." He pressed her hand. "We met on an app, went on a lunch date, fell hard for each other, and I decided to spend the rest of my off-season in Destin to see where this might go. And, of course, I'll meet your friend and boss."

"And then what?" she asked, shaking her head at this outrageous scenario.

"Then...I've satisfied my curiosity. I'll go back to playing ball, but instead of wondering, I'll know who gave me life. We don't have to tell her or my parents, you save face, and I get my answers." He finally lifted his hand after he'd basically seared her down to her DNA. "Good idea, huh?"

She tried to breathe, but it wasn't easy. "It's..."

"I know, crazy, Cocoa Puffs, whatever. But deep down, you know it's genius." He grinned at her. "I bet Tessa would love it."

She'd love it if she wasn't on the receiving end of complete and total duplicity.

"I don't think so," she said, glancing at her watch, aching to leave and think and then think some more. "I'm going to slip out, okay?" She picked up her bag and opened it to find her wallet, but he held out his hand.

"I've got it. Can you DM me your number? An address? I'll look for a place—"

"Let me think," she said, slipping out of the booth. "I'll...talk to you."

She darted out on shaky legs, stepping into the sunshine and practically colliding with a tourist.

"'Scuze me," she muttered, looking left and right to get her bearings. After a second, she started walking toward the beach, not sure where she was going or why.

How did she get herself into this? *Date* him? Well, yeah, in another life and for another reason, it would be an absolute dream. Guys like Roman Matteo came along exactly...never.

But to deceive Tessa? And her mother, grandmother, and every other Lawson or Wylie floating around the Summer House? It would be too much.

She hustled toward a wide-open town square, all grass leading to a wooden boardwalk high on a dune. She needed to see the water, to soak in the sun, and think about—

"Lacey!"

Oh, God. He'd followed her.

"Lacey."

She turned slowly, hissing a soft breath as he strolled across the grass toward her, a tall, golden, gorgeous lunatic in a tight gray T-shirt and faded shorts. His hair fluttered in the breeze and his smile grew with each step.

He oozed confidence and playfulness and sincerity and warmth and, oh, man, he *was* Tessa.

She stood stone still, brushing back some hair the Gulf breeze blew over her face. He reached her in ten seconds. Of course. He was a wide receiver. He ran and caught long shots for a living.

Without a word, he extended his arms, wrapped her in a hug, and pulled her straight into a chest of granite.

She looked up at him, lost for a moment, dizzy and confused and...warm.

"I don't know your last name," he muttered.

"Knight."

"Lacey Knight." He squeezed her tighter. "Be my girlfriend, Lacey Knight."

"Roman, I ca—"

He put one finger under her chin and lifted her face a centimeter closer, the gesture sending a bolt of electricity right down to her toes. It was fake, of course, a game of pretend that would end before it could get too real. But right then, it felt...kind of real.

"Please," he whispered. "You won't regret it."

Something told her she very much would. But all she could do was sigh and accept defeat.

Chapter Eight
Tessa

Tessa sat at the dining room table, a cold Pellegrino Essenza in one hand, her laptop open to the Kaplan event. Yes, she had an office in the back now, but it was so bright and cheery out here, with the water view and endless sky. She needed to bask in the beauty of it all while she made her little business happily hum.

Plus, the Summer House was unusually quiet this late afternoon. The only sound was the rustle of the palm fronds outside and the distant waves providing a steady rhythm to her thoughts. Vivien was out running design errands, Mom had gone for a walk, and Maggie was upstairs napping.

And her darling Lacey had gone hours ago to meet a friend from college somewhere down on 30-A. Forcing herself to concentrate on the Pinterest board full of overpriced centerpieces, she put her head back into little Naomi Kaplan's Bat Mitzvah.

A dog? Really, Jennifer?

Naomi's mother's latest idea was a stretch, but it could drive the theme. Apparently, she wanted to get a rescue that Naomi loved as her big "surprise" gift...so an animal-themed party was perfect. But how to pull that off?

She looked up again, squinting at the driveway. Lacey would know. She'd have some good ideas. Where was that girl? She hadn't called or texted all day.

Not that Lacey owed her a minute-by-minute accounting, since she was the world's most underpaid assistant. Tessa had fully approved of her taking some time to herself, but still. It wasn't like her to disappear for hours without checking in.

A while later, Tessa was on an animal-theme roll—was "Stay Wild" too much for a Bat Mitzvah?—when she *finally* heard the front door open.

"Lacey? That you?"

"Yep! It's me!" She sounded breathless and high-pitched as she breezed around the entryway wall, bright-eyed—very bright—with her dark blond locks wild as she dropped her bag on the table.

"Did you drive with the windows open?" Tessa asked. "Or have a drinky lunch?"

She inched back. "No. I didn't drink. And I didn't..." She tried to smooth her hair, her gaze darting around the room, the floor, the kitchen...but not at Tessa. "We walked around Rosemary Beach and went down by the water. That place is so stinking cute. Have you been?"

Well, well, well. Someone looks guilty.

"To Rosemary Beach? Yes. It's very...intentional. And precious." Tessa lowered the laptop screen, eyeing her young protégé and good friend who seemed...nervous. "Did you have fun?"

"So much," she said, heading into the kitchen to grab a glass and fill it with water. "Where is everyone?"

"Out and about." Tessa watched her lift the glass to her lips and could have sworn her hand was shaking. What was up? "So, tell me about your friend, Lace."

Lacey choked a little, but managed to get her sip down. "Oh, he was..."

"He?" Tessa raised a brow. "I thought you said it was a girl from college."

"No...a guy." She took another drink and stood awkwardly in the kitchen, like she wasn't sure if she should sit or keep walking.

Tessa leaned back on two legs of the dining room chair, trying not to snicker. "Do you really think you can keep it from me?"

Lacey paled. "Keep...what?"

"Was it...Romeo?"

Her eyes widened to shocked blue saucers.

"Whatever his name was," Tessa said. "The guy you're talking to on the dating app."

"Roman." Lacey croaked the name and took another drink, making Tessa chuckle.

"Did you have a date with him?" she asked.

Lacey kept drinking. Gulping, actually.

Tessa let the front legs of the chair hit the floor.

"You did! And you're keeping it from me, you little brat!" She snapped the laptop fully closed, officially ending work in exchange for good old-fashioned fun. "I want every single detail, not a thing left out. Everything."

Lacey lowered the glass and tried to swallow. Finally, she shook her head. "Not much to—"

"Lacey Knight!" Tessa shot up. "What was he like? Is he nice? Do you like him? Are you going to see him again?"

Lacey groaned and came toward the island. "Fine. Yes, I had a...date. I guess I like him. And, uh, yeah, I will see him again. I think."

Tessa crossed her arms, proud of herself. "I totally knew it. You should never play poker, Lace. You're the worst liar."

Lacey winced. "Really?"

"That's a good thing." Tessa dropped onto a barstool, spinning it around and propping her elbows on the counter, chin on knuckles. "Tell me about him."

"Tessa! Why does it matter so much?"

"Because I'm bored, haven't had a date in a thousand years, and you look like this was fantastic with a capital fan." She waved her hand around the island and gestured to the next stool. "Come, sit, spill the tea until I'm drowning in it."

On a huff, she came and sat down. "Well, it was..."

Before Lacey could finish, Vivien walked in through the side door, grocery bags in her arms.

"Who taught my mother how to text?" she asked. "I got sixteen messages at Publix. Apparently the Bolognese was such a success, they're trying their hand at stroganoff tonight."

"Do you need help with the bags, Mom?" Lacey asked, already up and obviously looking for an escape.

"Not so fast." Tessa snagged her T-shirt sleeve. "Now you have to spill to both of us."

"Spill what?" Vivien asked, unloading the bags. "And, no, I don't need help. This is everything."

"Lacey's been on a secret lunch date that lasted..." She glanced at her watch. "Many hours."

Vivien's eyes widened. "You met someone? How?"

"On an app," Tessa answered for her. "His name is Romeo."

"No!" Vivien gasped.

"It's *Roman*," Lacey said with an exasperated laugh. "Not Romeo."

"I like Romeo," Tessa joked, sliding off the stool to help Vivien with the groceries. "And, apparently, so does your daughter, because she's been stammering and blushing since she walked in the door."

"I didn't even know you were on the dating apps, Lace," Vivien said.

"I did." Tessa gave a smug smile. "See? She's more my daughter than yours."

Vivien shot a playful dirty look. "Fine. But I get to wear the mother-of-the-bride dress."

"Have at it," Tessa said. "I'll do the toast, 'cause I'm funnier."

"I can—"

"Stop!" Lacey exclaimed, holding up a hand and looking truly troubled.

Instantly, their smiles disappeared and Vivien put an arm around her. "Honey, we're just having a little—"

"No, no. Just...don't." She exhaled, visibly upset. "It's not funny."

Vivien squeezed her. "I'm sorry, Lace. We won't tease you about him."

Tessa just smiled. She might tease her, but only because this reaction? The girl had it bad.

"Okay, I'll tell you about him, but don't...we're not getting married, okay?"

"You never know," Tessa murmured.

"*I* know," Lacey shot back. "But as for Roman-not-Romeo, he's...he's..." She dug for a word, some color leaving her face again as she stared at Vivien. "He's great," she finally breathed.

So, so bad.

Vivien tried not to react, but her expression said she was thinking the same thing. She stepped away from Lacey and tried to busy herself with groceries. "So, what does he do?"

Lacey sighed, then relented with a small smile. "He plays football. For the Jaguars."

Vivien nearly dropped a loaf of sourdough. "Wait, *seriously?* Like, *professionally?*"

"Oh, I forgot you told me that," Tessa said, remembering when Lacey dropped her phone and admitted she had another life—a real one.

"You knew?" Vivien asked.

Tessa gave a smug shrug. "Of course I knew."

Vivien ignored the flex and concentrated on Lacey. "So you're dating an NFL player."

"I guess." Lacey tried to sound like it was no big deal.

"He's second-string right now, wide receiver. But he played at UF and was kind of a, um, big thing there."

Tessa let out a low whistle because who *wouldn't?* "Set the bar high, I say."

"I thought those guys went out with, like, movie stars and famous singers," Vivien said.

"Right?" Lacey threw her hands up, as if equally stunned to have caught this guy's eye.

"Well, he has good taste," Tessa said. "Who wants a movie star when you can have Lacey Knight?"

Vivien reached over the counter to give Tessa a high-five and a grin. "You bet, co-mama."

Lacey groaned.

"Just accept it, Lace," Tessa said. "You have two mothers now and we're you're biggest cheerleaders. Also, how can you date a guy who lives in Jacksonville? Is that where the Jags are?"

She nodded. "It's the off-season and he's thinking... well, he is coming to Destin. Soon. Like this week. He's going to rent a place, I think."

"Why?" Vivien asked. "Just to...see you?"

"You don't have to sound shocked," Tessa said. "She's a catch."

"He likes the water and likes to...fish," Lacey said. "So that's what he's catching. Trout. Not...me."

Vivien snorted and shared a look with Tessa.

"That's what he said," Lacey told them. "He grew up on the water over on the east coast, lived in a house with a dock, and now he wants to spend a month in Destin. Fishing."

"I like a guy who can fish," Tessa mused, crossing her arms. "Like my dad. It's so down-to-earth and humble. Is he?"

"Surprisingly, yes," Lacey said. "And, oh, I forgot you said your dad liked to fish. That's...yeah. Cool."

Tessa eyed her, not sure why that sounded weird, but it did.

"A humble NFL player," Vivien mused as she opened the fridge to fill it with some more food. "That's got to be unusual."

"He is...unusual," Lacey said, unable to fight a smile. "Really nice."

"To look at," Tessa teased.

Lacey just shrugged. "He's...yeah. A ten. And a half." She let out a sigh as if the whole conversation was just too much for her. "You'll see," she added.

"Oh?" Vivien turned. "We get to meet him?"

"I think so." She pressed her hands together and then wiped them on her jeans. "Why not? And, um, Tess. How's the Bat Mitzvah planning? What was Jennifer's 'outrageous request'? Did you pick a theme? Find the DJ? I bet I have a ton to do."

"What you have to do," Tessa said, sliding off the barstool, "is go for a boat ride with me."

"Now?" Lacey asked.

"End of a busy day and you, my darling girl, need to unwind. And I need air, sunshine, and salt spray. I'll fill you in on the Kaplan event—brace yourself, because there's a trip to a dog refuge in your near future. But let's hit the harbor and sip some G&Ts. You in, Viv?"

"I would, but I promised my mother I'd be here while she and Jo Ellen tackle stroganoff. Is she still napping?"

"Yeah, but she'll be down any minute," Tessa said. "So, Lace, boat?"

Lacey hesitated for half a second, then shook her head. "I can't, Tessa. I have...so much to do."

Tessa lifted a brow, not believing her, but she let it go. If she wanted to hide in a new love bubble and skip a sunset cruise, it was up to her.

"I'll be upstairs," she said, slipping away before Vivien or Tessa could stop her.

When she was gone, they just looked at each other.

"She's finished," Tessa whispered.

"I haven't seen her this way since Spencer O'Keefe asked her to prom."

Tessa clapped her hands and gave a little squeal. "Our girl's in love!"

Vivien beamed. "I just want her to be happy and with a great guy."

"Right? And don't wear pink to her wedding. I want to wear pink," Tessa said. "It's my signature color."

Vivien rolled her eyes and then they hugged like two happy moms with high hopes and big dreams for their favorite girl. Tessa added a squeeze, wishing she could tell Vivien how much this meant to her.

She'd given up her baby years ago, but her dear friend was generously letting her share this special, special daughter. What a treasure they both were.

July 2, 1991

OH. MY. GOSH. Today was maybe the BEST DAY of the summer so far. I am writing this on my bed and I'm smiling like a total dork!!!

So after breakfast, all the parents decided we should have some "family fun" together. (Dad was here, too. He's usually only here on weekends but he's taking this week off for July 4th.) Anyhoo, "some family fun" can possibly mean "something lame" but this time they picked GOOFY GOLF!!!

It's that mini golf place near the highway in Fort Walton Beach with the giant dinosaurs and Humpty Dumpty and all the weird statues that are probably haunted. Tessa and I screamed when we found out, because it's basically our FAVORITE place ever. I've wanted to go back since last summer when a little kid got stuck in the gorilla mouth and they had to call the fire department.

Kate pronounced it "iconic" even though Tessa and I don't even know what that means.

We all piled into two cars but I got stuck in van steerage with Crista who brought a whole backpack of Barbies and took up 85% of the space. Who needs Barbies at mini golf?

We got to the course and it was SO HOT I thought my hair was going to catch on fire. But it didn't matter because the second we got our rainbow-colored golf balls (mine was purple, well known by all as my favorite color), I knew this was going to be a fabulously awesome day.

Peter (♥) looked SO CUTE in his backwards Braves cap. He always smells like spearmint gum and sunscreen. I made Tessa go behind me in the order because I didn't want to be stuck between her and Kate while they were arguing about whether or not putting is a real sport.

Peter went first and got a par, then I stepped up and WHAM—hole in one. Not kidding. ON THE FIRST HOLE. He smiled at me and said, "Nice shot, kid." KID. UGH. But also...he noticed!!!

Tessa kept cheating (she says it's "strategy" to move her ball four inches closer to the hole) and Kate was SO SERIOUS like we were on a real golf course. Eli mostly tried to act cool and didn't care, but he DID yell at Peter for putting too close to the edge and almost knocking Crista into the hippo pond. It was chaos.

By the 18th hole, we were all sweating buckets and Eli tried to convince us that moss was edible (it's NOT). But guess who had the best score? ME!!!! VIVIEN LEIGH LAWSON.

Even better than Peter. By two points. And when I told him, he did this cute smile and said,

"Well, guess I've been dethroned. You're officially the champ."

Then (I CAN'T BELIEVE THIS HAPPENED) he took off his Braves hat and put it on my head and said, "Champ gets the crown."

I wore that hat the WHOLE ride home and kept it in my room since he didn't demand to get it back. Tessa said it smells like a locker room but I don't even care.

Anyway, I'm going to try and sleep now but I might just float away because the boy I've been crushing on gave me his hat and called me champ and didn't even make fun of me when I tripped on the sidewalk (which happened, by the way. Not my finest moment).

BEST. DAY. EVER.

Viv

P.S. Tomorrow we're going to the water park and I swear on Peter's Braves cap I'm going to finally go down the big slide. Even if I scream the whole way.

Chapter Nine
Vivien

"Now what?" Peter drove with one hand resting on the steering wheel, the other lazily tapping his thigh to the beat of a classic rock song that hummed from the speakers. The glow of a lovely dinner lingered over both of them and the sun had just disappeared over the horizon, painting the sky in a mix of coral and the soft purple of twilight.

"It's still light," she said. "We should do something fun."

Something fun. The words instantly reminded Vivien of the diary entry she'd read last night. Silly, childish, but now so crystal clear in her memory.

"What?" he asked, catching her smile.

"Does the name Goofy Golf mean anything to you?"

He choked a laugh. "It's still here, you know."

"No! Seriously?"

He glanced into the rearview mirror and pulled into the far left lane. "Wrong direction, right idea."

"We can go? Now?"

He laughed. "You sound like little Vivien, all excited to go to the putt-putt place."

"Do you remember when we used to go?" she asked.

"Because I just read all about one of those unforgettable days in my decades-old diary."

"Oh, that diary again." He grinned at her. "Did I brush sand from your face or help you up after a fall?"

"Worse. I beat you by two strokes and you put your Braves cap on my head. I might not have washed my hair for a week."

He belly laughed. "It is so time for a rematch. I do have a distinct memory of you wearing that hat for three days. I had to steal it back when you weren't looking."

"And you called me 'champ.'" She reached over and put her hand on his shoulder. "*Champ.*"

He took her hand and threaded their fingers, giving her knuckles the lightest kiss. "That'll be the last time for that. I'm very competitive, you know."

"Oh, I remember."

"I took my boys there when they were little," he said after making a U-turn and heading toward Fort Walton Beach. "We were in Destin for some reason and I remembered it was fun. I swear Humpty Dumpty still has that chip on his foot."

"How are your sons doing?" she asked. "Any chance they'll come over to see you while you're here? I'd love to meet them."

"They're busy but I'd love for you to meet them," he said. "Cam's doing a special assignment at the police academy, so when that's done, he could come over."

She loved that his older son wanted to follow in his footsteps with a career in law enforcement. It said a lot about his parenting. "And Connor? I guess he can't just slip away from dental school."

"He's up to his eyeballs in finals."

"Which I imagine are no joke at UF."

"Connor doesn't joke—he studies. But when the semester ends, he'll want to leave Gainesville, so maybe he'll come, too." He added a squeeze to their joined hands, resting on his thigh. "That is, if I'm still here this summer."

True. He was here for work, and that could end. "I know you want to find a lead, but maybe you'll still be tracking your missing man."

"Case is cold," he said. "The PD might call me back at any time for bigger problems."

Her heart dropped. She didn't want him to leave, but his home was in Pensacola, an hour away. They'd find a new normal. Wouldn't they?

She just wasn't sure what it was and from the look on his face? Neither was he.

They didn't get a chance to discuss it because the massive red Goofy Golf sign grabbed their attention.

Mid-week, with most of the spring break crowds finally thinning, the parking lot at Goofy Golf was only half full. There were some families and a group of teenagers taking pictures with the enormous green dinosaur.

Still holding hands, they walked toward the entrance.

"Wow." Vivien sighed out the word, a hundred different emotions bubbling inside.

"I know," Peter said. "It hasn't changed."

She looked up at him, focusing on one of those emotions—the strongest one. "It's so comfortable," she whispered.

"Goofy Golf?"

"No. Us—our shared history. It's so nice to know someone that long and have all those old memories."

He narrowed his brown eyes and leaned in. "Not too comfortable, I hope." He closed the space with the lightest kiss. "Don't trap me in the Friend Zone, Viv."

Her heart tumbled around, wondering if that's what she was doing. She inched back and looked up at him, not exactly sure what to say. "Depends on if you let me win or not."

"*Not*," he said. "You are not stealing a favorite article of clothing for another three days."

"Okay...then let's see who the champ is now."

Laughing, Peter ushered her to the entrance, paid for their round and handed her a purple ball. "I seem to recall you like this color."

She took it from him, inexplicably pleased that he remembered that one little detail about teenage Vivien. "The color of champions."

They set off down the first hole, weaving through a fiberglass jungle of oversized animals and strange fake buildings. Every statue was just as bizarre and delightful as she remembered—creepy clowns, off-kilter castles, and a kangaroo with a golf club glued to its paw.

Peter took his time lining up his first shot, shimmying his shoulders like he was on the opening hole of the Masters. "You ready for this level of skill?"

"Please. You peaked in 1990."

He laughed and took his shot, brushing against her as he stepped aside to let her line up. "Let me know if I can put my arms around you and help you with that weak-sauce stance."

"Hush your smack talk, Detective. Don't mess with the champ." She tapped the ball, which barely made it toward the green. "Okay, okay. I need to warm up."

"Take all the time you need, Viv." He gave her another light kiss on the top of her head just before taking his shot—and sinking it—but something was tugging at the back of her mind.

Not something—someone.

Danny.

Now, *he* wasn't comfortable. Was that good—or bad? And why was she thinking about him?

She was on a date with Peter, a man she adored. But she kept thinking about Danny, with his roguish grin and easy wit and million-dollar lifestyle. He made her feel like she was twenty-five and giddy, not a fifty-year-old divorcee trying to rebuild a fairly shattered life with an old...friend? Crush?

Really, what *was* Peter in her life?

Peter gave her a playful nudge as she put her putter behind the ball. "You're over-thinking, Champ."

Was she ever.

She blew the putt just as the phone she'd slipped into her pocket hummed. "That doesn't count. My phone's ringing."

"Champs don't cheat."

"Tessa did," she said on a laugh, pulling out her phone. "It's Eli. I better take this."

"I'll shoot for you," he said, stepping to her ball.

"Thanks. Hey, Eli," she said as she brought the phone to her ear. "You will never believe where we are right now! Goofy—"

"I'm a grandfather," he said, his voice thick with emotion.

"What?" she shrieked just as Peter sunk the ball. "The baby was born?"

"A boy. Seven pounds and...some ounces. I don't know. Healthy and good. They're naming him Atlas."

"Atlas? That's ambitious and beautiful, Eli! So awesome! I'm happy for you and Jonah. And Carly— maybe we'll get to meet her and the baby soon."

Peter came to stand next to her, and she tapped the speaker button so he could congratulate his friend.

"Way to go, Pops," he said with a huge smile. "Now which one of us is officially old?"

Eli laughed. "It's surreal, you know?"

"How's Jonah?" Vivien asked, thinking of her passionate and extraordinary nephew. "I sure hope this doesn't change his mind about the culinary arts program here in Destin, but I couldn't blame him if it did."

"I don't know. He's dazed. Long labor, but he was there and got to cut the cord. He's over the moon and probably has no idea what hit him."

Vivien laughed softly. "I can believe it. I'm so happy for you. And welcome to the family, little Atlas. Hope the weight of the world isn't on his seven-pound shoulders."

"Right? So, where are you guys?" Eli asked.

"Goofy Golf," they answered in unison.

Eli hooted. "Oh, you kids. Have fun. I want to call Kate and share the news."

"All right. I'll be home in a bit," Vivien said. "How's Mom?"

"Great-grandma Maggie? On a stinking cloud. She and Jo have decided to tackle baking, so I hope you want baby celebration cake when you get home."

Smiling from the call and the news and the rightness of the world at that moment, Vivien slid her arm around Peter's waist as they walked to the next hole, talking about the new arrival.

The call brought an even brighter spirit to the competition, the two of them laughing non-stop until they finished the seventeenth hole, when they realized they were tied.

"Okay, this is serious business," Peter said at the entrance to a narrow tunnel guarded by a ridiculous goblin statue. "I cannot let you whip me again."

"You can and you will." She angled her head. "You want to go first?"

"Sure." Peter lined up his shot, tongue between his teeth, full concentration. She took the chance to just... look at him, and appreciate that Peter McCarthy was still as attractive to her as he'd been when he was seventeen and crowned her a champ.

He was in good shape at fifty-three, a tall, strong, protective man who cared deeply about people, and his purpose in life.

He still made her feel things. She just didn't quite know what they were.

He took his putt and watched the ball roll close to the hole and...stop, making him grunt in frustration. "Okay, Viv. You're up and you need a hole in one to win or a shot that great to tie."

She inhaled as she walked to the tee. "What do I get if I win?"

"A kiss."

"And if I lose?"

"You have to answer a very serious question."

She looked up from the ball, surprised by the somber note. "Okay. What's it about?"

He didn't answer, so she pulled her putter back to take the shot.

"Us."

She tapped the ball sideways, glaring at him. "You did that on purpose."

"All's fair..." He walked to his ball, knocked it in, then bent over to retrieve it from the cup. "In love and friendship." He straightened and looked right at her. "I just don't know which one this is...yet."

She stood very still, holding his gaze, aware that her palms were damp and her world could very easily shift depending on how she responded to that.

"Is that the question?" she finally asked.

"No." He tipped his head toward the ball. "If you make this shot, we tie and you don't have to answer my question. If you miss, I'll ask."

As she put her putter behind the ball, her heart

slammed against her ribs, and not because she gave a hoot about this game.

But she cared very much for Peter. This wasn't just a summer crush anymore. He was a man with a life, with roots. What was he going to ask her?

She took her shot, missing by a foot. From behind her, he slid both arms around her and pulled her into his chest. She could feel his heartbeat, too, and the sheer strength of a man she trusted.

"Viv," he whispered into her ear. "I want to be more than your friend with history. I want to be with you. I want...us." He turned her around slowly and looked down at her. "Is that possible or am I dreaming?"

She inhaled softly, lost in his gaze, vaguely aware of the next group of golfers coming to the eighteenth tee. She swallowed, silent. After a moment, they heard the others' laughter, waiting for them to leave the green as they teed up.

"Come on," he said gruffly. "We'll finish off the course."

They walked to the car in a companionable silence, holding hands, the weight of his question pressing on her.

As they reached his car, he stopped at the passenger side, pulling her into an embrace. "Listen. Just so I'm clear. I don't have to go back to Pensacola."

She drew back. "You don't?"

"I've infiltrated the Destin PD—in a good way. The chief offered me a job here, which is very alluring. I could stay—sell my house, buy something here. I could stay. For you."

For *her?*

"Peter, I..." She exhaled slowly. "That's...wow."

"I've been holding back, Vivien. I know you're just out of a long marriage and I know exactly what's involved with a divorce. But this opportunity came up and I wouldn't consider it, if not for you."

"That's a lot to put on me."

"I know," he agreed instantly. "But I care about you. I think—no, I know—we could be happy together."

"Oh." She tried to breathe again. "But Cameron's at the Pensacola police academy. And when Connor finishes dental school, won't he go back home near you?"

"They're grown men," he said with a shrug. "I'm not going to choose my home base because of where they are."

"But you'd choose it because of me?"

"Yes," he said without hesitation. "At least I would if I believed there is a real future for us."

"Of course there is," she said. She just didn't quite know what it looked like.

She wanted to say yes. She wanted to leap into this moment, let herself believe that the boy she'd once fantasized about had somehow grown into the man she could love.

But Danny's face flashed through her mind. That reckless spark. That inconvenient flutter of excitement she hadn't felt in years. Not to mention, her divorce papers had barely just been signed. And that was honestly far more of a deterrent than a flirtation with a client.

"Peter," she said softly. "I... I don't know what I'm ready for. I'm still figuring everything out. I love spending time with you. I just... I need a little more time."

He nodded. "Take all the time you need. I'm here for a while, then..." He pulled out his phone. "Hang on." He frowned, reading the text. "Oh, wow. This is big."

"You found the missing guy?" she asked, her heart tumbling. That meant he'd leave, unless she—

"Do you think Maggie and Jo Ellen are still up?" he asked, the question throwing her a little.

"Yes—baking a great-grandmother celebration cake, according to Eli. Why?"

"I have news about your father's case. We should go see them."

"Okay." She broke away as he reached to open the car door.

"And Viv," he added, smiling at her. "I don't mean to pressure you. Take your time. I got carried away with the thrill of victory."

She just smiled at him and slid into her seat, her heart full and confused. Had her teenage heartthrob just asked her for...a future?

She glanced at the Goofy Golf sign as he rounded the car to climb in. Iconic, indeed.

VIVIEN OPENED the front door to the Summer House and frowned at the muffled sound she heard. Was that... someone crying?

The strangled noise was followed by a deep gasp, a wheeze, and...a snort?

"Jo! Get ahold of yourself!" Maggie exclaimed, but she didn't sound like Maggie. She wasn't mad and she certainly wasn't crying.

Was Jo Ellen? Had a bout of grief—

"I can't!" Jo Ellen shouted, then a gale of giggles followed. "Look at that! Mags! I've seen five-year-olds do better! And that color! You had a great-grandson, not a Smurf!"

Maggie choked a laugh. "Fine. Icing isn't my forte. And that's supposed to be a globe, for Atlas. You want to do—" She looked up and saw Vivien come in from the entry. "Oh, hello."

"Hello." Vivien paused at the sight of Maggie and Jo Ellen smearing bright blue icing on a sheet cake, wearing the aprons that Kate and Jonah used to love when they cooked. "This looks like fun."

Her mother almost looked embarrassed to be accused of having fun. But she didn't deny she'd been caught in a moment of sheer abandon with her former best friend.

Jo Ellen didn't look guilty or ashamed. She wore a huge smile, a dab of blue icing on her cheek, and the first real glint Vivien had seen in the grieving woman's eyes.

"We baked a cake!" she announced. "A baby boy cake. With...a globe. Or something."

"I see that." Vivien came closer, glancing at the ... creation. "It's a masterpiece."

Maggie gave her a dark look. "It's a mess," she shot

back, sounding much more like the mother Vivien knew and expected to find. "We attempted baking."

"We should stick with cooking," Jo Ellen said dryly, then elbowed Maggie. "Nothing ventured, right?"

Maggie rolled her eyes and tried to smooth the icing some more, then looked over Vivien's shoulder. "Hello, Peter."

"Maggie, Jo Ellen." He came to the island counter and took a long look at the cake, then up at them. "Looks delicious. I say you should never judge a cake by its icing."

"Smart man." Maggie took her icing tool to the sink to rinse it off. "How was dinner?"

"We need to talk," Peter said, making Maggie freeze in the act of flipping the faucet. Slowly, she turned, dropping the icing knife in the sink unrinsed.

"Is something wrong?" Jo Ellen came around the island. "Is it about Artie?"

Peter angled his head. "I just got a message that kind of changes the game."

"Hardly a game," Maggie said under her breath, coming closer and leaning on the counter to look at him. "What is it?"

"I have a friend in the FBI, based in D.C. He's pretty high up the food chain, so he was able to access some rather, uh, elusive information."

The words touched Vivien—how sweet of him to care so much about their situation that he'd pressed a friend for sensitive information. Points for Peter, who opted not to tell her whatever he'd learned while they drove home. He said he wanted to tell Maggie and Jo Ellen first.

But Maggie didn't look grateful for his effort, or his secrecy. "The FBI? This wasn't a federal case, even though there was tax evasion. Roger was charged by the Atlanta police department. Why would the FBI get involved?"

"I don't know, but there's a case file," he said. "And normally I would think that meant Roger's crimes were worse than you thought and crossed state lines. And, of course, federal tax evasion, but I hear what you're saying. This is the first I've heard of the feds being involved, so I'm surprised, too."

Jo Ellen turned to her friend. "Surely you would know if your own husband was investigated by the FBI, Mags."

"Not at all," she countered. "He protected me from the whole thing. He didn't want me included in the slightest. He was absolutely insistent that the less I knew, the better."

Vivien made a face as she pulled out a stool to sit at the counter. "I would think he'd have wanted your help, Mom. You're so smart and resourceful."

"Well, he didn't." She looked hard at Peter. "What else did you find out?"

"That the investigation team was CCSG, out of Biloxi, Mississippi."

All three women just stared at him.

"Crime and Corruption in Sport and Gaming," he explained. "Did Roger gamble?"

"No!" Maggie pressed her hands to her chest, aghast at the suggestion, which almost made Vivien laugh.

He'd committed fraud five ways from Sunday, stole from clients, and laundered some cash, but the man did not gamble. Maggie's defense of her late husband was consistent, if nothing else.

"He would never gamble," Maggie insisted. "He didn't bet on races, or...or associate with people who did."

"Yes, he did," Jo Ellen said, making them all look at her. "We all did, even if we didn't know it."

"What are you talking about?" Maggie demanded.

"Frank Cavallari had his fingers in all that stuff," she said.

"Of course," Peter said, nodding. "I had heard a rumor that the deli was a hot spot for illegal lotteries and betting. Years ago, it wasn't unusual for small businesses like that to be a central receiving place for bets and payouts. Frank was likely a bookie who got a cut of the numbers they ran."

"What does that have to do with Roger?" Maggie asked, looking from one to the other, and settling on Jo Ellen. "We bought Italian food from that store and went out to dinner with Frank and Betty. No...gambling."

"But plenty of drinking," Jo Ellen murmured. "Frank and Betty could put it away."

"But that doesn't mean my husband was a gambler." Maggie took a deep inhale, the first sign that she was about to lose her temper. "And Frank Cavallari had nothing to do with Roger's...problems. The situation was in Atlanta, around Roger's business. When he was here, he was free of it all."

"Maybe, maybe not," Peter said. "If Frank was somehow part of organized crime, maybe he roped Roger into working with him, even starting an arm of the gambling business in Atlanta. That would explain the FBI's involvement."

"How does it change the game?" Vivien asked, remembering what Peter had said earlier. "Does this mean my mom and Jo Ellen can't get the answers to what Artie did and why?"

"Artie didn't do anything," Jo Ellen said.

Maggie sniffed. "Except turn my husband in to the police."

The two of them glared at each other, tumbling right back to square one.

"It means getting background information or files will be impossible," Peter told Vivien. "My contact said the files were transferred to federal offices and sealed, which explains why the attorney can't find them. It's essentially a brick wall that will not come down."

For a moment, no one said anything, but Maggie looked at Jo Ellen, that silent communication they always seemed to share ricocheting between the two women.

"I know what we can do," Maggie said softly.

Jo Ellen nodded. "Yeah."

Peter and Vivien glanced at each other, lost.

"We'll have to talk to Frank and Betty," Maggie said. "They're the only stone we haven't turned over."

"But don't get your hopes up, Mags," Jo Ellen warned her. "Frank never talked about that unsavory stuff."

Maggie lifted a brow. "But Betty talked. At least she did after three glasses of chianti."

"Then let's go," Jo Ellen agreed. "And we'll take a bottle."

"I think it's good to go on a fact-finding mission," Peter said. "But be careful and subtle."

"You think it's dangerous?" Vivien asked, a skitter of fear going up her spine.

"No, but...I wouldn't want to wake up the FBI any more than we already have. The last thing you need is to have them come sniffing around this house and the profit it represents."

Maggie paled at the words. "You're right. But I still want to talk to them. We'll be subtle." She threw a look at Jo Ellen. "At least I will be."

"Yeah, you're so subtle, Mags," Jo Ellen said dryly. "As understated as Smurf-blue icing."

The air of friendship blew through the room again as they offered Peter a piece of cake. He politely declined cake, and after a few minutes, Vivien walked him to the front door.

Stepping outside, she looked up at him. The night air felt heavier now, thick with old secrets and fresh uncertainty.

"You okay?" he asked.

"A little overwhelmed," she admitted. "It was a lot tonight—feds involved and a baby born and..."

"Losing at mini-golf," he finished for her.

She laughed. "Yeah, a champ no more."

He wrapped his arms around her and gave her a light kiss. "You still won my heart."

"Oh, Peter." She dropped her head on his shoulder and sighed.

"We'll figure it out," he whispered, giving her such a classy way out.

After one more sweet kiss, she watched him walk to his car and drive off.

Vivien stood outside a moment longer, staring out into the dark, wondering as much about the past as the future.

Chapter Ten
Maggie

"Don't you think it's rude to just show up unannounced and uninvited?" Jo Ellen asked from the passenger seat, one arm around her handbag like it was a baby, the other gripping the door as though Maggie's driving was going to kill them both. "You always follow social protocol, Mags. Also, would it kill you to use a turn signal?"

"This isn't a social protocol situation, and I haven't seen a turn signal since we got on the road," Maggie replied as she navigated—rather well, in her opinion—the heavy traffic. "I don't want to stand out as a tourist."

Jo snorted and let it drop. "But we're just going to knock on their front door?"

"That's what Kate and Eli did," she said, recalling her conversation with her son this morning. "No one had a heart attack. It's fine if we just arrive."

Jo Ellen sighed and studied the shops going by. "Kate and Eli. Who'd have ever thought that would be a thing?"

"It's not a *thing*," Maggie said quickly. "They're friends."

"Friends who kiss, talk on the phone every day, and can't wait to see each other again."

Maggie let her eyes shutter, not quite ready to accept that relationship yet. What would Roger say? After he stopped spinning in his grave, that was.

"What? Why don't you like them together, Mags?" Jo Ellen pressed when she didn't answer.

"You know why," she finally replied. "It's bad enough that the kids have all become friends again and you and I are spending endless hours reminiscing and laughing and cooking and falling back into old patterns. But if Eli marries a Wylie..."

"You think they'll get *married*?" Jo couldn't keep the note of excitement out of her voice.

"No. Maybe. I don't know." Maggie shot her a look. "We made promises, Jo. Both of us."

"Did that include our kids?"

"I don't *know*," she repeated on a huffed breath. "But that's why we're going on this mission."

"To solve *The Case of the Mysterious Promise*." Jo sang the words, making Maggie smile even though she didn't want to.

"I hate to break it to you, Jo, but at seventy-eight? We're more *Murder She Wrote* than Nancy Drew."

"I hope there's no murder," Jo muttered. "Just a dumb promise."

"We don't know if it was dumb," Maggie said, spying her next turn—and using the signal this time. "Here's the bridge to Santa Rosa Beach, so maybe we'll find out soon."

"What are we going to say?" Jo Ellen asked. "Do we tell them everything?"

"I don't know," Maggie admitted. "But I sure want to know why Frank told Eli that you and Roger had an affair—"

"And Betty told Kate that you and Artie did."

They both chuckled at how preposterous either scenario was, but their smiles faded after a few seconds.

"Maybe they were sauced," Jo Ellen said as she shifted in her seat. "Kate said they broke out the limoncello."

"Frank's favorite," Maggie recalled. "Betty liked her wine. Remember how she'd bring it to the beach in a thermos? I was always so afraid Crista would drink it by accident."

"She was fun, though," Jo Ellen said. "Remember the disco ball in the middle of the deli?"

"Do I remember? I told her it was the definition of tacky and you know what she said?"

"No, what?"

"My 'obsession' with *Gone With the Wind* was tacky. She told me I shouldn't have named Vivien after a movie star." She gave a sly smile. "So I threatened to hit her with my gold-dipped brick from Loew's Grand Theater in Atlanta."

"You have one?" Jo Ellen asked.

"Roger bought it for me at a silent auction fundraiser. It's got a plaque on it with the date of the premier in 1939." She sighed. "There was nothing that man wouldn't do for me."

"Except, you know, not commit crimes."

She fumed at Jo Ellen's whispered comment, biting back a response. She was right, and Maggie knew it.

"They live on the next corner," she said, turning onto a tree-lined street and slowing at a one-story brick house with a gaudy red front door.

"Way to be subtle, Betty," Maggie muttered as she pulled into the driveway.

"The landscaping is gorgeous," Jo Ellen mused, taking in a riot of bougainvillea and well-tended plant beds. "Frank must still like to garden. Glad they're not too old for that."

"Just pray their memories still work," Maggie said.

As they climbed out of the SUV, the front door opened and a much older version of Frank Cavallari stood peering suspiciously at them. At eighty-seven, his hair was thinner and all white, and his bushy brows more salt than pepper. He'd never been a tall man, but he'd shrunk to about Maggie's height of five-foot-six, and the sorry-looking overalls he wore just made him look shorter.

He took a step out to the small porch, clearly wary of them. "You ladies sellin' something? 'Cause I ain't buyin'."

Maggie stiffened, lifting her chin as they reached him, noticing that his brown eyes were still penetrating, if a little cloudy and surrounded by deep wrinkles. Did she look that much older, too? Probably, but in true Scarlett O'Hara fashion, she didn't want to think about that right now.

"Frank Cavallari," she started. "You don't remember—"

"Maggie!" He spread his arms and swooped her into a hug, surprisingly strong for his shrunken body. "And Jo Ellen?" Another hug, then he yelled over his shoulder, "Betty, get yourself out here, woman! Maggie and Jo Ellen are here! In the flesh!"

Maggie couldn't help smiling at the response, but she didn't know why she'd be surprised. They'd left on fine terms that last summer. She and Roger had had one more dinner with Frank and Betty after the Wylies left in such a hurry. Neither one of them breathed a word about the big fight, or that the Wylies had left for any reason other than Artie's job.

They'd all lost touch shortly after the hurricane that hit in September, so there'd be no reason *not* to have a loving reunion.

"Mags and Jo?" Betty called from inside the house just before appearing in the entryway. She gasped and covered her mouth. "Are you kidding me?"

She came out and they hugged again, a little more effusively than Maggie liked, but there was never any stopping Betty Cavallari. She'd aged a little better than Frank—pickled from all that chianti, no doubt—though her hair was white and she'd put on a decent amount of weight, most of it in her bosom.

But her laugh hadn't changed, nor her bright and warm smile, flashy earrings, or the bubblegum pink top they matched.

After the infernal hugging finally ended, Frank invited them in, sweeping them past a formal living area into the kitchen. With non-stop chatter—mostly from

Betty—they eventually took seats around a breakfast table in a nook overlooking one of those fake Florida reservoirs that people called "lakes."

Betty insisted on bringing out her powdered sugar cookies and Maggie and Jo Ellen accepted her offer of some coffee. While she brewed a pot, Betty beamed her huge smile at them.

"So I guess you heard your kids were here a while back," she said. "Surprised us just like you two."

Jo Ellen nodded. "Kate told me all about your visit."

"And everything you said," Maggie added, getting a raised eyebrow from Betty. Well, too bad. She was not interested in beating around the bush with small talk. They could do that later, but she had too many questions that had to be answered.

"I don't know what all we said," Betty responded. "But they told us you two hadn't talked in thirty years. Happy to see you're best girlfriends again."

"I wouldn't go *that* far," Maggie said dryly.

Frank gave her a smirk. "So you haven't lost your, uh, sarcastic sense of humor, Maggie?"

"No, but I have lost my husband," she said. "I assume you heard that Roger was incarcerated and passed away in prison."

Anytime she spoke the words it felt like gravel in her mouth, but today was particularly bad. These people had known Roger, and loved him. But the elephant was too big in this kitchen to gloss over it.

For a moment, no one spoke, then Frank let out a soft groan. "It's so sad, Maggie. I'm sorry. And Kate told us you've lost Artie, Jo." He reached over the table and put a hand on hers. "We were so devastated to hear that."

"Thank you," she murmured as Betty came back with a small tray holding four coffee mugs and fixings. "Kate and Eli told us your families are sharing that old beach house after a renovation. How exciting!"

"Very," Maggie said as she fixed her coffee.

Betty fussed with the cookies and, finally, the four of them sat facing each other in an awkward silence.

"Oh!" Betty exclaimed, pushing her chair back. "I have to show you pictures of our grandchildren."

"No." Maggie underscored the single syllable by putting her cup down with a thud. At their looks, she shuttered her eyes in apology.

"As much as we're enjoying this reunion," she began, hearing her clipped tone, but not caring, "Jo Ellen and I actually came here for a reason."

Jo Ellen leaned in. "Maggie's right. We need to find out a few more details of...some things we don't understand. We hoped your memories would be better than ours."

"My memory is fine," Maggie interjected. "But the fact is, our husbands both made us promise not to speak to each other. We accepted that edict, but now, thirty years later, both men are dead. We are trying to find out why they wanted us separated."

"We certainly don't know," Frank said quickly.

"And what difference does it make?" Betty added. "Be friends if you want to be friends! As you said, both men are dead, rest their souls."

"It makes a world of difference," Maggie insisted, impatience crawling over her. "If it was something awful, then Jo and I shouldn't be friends."

"We have no idea," Betty said.

Frank just looked down at his coffee and uneaten cookie, quiet enough that Maggie thought he *did* have an idea, but didn't want to say. Something he was hiding from his wife?

Well, too bad. The truth, whatever it was, had to come out.

"We've recently learned that Roger's case wasn't just a police matter," Maggie said. "The FBI was involved, making it a federal investigation. All the files —every last one—went missing from his attorney's office."

Frank still didn't look up.

"Do you have any idea why, Frank?" Maggie asked.

"Course not," he said quickly. "But I don't know why you can't let the past be past. Who gives a hoot what happened thirty years ago?"

"We do," Maggie and Jo replied in perfect unison.

"Well, we just don't know," Betty said, trying again to push her chair out. "But we have three grandchildren who—"

"Look, Frank." Maggie narrowed her eyes at him. "We know you used to run numbers at the deli. And we're not here to judge, but was Roger ever involved in that? Was Artie?"

"Artie?" Frank snorted so hard, he coughed. "Mr. Goody Two-Shoes?"

Jo Ellen smiled. "He was ethical, but we have to know everything."

Another long silence pressed on the room until Frank sighed then looked at his wife with a question in his eyes.

"Go ahead," she said softly. "They want answers..."

Finally, Maggie thought with a huff of breath.

He closed his eyes, looking trapped. "Yes, I was a bookie," he said. "I ran a side hustle at the deli. Took bets on horses, football, you name it. I'm not proud of it, really."

"Well, I was proud of the fur coat it got me," Betty said sheepishly.

"I'm sure you got so much use out of that in Florida," Maggie cracked. "Please, go on, Frank."

"I never got caught," Frank said. "I skirted the law and I swear to God this had *nothing* to do with either of your husbands. Well, Roger..."

Oh, heavens. "Roger what?" Maggie demanded when he didn't finish.

Frank shifted in his chair. "It doesn't matter, Mag—"

"It matters!" she exclaimed, the sound of her voice reverberating through the kitchen. "We want to know."

He groaned, leaned back, and scratched his chin. "It really doesn't matter, 'cause Cotton Ramsey is deader than a doornail now and his whole operation has been gone for years."

"Cotton...who?"

"And I honestly don't know what happened between them, but—"

"Make some sense, honey," Betty said, putting a hand

on her husband's arm. "These ladies don't know what you're talking about."

He nodded and took a sip of coffee, looking like he'd kill for it to be something stronger.

"The gambling operation was run—and owned—by a group out of Biloxi."

Jo Ellen and Maggie exchanged a look. *Biloxi*. That was where the FBI investigation was based.

"They were what used to be known as the Dixie Mafia," Frank said softly. "Have you heard of them?"

Maggie choked. "The *Mafia*?" Chills blossomed on her arms. "You were involved with the Mafia, Frank?"

"The Southern version, which is mostly good ol' boys who used to make moonshine and then they moved into betting and...you know, other stuff."

Maggie had no idea what "other stuff" meant and wasn't sure she wanted to.

"Anyway, the guy at the top of the food chain was a fellow named Cotton Ramsey, and he went to jail a few years after Roger and the whole thing fell apart, thank God. Betty and me, well, we just wanted to lay low. Closed the deli, moved out here...very sorry for anything we'd done."

No one spoke as both Maggie and Jo Ellen tried to process this unfathomable news.

Then Betty got up, taking the untouched plate of cookies, and walked toward the counter.

"What on Earth was Roger's involvement with these people?" Maggie managed to ask.

"He, uh, he came to me once," Frank said, running

stubby fingers through his white hair. "I think it was not that last summer, but the one before. Maybe 1994. He was in a bind. Something about moving money from one client to another and things getting lost and...I can't recall all the specifics."

Maggie stiffened. The specifics, she thought, were no doubt listed in excruciating detail in the missing federal files. As she understood his crimes, her husband had essentially stolen from one man to pay another, and couldn't pay the first one back.

"Anyway, he needed some cash. A lot of it. I put him in touch with Cotton."

"And?" Maggie asked.

"I never heard another word. Honest to God, I swear, Maggie." He raised his right hand, his expression pained but serious. "I have no idea if anything happened between them. Roger never mentioned it again and neither did Cotton's guys."

Maggie narrowed her gaze, her heart rate skyrocketing. "You sent my husband to the *Mafia*? For a loan?"

"I didn't send him. I gave him a name. He made the choice."

Maggie wanted to argue, but couldn't. Every bad decision Roger made was his own, and she could look past her love for her late husband long enough to see that.

She looked over at Jo Ellen, who was staring at her with the same stunned expression, proving she'd known nothing of this.

"Does that help you girls?" Betty asked as she returned to the table.

"I don't see how," Maggie replied, pushing up, since she just wanted to get away as far and as fast as possible. Forget small talk and grandchildren and memories.

Jo, bless her heart, was already gathering her bag for the same speedy escape.

No one tried to stop them as they pushed their chairs in and muttered their thanks.

Frank looked a little shellshocked, and stayed seated when they walked out of the kitchen with Betty, mumbling his goodbyes.

"I'm sorry if you found out some upsetting things," Betty said as she opened the front door.

"Well, I have one more question," Jo Ellen said, pausing to turn to Betty.

"I'm not sure I can—"

"Yes, you can," Jo Ellen interjected, proving that she sure could have a backbone when she wanted to. "Why in God's name would you tell Kate and Eli some trumped-up nonsense about us having affairs with each other's husbands?"

Betty stared at her. "Well, me and Frank agreed that for the rest of our lives, which might not be that many more years, that would be our cover story if we were ever asked by any of you."

"Why would you need a cover story that involves us?" Maggie demanded.

Betty looked hard at her, her eyes sad...and scared. "Yes, the Dixie Mafia is long gone. Cotton Ramsey is dead. But we don't ever want anyone coming after us. And if Frank's associated with Roger...well, we were just scared. So that was our excuse for why we didn't talk to you anymore."

"Well, that's just dumb," Maggie said. "And it makes no sense."

Betty sighed and stepped back, ushering them out the door with one hand. "You be careful, girls. You dig deep enough, you're bound to find things you don't like."

With that, they left, cold and unsatisfied despite the May sunshine that poured over them.

A moment later, they got into the car and shut the doors, silence pressing between them.

"Have you ever heard that name before?" Jo Ellen asked. "Cotton Ramsey?"

"Never in my life," Maggie said. "I thought I knew everything about Roger. Turns out I know...nothing."

"We'll tell Peter about it," Jo Ellen said. "See what he can dig up."

Maggie started the car, noticing that her hands trembled, making the mottled surface of her skin look old and fragile.

They weren't Nancy Drew or the *Murder She Wrote* lady. They were just two aging women with sunspots and aching backs and stubborn hearts. Just two old ladies who wanted answers.

But for the first time since she laid eyes on Jo Ellen after thirty years of missing her, Maggie wasn't sure if she wanted these answers anymore.

Chapter Eleven

Lacey

The conversations by text and phone that Lacey had been having with Roman had somehow given her a false sense of readiness for tonight's family dinner. She'd only seen him once since they met in Rosemary Beach a week ago.

He'd taken a one-month lease on a three-bedroom house on Lagoon Drive, not five minutes inland from the Summer House. Lacey had stopped by to see him and the house, which was clean and recently remodeled, situated on a canal with lovely sunset views. When he showed her around, he was most excited about the dock...well, second-most excited.

He'd practically jumped out of his skin when she told him he was formally invited to the Summer House for dinner to meet her mother, grandmother...and his biological mother and grandmother.

Now they were minutes from the start of that evening, and all her mental and emotional groundwork seemed to evaporate into thin air. What would happen? Would Tessa know? Would he blurt out the truth?

Stepping outside when she heard the rumble of a

sports car pulling into the driveway, she felt flushed despite the cool white sundress she wore. Nerves stretched across her chest every time she thought about what she was doing.

Breaking promises. Telling lies. And pretending to have a boyfriend.

The engine of a navy blue Porsche—*what else?*—quieted as she reached the bottom step, where she paused to watch him climb out of the car.

Holy...moly. Forget whether or not Tessa would recognize her own son—who in that house, or the world, would believe that Lacey Knight would attract the attention of this guy?

He wore a loose-fitting white linen shirt that somehow made his shoulders even broader, and khaki pants that looked clean, pressed, and wildly expensive. His hair might have been combed, but the Gulf breeze tousled his soft golden waves. With his sunglasses on, all she could really see was his smile, which blinded even from twenty feet away.

"Hey, can you help me with my gifts?" he called.

"You brought gifts?" she asked, hating that her voice sounded slightly high-pitched as she approached the car.

"Of course. I know there's a slew of women waiting in there, so I did my best. Flowers for your mother because that's what my mom would want." He handed her a fat bouquet of sunflowers and white lilies. "And this cute little plant because you said your grandmother liked roses and this is a miniature rose bush."

She gathered the bouquet and took the handle of a sweet bucket that held a tiny bush with delicate pink buds.

"And for the others, chocolate. Not so creative, but what woman doesn't like chocolate?" He produced a gold bag emblazoned with the logo of a high-end candy shop in town. He leaned down and whispered, "I still can't wrap my head around the fact that my birth mother and *her* mother are both here."

Here and about to be blindsided, she thought.

"Roman, this was all very thoughtful." She raised the bouquet and bucket as he hooked the bag on her free finger. "They'll be so grateful."

"I didn't forget you, of course." Once again, he reached into the car and produced a small bag. "I hope my girlfriend will wear my jersey."

He pulled out a turquoise football jersey, holding it open to reveal "Matteo 14" on the back. "It's big but..." His lips lifted in a smile that could melt the chocolate she held. "You'll look spectacular in it."

All her stress instantly morphed into a different sensation—this one making every female cell in her body tingle right down to her toes.

"I'll wear it with pride," she said with a breathless laugh. "Gifts weren't necessary. They're all pretty excited to meet you."

He pushed the sunglasses up and she got a good look at his whiskey-colored eyes trimmed with thick lashes. And...more tingling.

"What's our game plan?" he asked.

She drew back. "I didn't know we needed one."

"If she's suspicious, I mean," he explained. "Flat-out denial? Laugh like hyenas? Or...change of subject? Anything but the truth."

She looked up at him, a little surprised to hear that proclamation.

"If the truth is ever going to come out," he explained, "I have to be straight with my parents first. They deserve to know before anyone else."

She thought about that, nodding. "I get it."

"So?" He inched back and made a casual gesture toward his face with the bag he held. "Look hard. Would you know instantly? Is it that obvious?"

She did look, hard and long, happy for the excuse to drink in every delicious detail of the man's face. He wasn't GQ model perfect—his nose was a little crooked and he had a light scar above one brow, but *oof.* He looked good.

But that wasn't what he'd asked. Would Tessa know she was staring into the face of her own son? Other than the golden-brown eyes and light hair, he didn't look *exactly* like Tessa. Strong bones and a wide smile, but her face was so feminine and beautiful.

"She'd have to be looking for it," Lacey finally said. "She doesn't know your name, or she would have reacted to it the first time she saw you on my Instagram account. There wasn't so much as a flicker of recognition. I'm sure they'll all be too...distracted by you."

He gave an easy laugh. "I'll pull out all my charm."

"Don't overdo it," she warned. "I don't think I can handle too much."

Still laughing, he put his arm around her, taking the rose bucket and flowers.

"Come on, Lacey. Lead me to the women wolves." He finally slowed his step and looked up at the house. "Nice crib, by the way. I love this place. But you know, my mom always says the real beauty of a house is the people inside."

"Oh, I like—"

The front door opened and Tessa stood there, a G&T in one hand, the other stretched out in greeting. "'Romeo, Romeo, wherefore art thou?'"

Lacey sucked in a soft breath as she felt the man next to her freeze mid-step, looking up at...his biological mother. For what felt like an eternity, he didn't say a word. Lacey waited, her heart hammering, suddenly very, very uncertain that this was such a good idea.

No, of course it wasn't. It was madness, pure and—

"'Deny thy father and refuse thy name,'" he replied as he climbed the stairs.

What? What did he mean? Was he—

"And he quotes Shakespeare," Tessa said, throwing her head back with a laugh.

"My high school English teacher was married to the football coach. They thought it would be hilarious if the team did a production of *Romeo and Juliet*." He held out the bag of chocolates. "You must be Tessa."

She blinked up at him, speechless for a split second. Long enough for Lacey to feel her whole body tense.

"I am," she said, her eyes flashing. "And you"—she opened the door wider to invite him in—"are just what the doctor ordered around here. Come and make all the ladies swoon."Laughing, he walked in and stepped toward the living room. Behind him, Tessa whipped around to Lacey and mouthed, "Oh, my gawd!"

Woman, you have no idea.

But Lacey just smiled and tried to relax into the evening. It would either be the best night she'd had in a long time...or a nightmare.

Jo ELLEN WAS downright giddy in the presence of NFL "greatness" as she put it. Mom acted just weird enough for Lacey to know she was under the Roman Matteo spell, too. Even Maggie's icy exterior thawed under the warmth of their guest.

And Tessa?

Well, she certainly had no idea that the center of attention at their outdoor dining table was the baby she'd given up for adoption twenty-five years earlier. And that gave Lacey mixed feelings—guilt, remorse, excitement, and an overwhelming desire to tell her the truth.

Lacey hadn't expected that last sensation.

She'd been so wrapped up in the fact that she'd broken her promise, so fearful that Tessa would take one look at the guy and burst into tears, that she didn't realize how much she *wanted* Tessa to know. How could she not?

Roman was nothing short of amazing.

They all chattered through Maggie and Jo Ellen's Bolognese reprise, which was even better this time. He regaled them with stories about life in the NFL and several about his childhood in a beach town that sounded as magical as this one.

Classy right down to his last strand of DNA—shared, as it was, with a few people around the table—he consistently asked questions and listened to every answer.

He had Lacey's mother talking animatedly about her design business, absorbed every detail of Grandma Maggie's recent trip to Europe, and was genuinely sympathetic when Jo Ellen talked about the late, great Artie Wylie.

Well, after all, that *was* his grandfather, although not one of the other women seemed to suspect anything. Even Tessa. Especially Tessa.

And that made the longing to tell her the truth even stronger.

"Lacey tells me you grew up fishing," Tessa said as the meal came to an end.

"Had a rod in my hand at two," he said. "I was really lucky to live in a house on the water with a boat dock, just teeming with redfish, trout, and so much snook it was a joke."

"Did your father fish?" she asked.

"I taught him," Roman said with a laugh. "I don't know how but it was like I was born knowing how to catch a fish."

Lacey stared at her half-eaten food, slowly setting her

fork down before she had the courage to look at Tessa. Was this it? Was she going to put two and two together and come up with...Artie the fisherman?

"And you want to fish while you're here?" she asked.

"Like I want to breathe," he joked.

"You're in luck," she said brightly. "My sister just sent my father's old rods and reels down for a local charity. You two up for a fishing trip tomorrow on the boat?"

A whole day on the boat with Tessa and Roman? Maybe that's when they'd tell her.

"I'd love that," Roman answered without hesitation, reaching for Lacey's hand. "Our first fishing date. Should be fun, huh, Lace?"

She slid her fingers into his and tried to ignore the jolt of his touch. "Absolutely," she agreed.

"Let's clear this for dessert," her mother said, standing. "You two take a walk on the beach. It's too pretty a sunset to miss."

"Let me help—"

Tessa put a hand over his. "Walk with your girl, Romeo. Mother's orders."

The words gave Lacey a different kind of jolt. She shared a quick, secret look with Roman, who barely hid his smile. "I never argue with a mother's orders."

He stood and thanked Jo Ellen and Maggie for the best Bolognese he'd ever had, took a few dishes into the kitchen, then put his arm around Lacey's shoulders.

"Let's take that walk now."

And every hair on the nape of her neck stood up.

A few minutes later, they were hand in hand on the boardwalk, headed to the beach.

"So..." She looked up at him, trying to gauge his expression, but she simply didn't know him well enough to get a read on his thoughts. "Is she what you expected?"

"She's..." He blew out a long, slow breath as they reached the end of the boardwalk. "Wow. I just have to process this for a minute. I just met the woman who gave me life."

She sighed. "I imagine that shakes your foundation."

He peered out to the water, quiet for a good thirty seconds.

"Yes and no," he eventually said. "It's kind of weird to think about it, and wonder, you know, why she didn't keep me. She wasn't a teenager."

"No, she was twenty-five, single, unsettled, unmarried, and a person who runs from conflict or trouble," Lacey said, instantly needing to defend her decision. "And, you know, she had other options."

"I know." He closed his eyes. "Believe me, I've thought of that. And I want you to know that. I have no bad feelings toward her—in fact, I admire her for the decision. It's just hard not to wonder what life would have been like if she had raised me."

"Fun," Lacey said quickly, making him smile.

"For sure. And, to answer your original question, no. She's not anything like I expected."

"Really? You're so much like her. I mean, obviously, there's a family resemblance, but she has your warmth and joy."

He gave a smile. "She's a thousand times better than I'd ever dreamed, Lacey. I'm overwhelmed by her. And, I might add, you."

"Me? I didn't do anything except...you know, lie, betray, pretend, and otherwise break the rules of ethics."

He draped an arm around her as they stepped down on the sand and kicked off their shoes.

"You did that for me," he said. "You facilitated this meeting and I know it wasn't easy for you. Your nerves were singing loud when I got here."

"But you relaxed me," she said. "You'd put anyone at ease. Heck, even fearsome Maggie was panting for your next story."

He laughed, and the sound came from deep inside his chest, real and warm. "She's not so bad. And Jo Ellen? Wow, that Artie guy must have been something. But every time his name came up, Maggie shot daggers. What's up with that?"

"There's a lot of drama around him I haven't told you about. I will, later. But tell me more about your thoughts on Tessa."

He slowed his step, kicking the sand. "I wish I could thank her, you know? Her decision led me to a life with the two finest human beings who ever lived. Bob and Faith Matteo are..." He shook his head. "I'll get choked up, and you don't want to see that."

Oh, but she kind of did. "You're so sweet."

"I'm blessed beyond measure and it was Tessa who did that for me."

"And Artie," she said. "Apparently, he arranged the

adoption. Jo Ellen never knew. Neither did Kate, Tessa's twin sister."

He thought about that for a moment, walking slowly along the water's edge, no regard for the hem of his pants getting wet.

"Anyway, I never expected her to be so beautiful and alive and...awesome. I'm so happy I know her."

"Now what?" Lacey asked after a beat.

"Now I continue to get to know her." He looked down. "And you, my new girlfriend."

She rolled her eyes but he didn't laugh.

"Like I said, you get the credit for making this happen, Lacey."

"But if you spend a lot of time with her," Lacey said slowly, "will you tell her?"

"I might," he said. "I'm not sure how or when. Would that wreck your relationship?"

"I don't know, but..." She made a face. "I kind of want to tell her now, and take whatever happens."

"No, no, no," he said, shaking his head. "I *have* to tell my parents first and they just left on a cruise they've been planning for ages, and I don't want to...rock the boat, if you'll excuse the pun."

"Why would your meeting her ruin their vacation?" she asked.

"I just don't know how they'll take it."

That surprised her, considering they were "the finest humans alive."

"I mean, they'd understand," he added, maybe reading her expression. "But I think my mother really liked being my only mother. I feel like I owe it to them to be first."

Lacey sighed. "So...we keep on lying?"

"Who's lying? She didn't ask if I was her son."

"She thinks you're my boyfriend."

"I am." He squeezed her into his strong, solid side. "It's not a lie."

"Roman," she scoffed. "It's cute of you to say that, but let's be real."

"I am." Slowly, he turned her in his arms so she was facing him. "I really like you. I really want to spend time with you. I really rented a house in Destin to be your boyfriend."

"None of that is real."

He tipped his head and gave her a look. Then, without another word, he lifted her just an inch off the ground and kissed her lightly on the lips. His mouth was warm, inviting, and, yeah, really real.

When he very slowly let her feet touch the sand and drew back an inch, she nearly swayed into him.

"Lacey, you are—"

She put a hand over his lips. And not just to stop him from proclaiming whatever she was, but just to feel how soft they were one more time.

"Don't," she whispered.

"Don't kiss you?"

Don't break my heart, she wanted to scream. Because she could already feel how shattered it would be when this ended.

"Don't...take this too far," she said instead.

"I promise, Lacey Knight. I'll only take it as far as it was meant to be."

When they turned to walk back to the house, she realized that whole exchange was easily visible from anyone standing on the deck—and she knew that all four of them had been watching.

So was that kiss for her benefit...or theirs?

Chapter Twelve
Tessa

She didn't know what it was about Roman Matteo, but Tessa felt so comfortable around the young man. Familiar, even. And far less nervous than Lacey, who was a little on edge and jittery when he arrived for their fishing adventure.

First, Tessa took him into the garage to dig through the box that Kate had sent, and admired the way he handled Dad's fishing gear. With respect, but also with confidence. Most of it was in pretty good shape—good enough that they could use it to fish today before she donated a few rods and reels to The Abundant Catch. And those that were broken, he seemed certain he could fix when he had the right tools.

They opted to drive the short distance to the marina so they could bring everything they needed for a day of fishing on the boat, plus a cooler for lunch and cold drinks. He easily unloaded everything onto the dock, commenting on how nice the marina was and how at home he felt.

"I want you to meet Seamus," Tessa said. "He was a friend of my father's and runs the charity I mentioned. Let's make a quick stop in the marina office."

"Sure."

"Oh, I don't know about that," Lacey said quickly.

Tessa threw her a questioning look. "Why not?"

She froze, and gave the weirdest look to Roman. "Do you want to do that?"

"Why wouldn't I?"

Her eyes widened but then she shrugged and gestured toward the equipment and cooler. "We can't just...leave this."

"It'll be fine," Tessa said.

"No, no," Lacey said. "That's...too much. He'll want your autograph and...you're famous."

Was she out of her mind? Tessa just laughed and tugged Roman's T-shirt sleeve. "It'll take two minutes, no autographs. You stay with the stuff, Lace. Come on, famous guy. Let me show you off."

He walked with her, laughing. "Nothing to show off, really."

"I don't know about that or why"—she threw a look over her shoulder—"Lacey is acting so odd."

"She's just protective of me," he said. "I like it."

Tessa grinned at him. "You better stop being perfect, young man."

"Hardly," he scoffed.

"I mean it. You make that girl fall in love and leave us and I'll never forgive you."

He gave her a quick look, an unreadable expression in his eyes. But it was just enough to make Tessa uneasy. Why?

Was he planning to do just that? Leave her with a

broken heart? She really wanted to know what his motivations were and intended to find out. Was he too good to be true? Tessa could suss that out in no time.

At the marina office, she peered into the open door, only seeing Clay at the desk.

"Hey, Tessa. Taking your boat out today?" he asked.

"I am, but I was looking for Seamus." She stepped inside, inviting Roman to join her. "I wanted to introduce him to—"

"Oh, I know you. Wait. Are you...Roman Matteo?" Clay stood up, his jaw loose. "No way, man! It *is* you!"

Roman smiled and took a step closer, the picture of humility. "Hi. Clay, is it? Have we met? I'm Roman."

Clay took the hand Roman offered, shaking it way too hard. "This is insane! I'm a huge Jags fan! I make the drive to Jacksonville for at least one game every season and...*wow*. What are you doing here?"

Roman gave an easy laugh. "Fishing, I hope."

"How...what...I can't believe this." He came around the desk, looking starstruck. "Seamus is going to be bummed he missed meeting you. Although, dude, you need to get off the bench more."

Roman chuckled. "No kidding. Hey, I'm just glad I get to wear the jersey, but thanks. And I'll be back to meet everyone. I'm here in Destin until training kicks into high gear."

"That's awesome. How do you two know each other?" he asked Tessa.

Roman glanced at her, giving that odd look again, making something deep inside her ring out an alarm.

"I'm dating Lacey Knight," he said.

"Vivien Lawson's daughter," Tessa reminded Clay.

"Ooh." The other man's brows shot up. "That's cool."

And speaking of Lacey, she was probably melting in the sun with the cooler and gear. "Is Seamus going to be here today?" Tessa asked.

"He's not," Clay said. "But he'll be back."

"And so will I," Roman promised.

"And we have some equipment to donate," Tessa added.

Clay gushed some more and then they said goodbye and walked back out into the sunshine. Before they took a step, Tessa put a hand on Roman's arm and looked up at him.

"I have to know," she said. "I have to know and you cannot lie."

She could have sworn all the color faded from his tanned skin. "What?"

"Are you for real?"

"I'm...I'm..." He blew out a breath. "Yeah. I mean, yeah."

"I'm serious," she said. "Are you too good to be true? Are you going to break that girl's heart? Are you for real, Roman Matteo?"

His smile disappeared. "I'm real. I'm not too good to be true. And, please remember this, Tessa, no matter what happens—I'm not here to break any hearts."

She let out a breath she hadn't realized she'd been holding. "Okay. I'm going to believe you. But you better be telling the truth."

"I am," he said, turning away so fast she couldn't quite catch the expression in his eyes. But he walked a few steps ahead toward Lacey, leaving her standing in the sun wondering if he was all that...or a big fat fake.

THEY HAD the boat underway in no time, with Roman showing a natural affinity for managing the lines and helping them off the dock. Shocking no one, he was as at home on the deck of a cabin cruiser as he was on a football field.

He inspected every inch of the vessel, above deck and below. Afterwards, he settled in next to Lacey on the bow bench, tipping his head back to get sun on his face as he draped an arm around her.

And she stiffened as though she hadn't been expecting it.

Maybe Lacey was just being cautious, too. After all, the guy was textbook perfection. Surely there was a red flag, a fatal flaw, a reason to run.

Could it be he was a kind, considerate, humble, warm, gorgeous NFL wide receiver who made millions and could do anything during the off-season but chose fishing with Lacey and Tessa?

Nah. Nobody was *that* perfect.

"How long have you had this boat, Tessa?" he asked.

"About a month and a half. Smartest negotiation I ever made."

His brows lifted behind his sunglasses. "Negotiation?"

Tessa grinned, flipping back the ponytail that had fallen over her shoulder with purposeful smugness. "I persuaded a rich client to include it in my fee because he owed me this and a lot more."

Roman choked on a laugh. "That's hilarious."

"That's Tessa," Lacey said, looking bemused and still proud. "Fearless, cool, and gets exactly what she wants."

"I love that," Roman said softly, regarding Tessa for a moment. "I mean, if you know what you want."

"I usually do, and in this case? It was a boat. Do you know what you want, Romeo?" she asked with a tease in her voice. "I mean, beyond a good season of football and a renewed contract."

"A good catch out here," he answered glibly. "I did some research and heard that Destin is called 'The World's Luckiest Fishing Village.' Is that true or just good PR?"

"You should know about good PR," Tessa said. "You have it down to an art."

He sat a little straighter, the arrow hitting its mark as he slowly took off his sunglasses. "You want me to answer that question about what I want out of life?" he asked, all humor gone.

"Yes, I do."

Lacey looked concerned. "Tessa, don't—"

She held up a hand to quiet Lacey. "I really do want you to answer the question, Roman. Honestly and without...spin."

He leaned forward, dropping his elbows on his knees as he squinted with lush lashes and a direct gaze.

"I do know what I want. My parents pounded it in my head."

"What's that?" Lacey asked, her voice soft enough to barely be heard over the wind and the inboard engine now that they'd picked up a little speed.

He didn't answer right away, but glanced at Lacey. "You sure I can be honest?"

"If you don't want to be thrown overboard," Tessa answered for her.

Lacey nodded, staring at him with a question in her expression, as if she had no idea what he was about to say and might be a little nervous about it.

He looked from one woman to the other. "My parents, Bob and Faith, have an amazing marriage. They're connected in a way that very few people enjoy. I'd like that one day, and kids. Several of them, if I had my way. I think family is the most important thing in the world and I also think it's not valued enough today."

Lacey stared at him, silent. Tessa felt her jaw loosen.

Really? He was...looking for love? A family?

"I can imagine you meet a lot of..." Tessa left the question unfinished and drifting in the sea breeze.

"Yeah, I do," he said, obviously knowing where she was going. "Haven't met someone who's down-to-earth enough for my taste." He gave Lacey a little squeeze. "Present company excluded, of course."

She just smiled, quieter than Tessa could ever remember.

"That's it," he said. "That's my thing. Family."

Wow. That was...a good thing. "Do you have siblings?" Tessa asked.

"No, no. I was...um, an only child," he said quickly, as if correcting himself. "So that's why I want a big family."

"How old are you?" she asked.

"Just twenty-five. Plenty of time, but that doesn't mean I don't think about it."

Twenty-five. Tessa felt a jolt as if she'd driven over a wave, not the glassy harbor water.

That was exactly the age her son would be—*was*—somewhere in this world. Good heavens, she hoped that baby had turned out as fine and strong and impressive as this young man.

She felt Lacey's gaze on her, intense and knowing. Of course. Lacey knew her secret and she had to guess exactly what Tessa was thinking.

"Okay, kids," she said brightly, happy to see the break to the bay and change this subject. "Hang on to your hats and each other. We're getting underway!"

With that, she kicked the throttle and the bow rose from the water, getting a hoot of happiness from Roman. He threw his arms around Lacey and gave her a hug as if protecting her. Tessa's heart crawled into her throat, her emotions as wild as the wake behind her.

Was her son—the one she'd held exactly one time in her whole life—anything like this boy? Was he falling in love right now? Living his best life? Wondering about her?

She hoped so. And just thinking about it kind of hurt her heart.

So, she pressed the old pain away and took them for a fun joyride around the picturesque bay, then found a cove Seamus had told her was teeming with speckled trout and redfish. The spot was in the shadow of the bridge, tucked into thickets of mangroves and pepper trees.

"This is exactly like my backyard growing up," Roman told them as they dropped anchor.

"Nice life," Lacey said. "Beats the suburbs of Atlanta."

"It beats everything."

"Where exactly was that?" Tessa asked. "Near Jacksonville?"

He looked up at her as he pulled a rod from the collection. "A few hours south, near Cape Canaveral," he said. "Close enough to grow up seeing space launches."

"That's cool," Lacey said.

"It was awesome. Our house had a fat canal in the back, lined with these mangrove trees. There were dolphins, manatees, and pelicans everywhere. And so many fish it was crazy."

Roman took some of the gear and the bait box to the back of the boat to set up, leaving Lacey and Tessa on the bow.

Tessa pulled her sunglasses down to get a good look at her young friend and protégé, who still seemed like she could snap at any moment.

"You okay?"

"I'm good," Lacey said, fidgeting with some threads of her cut-off shorts.

"You're really freaking out, aren't you?" Tessa whispered.

"No." Lacey shot her a glare. "I'm not freaking out."

"You totally are. You've got the new-boyfriend jitters. Classic."

Lacey groaned. "Can you not?"

Roman, clearly catching the tail end of their exchange as he came back, slung an arm around Lacey's shoulders. "Don't worry. I'm super low maintenance."

Tessa grinned and pulled out the bait box. "Yeah, yeah. We'll see how low maintenance you are once you have to get a hook from the mouth of a flounder."

"I should be so lucky." He handed Lacey a rod. "This one's perfect for you, Lace. Let me show you my lucky cast."

A minute later, the two of them were side by side, laughing and talking while Roman guided her through the process...exactly as Artie Wylie had guided little Tessa. He actually cast with the very same hitch at the halfway point, and lifted his chin like it would help the bait and hook go farther.

It was like her dear departed father had come back from heaven to be with her for the day.

Which was the silliest, stupidest thing Tessa had ever thought, but for some reason, the very idea comforted her. He wasn't Artie reincarnated, but he was a great guy and all Tessa could do was hope he kept that promise and didn't break Lacey's heart.

Chapter Thirteen
Vivien

Vivien spread the last of the wallpaper samples across the floor in Danny's upstairs loft, then stepped back to make a final selection. Pale sea-glass green textured grasscloth, a bold navy-and-white geometric, or a sandy linen weave that caught the late afternoon sun just right?

Any one of them would be perfect in this light. Or maybe she was just in a good mood, doing what she loved to do and getting paid well for it.

Glancing around, she gazed out onto Four Prong Lake, its glassy surface now glowing with gold and lavender reflections from the setting sun. Which made her realize she'd been up here working for a long time.

She glanced at her watch and blinked. Nearly seven. Not late afternoon—early evening. No wonder her stomach was growling.

Danny had been downstairs most of the day, holed up in his home office, leaving her to work in peace as she tested colors and wallpapers, and used interior design software to virtually create the space she wanted. She'd met with the window treatment company and had a few video calls with furniture vendors to make final selections.

But she had to be done now, so she gathered her swatches and samples into her tote and headed downstairs to find the shoes she'd left at the door and say goodbye to her client.

At the bottom, she stopped to inhale something...amazing. Something rich and buttery and irresistible.

And, oh—her gaze moved to the kitchen and landed on some*one* who kind of fit those descriptions, too.

Danny stood at the stove, sleeves rolled, wine glass in hand, lobster tails sizzling in a pan.

"That smells...unbelievable," she said, unable to hide the amusement or fascination from her voice.

He turned and grinned. "A man keeps his promises. I said I owed you dinner. Stay."

The command—not a question—sent an unfamiliar reaction right down to her toes. Well, maybe not so unfamiliar. He frequently had that effect on her.

Vivien opened her mouth to protest and come up with an excuse to turn him down, but...couldn't think of a thing.

"Come on, you've been working up there for hours." He notched his chin toward the stove, a divine smell of sizzling seafood filling the air.

"And I have several finished renderings so you can make a final decision on the built-ins and furniture."

He lifted a shoulder. "I trust your judgment, and you need to eat." He used a fork to lift a tender piece of lobster. "You need to eat this."

The aroma hit her nose as forcefully as his sly smile.

"I guess I could…" Vivien swallowed, walking into the kitchen. "Have dinner."

He poured white wine into a second glass and handed it to her. "Sit. You look like you've been rearranging the world upstairs."

She accepted the glass with a smile. "Wallpaper and flooring samples. I did a FaceTime call with a carpenter for the built-in, and I ordered a pool table. I left the samples all laid out for you. You have to make the final decision."

"Perfect. I'll tell you I love all of them, so we can skip the part where I pretend to have an opinion."

"You have a choice of soothing color palettes, but I'll do the rest," she promised, taking a sip.

The wine was dry and crisp. And tasted achingly expensive.

"Let's eat outside," he suggested, taking two plates from the cabinet. "The sunset over the lake is going to be almost as spectacular as my *fra diavolo*. I hope you like a little spice."

A few minutes later, they were situated at the dining area on the back patio, with plates full of an absolutely gourmet meal.

"Where'd you learn to cook?" she asked as she placed a napkin on her lap.

"Here and there. And Italy." He smiled, smoothing his own napkin. "It's just a hobby, but I find it very relaxing."

The sun was a slow-burning orange, setting over the lake like a spotlight made just for this dinner.

Danny poured more wine and leaned back in his chair, watching her with that easy, interested gaze he always seemed to have.

Then he lifted his wine glass. "To a woman who soothes with color palettes."

She smiled and met his crystal with hers. "To a man who relaxes with lobster *fra diavolo*."

"Bon appetit," he replied. "I hope you like it."

"I know I will."

With the first bite, they shared an easy silence, not counting her moans of pleasure as the fantastic tastes hit. That made him laugh, and his blue-gray eyes light with pride.

"This is amazing, Danny," she gushed.

"Thanks." After a beat, he leaned a little closer. "Permission to change the subject and ask a personal question?"

"*Oookay*." She dragged the word out. "If you must."

"Oh, I must," he teased, a different and far more flirtatious spark in his eyes. "Was it a wretched divorce?"

The question threw her, not expecting him to change to *that* subject. Or get that personal. She managed to swallow and dab her lips to buy some time.

"Truly divine," she said. "I mean the food, not the divorce."

"I figured." He curled some pasta around a fork and took a bite. "They're never divine. The best you can hope for is...relatively painless and not too complicated."

"It was," she said. "Well, the painful part is mostly behind me, and the papers are signed, so the complications are over. All in all, I'm glad it's in the rearview mirror. I'm on somewhat amicable terms with him, and my daughter is too old for a custody battle. She and I remain so close we are literally sharing a bed." She grinned. "That's temporary but really fun."

"I bet," he agreed. "So now what? How does the future look?"

"Like...a soothing color palette," she joked, attempting to get back to the business of design. "Short term, I'm living in paradise and building my business."

"And long term?" he asked. "Staying here?"

"Now *that* is complicated," she said.

"Tell me." It wasn't a question—a conversation style she'd noticed and chalked up to his low-key alpha-ness.

"Okay, but it's a bit of a tale."

"I have all night."

Oh, boy. That was a long time.

Taking the invitation to share, she dove into the whole history of the Summer House, trying to relate an abbreviated version. But he asked a lot of questions, not too probing, but thoughtful enough to show he truly understood just how thorny family history could be.

"So, it sounds like you'll keep the house and stay in Destin," he said as she finished.

"Not necessarily, but maybe." She smiled. "How's that for definite?"

"Do you like that uncertainty or does it bother you?" he asked, again taking the conversation a little deeper than she would normally want with a client, but...she liked his questions.

And, if she was being honest, she also liked his food, his looks, his beautiful waterfront deck, and this whole night. She liked *him.*

She lowered her fork, thinking about his question instead of his direct and interested gaze.

"Uncertainty doesn't bother me as long as I feel like clarity will eventually come," she said. "I am trusting the process."

"Which involves..."

"Other people's opinions, lives, finances, and relationships," she said, thinking about the scope of the whole Lawson-Wylie-Summer House saga. "For the moment, for the very short term, I'm taking it one day—and one job—at a time." She angled her head toward his house and gestured to the upstairs. "Thank you for giving me this one."

"You're quite welcome," he said, finishing by putting his knife and fork on his plate and leaning forward. "As you can see, I'm making this place a home, so..."

She looked up expectantly, not sure where he was going.

"I'll likely be staying here, too. I'm even considering selling my condo in New York."

"Really? That seems like a big change. Would you move here because of Fiona?" She thought of his sister, her difficult client.

"I know, hard to believe I'd upend my life for a person so...not wonderful."

She smiled. "You told me she had a good reason for her, uh, prickly personality. You also told me you'd share. Can you, or am I overstepping my bounds?"

"After you just gave me the whole backstory on your family feud? Of course I'll tell you. After we put all this away and settle in to watch the moonrise."

"Oh...I..."

He stood slowly, a smile pulling. "Or is that too much like a date and not enough like a business meeting?"

She gave in to a smile. "That obvious, huh?"

"Yep. And I don't want to make you uncomfortable, but when the sun goes down..." He jutted his chin toward the last vestiges of a golden glow on the water. "It becomes a date. So, you decide if you want to hang out here or grab your bag and samples and schedule our next business meeting."

For a long moment, she looked up at him, letting the offer settle on her heart.

"I'll stay for a while," she said softly, getting another shiver from his look of satisfaction.

After cleaning up together, they took decaf back to the patio, sat side by side on a comfy rattan sofa, and lost complete track of time.

True to his word, he delved into Fiona's story, sharing with great grief the fact that his sister had lost a child at a young age. She'd never had another, and it changed her completely.

The story not only broke Vivien's heart, it gave her incredible respect and sympathy for Fiona, and touched her that Danny could tear up when talking about a nephew who'd never made it to high school.

They talked more about families, work, books, art, movies, and marriage. Eventually, they returned to their decisions about where to live.

"I want to be near water," he said. "My other option is in the Hamptons, but it's so...Hamptons."

She laughed at that. "I would imagine."

"My buddy is selling his house up there and I actually considered buying it instead of this, but then Fiona's husband died and I felt responsible for keeping an eye on her."

And now she understood why.

"The house is gorgeous, though." He reached for his phone, which he'd left face down on the coffee table for hours. "As a designer, you'll appreciate this. Look."

He thumbed the screen, typed something in, and inched it away, laughing. "Where are the reading glasses when you need them? Oh, here. Check this place out."

She took the phone and angled it, then gasped at the rambling beachfront home featured on a real estate page. "Oh, that's gorgeous."

"Click through," he suggested. "You'll love what they've done with it."

She certainly did, getting no further than the entryway when she nearly dropped the phone. "That's it!" she exclaimed.

"The house you want?"

"The chandelier." She zoomed in on a pearl shell light fixture in the middle of the image. "It's exactly what

I want for the Summer House for the vaulted ceiling on the first floor. I saw it on a design site and have fantasized about it for a while."

"Want me to ask where they got it?"

"Yes and no," she said, smiling at him. "It's way out of my price range."

He shrugged. "You never know. My friend is a bargain hunter and might have found a knockoff. I'll ask."

"Would you?"

"Of course. If it makes you happy."

That simple statement did something to her heart—something like skipping a beat and rolling around and maybe cracking a little.

She looked away, her gaze landing on a sky full of stars, realizing the air had cooled. The corner of his phone showed that it was well past eleven, and she'd been here...way too long.

"You know, I better go," she said, handing the phone back to him.

Danny didn't move for a moment. Then he stood, too, heading inside with her and helping her pick up her bag and samples, then walking her to her Highlander in the driveway.

"Thank you for dinner," she said, unlocking the door.

"Thank you for making my loft not look like a frat house." He angled his head down. "But more than that, for your company. I didn't realize quite how lonely I was."

Vivien felt her breath catch. "No one should be lonely," she managed to say.

"I agree." He searched her face, his gaze intense. "And I can't remember the last time I enjoyed someone so much. I really..." He let out a breath that sounded like surrender. "I like you, Vivien. And I want to see you again—not professionally."

Her poor heart flipped again. "That's...nice. And unexpected."

He gave an easy laugh. "Is it? I've been attracted to you since the day I soaked you in sprinkler water."

She laughed, too, at that memory.

"And I'd like to take this...further. That is, if you will give a chance to...what did you call me? The Hapless Handyman?"

She grunted at the nickname. "I'm sorry."

"I'm not." He closed the space between them, brushing her lips with his. "Come back for more long talks and food and..." He sighed into the almost kiss. "Time together."

Her knees literally wobbled at the warmth of his breath on her lips.

When she didn't answer, he reached a hand out and tucked a strand of hair behind her ear, his thumb lingering on her cheek for several heartbeats. Then he opened the door for her and gestured for her to climb in.

"Drive safe, Vivien."

"I will."

What was she doing? Where was this going? And what about...*Peter*?

Somehow she managed to start the car, watching him step back as she pulled out and drove away.

What was happening? She had no idea...but it was the most fun she'd had in a long time.

VIVIEN CLOSED the Summer House front door behind her, turning the knob to keep it from clicking shut too loudly, grateful they didn't have an alarm set. Everything was still and hushed, dark except for the glow from the stovetop clock that read 12:17 a.m.

Vivien tiptoed barefoot through the kitchen, shoes dangling from her fingers, getting a punch of déjà vu from one hot summer night when she, Tessa, and Kate had snuck in late and walked right into Maggie.

She hadn't meant to stay at Danny's for so long. But she hadn't wanted to leave and the time with him had flown by. Still thinking of his parting kiss, she grinned to herself as she climbed the stairs slowly, slipped into the main suite she shared with Lacey, and closed the door gently and, she hoped, silently.

The room was cool and smelled faintly of her lavender pillow spray and Lacey's shampoo. The moonlight cast silvery streaks across the comforter. Lacey was bundled beneath it, sound asleep.

Behind the bathroom door, Vivien changed quickly into her pajamas, washed her face, brushed her teeth, and did her level best not to make a sound when she slipped into bed.

"That was a really...long client meeting."

Vivien sucked in a surprised breath. "You're awake?"

Lacey turned on her side, but it was too dark to make out her expression. "Kind of hard not to be when you come tiptoeing in like a teenager who just made out in the back of a car."

Vivien laughed, covering her mouth. "It wasn't like that."

"Mm...hmm."

Vivien giggled, oddly giddy.

Lacey reached for her phone to check the time. "Mom. It's after midnight."

"I know. I lost track of time."

"Is that what we're calling it now?" Lacey teased. "Losing track of time with a very handsome, rich client who flirts like it's a sport?"

"Says the girl dating a literal NFL player." Vivien pulled the covers up and rolled toward her daughter, seeing a smile now. "Do not make me regret telling you things."

"Did you kiss him?" she asked, a playful note in her voice.

"Kiss...are you...why would I..." At Lacey's pretend scowl, she gave up the fight. "One teeny-tiny, barely worth mentioning, light as air but still really mind-blowing kiss."

"Mom!" She shot up, throwing the covers off as if she simply had no words. "You *kissed* him?"

"To be perfectly accurate, *he* kissed *me*." A beat passed, and then Vivien exhaled. "And, Lacey Knight, I freely admit I don't know what I'm doing."

"With Danny?" Lacey asked.

"With Danny. With Peter. With...my whole love life." Vivien rubbed her forehead. "Not that I expected to have a love life a month after my divorce the year I turn fifty."

"Well, apparently you do." Lacey slid back under the covers and snuggled closer, like she did when she was a teenager and came home from a date that had to be hashed and re-hashed. "Tell me everything. I mean, I know he's hot—"

"Hot?"

"I guess you'd call it handsome," she corrected. "And wealthy. And into you. What else did you find out tonight?"

"So much," Vivien said on a sigh. "He's fascinating and successful and caring. But...Peter."

"Yes, Peter."

Vivien shot her a look. "They're such wildly different men. Peter is calm and solid and kind. He's been in my life for decades. He knows my family. My baggage. He wants to move here, Lacey, and, you know, be with me. As a couple."

Lacey bolted upright again. "Wait, what?"

"He said that a few nights ago when we went to mini-golf. He wants to be serious. Official. Real."

"Mom, that's huge. That's a *commitment*."

"I know," Vivien said softly, tugging her back down. "And he'd be wonderful. He's the kind of man I could build a life with. But Danny..."

Lacey groaned. "Oh, Danny. Hapless Handy turned Hedge Fund Hunk."

Vivien laughed. "Danny is magnetic and I'm drawn to him. I don't know him well, but I feel like I do. Like I could talk to him all night. He makes me feel...I don't know...like I'm twenty again. Not sure you can actually put a name to that feeling, but it's really nice."

"So, let me get this straight," Lacey said, leaning on her elbow and propping her head on her hand. "You're The Bachelorette now."

"Oh, stop it."

"Should I bring out two roses?"

Vivien jabbed her and made her head fall off her hand, and they both laughed again, then grew quiet as they lay in the dark.

After a minute, Lacey inched closer. "Can I say something? It's profound."

"Hit me, baby girl."

"You've spent so much of your life doing what was expected. Following Maggie's strict rules. Being Ryan's perfect wife and top designer. And, all the while, right next to me as the best mother in the world. Through it all, you've kept yourself exactly dead last."

Vivien closed her eyes. "That's not how it felt, honey. I loved all those roles. Well, maybe not being Maggie's daughter, but it wasn't that bad. I had Eli and Crista. But I never felt last in life."

"It's your time," Lacey said on a hushed whisper. "I mean it, Mom. This decade, your fifties? This is when you come first and you get to choose joy now. Whatever that looks like. If Peter makes you feel loved and secure, amazing. If Danny makes you feel feminine and seen, also amazing. You deserve all of it. You deserve happiness."

Vivien squeezed her eyelids against the sudden tears that prickled behind them. "You're really wise sometimes, you know that?"

"I have my moments."

A beat passed. Vivien turned her head on the pillow. "Thank you, honey. I'll hold on to that advice. Now can I turn the tables?"

Lacey stiffened. "Is this about Roman?"

"Yes. What's going on there? You've seen him several times this past week."

She let out a long exhale. "Yeah. Well, I'm choosing what makes me happy. It feels...right."

There was just enough of a defensive note in her voice that Vivien had to wonder if there wasn't more to this relationship than Lacey was sharing. She knew her daughter...and this one was different.

She just didn't know how or why.

But she knew one thing. So she reached across the bed and took Lacey's hand.

"I love you, Lace."

Lacey squeezed her fingers. "Right back at you, Golden Bachelorette."

Vivien groaned. "Don't call me that."

"You *are*, though. You've got options. Drama. Romance. I'm just waiting for someone to jump in the pool wearing a tux."

Vivien laughed quietly. "Go to sleep."

They both lay there in the dark, smiling, hearts a little fuller than before.

July 10, 1991

Today we went to the community pool, and it was a thousand degrees outside but also PERFECT. Like, the sun was just right, and the breeze made the umbrellas do that flappy thing, and everything felt summery and delicious.

Kate and Tessa and I all wore big, floppy hats and sat together by the deep end with our feet in the water to stay cool and drank something Aunt Jo Ellen called a "mocktail" which totally looked like a real drink.

I put lemon-scented Sun-In in my hair (shhhh don't tell Mom) and Tessa braided a little section of hers like she always does when she's bored. Kate was reading _To Kill a Mockingbird_ AGAIN because she's an actual genius and said she forgot what happened to Boo Radley. Like... okay, nerd.

But what I really want to write about is our moms.

They were sitting off to the side of the pool at this little round table with their drinks (maybe not "mocktails") wearing sunglasses that made them look like movie stars. Who knows what they were talking about, but, man, those two can yak.

But more than that, they were LAUGHING. Loud. The kind of guffawing where they had to take their sunglasses off to wipe their eyes and were leaning in so close I thought they were going to fall out of their chairs.

We were picking up bits and pieces that made no sense but were still hilarious.

Aunt Jo Ellen said something like, "Remember that time we snuck out of the Sigma Nu party with all that food stashed in our purses?" and my mom—M_aggie_Lawson_, the queen of Southern perfection and "posture is character"—laughed so hard she SNORTED.

Repeating for those in the back: _SHE_ _SNORTED_.

I didn't even know she could snort.

And I swear she looked so HAPPY. Also she corrected Aunt JE—apparently it was Sigma _Chi_ not Sigma N_u_. And that brought on more unex-plained gales of laughter about a guy they called Bruce the Moose. Not kidding.

I pointed it out to Kate and Tessa and we all watched them for a second. Just sitting there, best friends since college, looking like they were connected at the soul.

Kate reminded us that they've been best friends longer than we've been alive. Isn't that wild! And Tessa kept pointing out how they didn't even have to say anything, but just look at each other and start laughing.

We all decided we want that kind of friendship with each other for the rest of our lives. So, right then and there, under our floppy sunhats with our feet in the pool, we took each other's hands and we made a pact.

We promised that no matter what happens, we'll all stay best friends forever.

That even when we're ancient (forty!!) and married or not or moms or not or whatever—we'll stay close. No exceptions. We'll drink (real) cocktails and wear big sunglasses and laugh without even saying words.

We pinky swore. That means it's legally binding. And I really believe it. I do.

Because me and Tessa and Kate—we're meant to be best friends. Just like Jo Ellen and Maggie.

Forever.

Love,

Viv

P.S. Crista was there too but she was in the baby pool with her Barbies and cried so Tessa had to braid her hair just to calm her down. So. Yeah.

Chapter Fourteen
Maggie

Maggie was just starting to truly relax when she heard a knock on the Summer House front door. She and Jo had been outside for hours, talking and reminiscing like the two old ladies they were.

But with every shared memory or bawdy laugh—much louder than Maggie really liked to laugh, but when Jo said "it bears repeating" for the fifteenth time, she lost it—guilt pressed a little harder. Roger would be furious. And when the smile faded from Jo Ellen's eyes, Maggie knew she was thinking the same thing about Artie.

"That's Peter," Vivien called, poking her head out to the deck. "He said he wanted to talk to you two, remember? Is this a good time?"

"Is anyone else home?" Maggie asked, immediately rising from the sofa and smoothing her linen trousers. "Because I'd like complete privacy for this conversation."

"No one, Mom," Vivien assured her. "Tessa and Lacey are running around town finishing whatever they need to do for the Bat Mitzvah, and I'm up in my room working on a client's project. You are alone out here."

"Good. We'll see him now."

When Vivien stepped away, Jo Ellen stood and came closer to Maggie. "Maybe now we'll get some answers, Mags. We gave him that Cotton Ramsey name darn near a week ago."

Vivien nodded, suspecting that's why Peter wanted to talk. They'd told him everything that Frank had shared and he said he'd "look into it."

She dreaded what he might find. Roger and the Mafia? The *Dixie* Mafia, whatever abhorrent thing that was.

It pained her to think about.

A moment later, Vivien and Peter stepped outside, and instantly, Maggie felt a prickle of warning. Peter's expression was wary and worried, far more serious than the affable detective usually was. Just looking at him, she sensed a sudden shift in pressure before a storm.

"Hello, ladies," he said in a fairly solemn greeting. "How are we today?"

"I don't know," Maggie replied, not interested in niceties. "You tell us."

Vivien put her hand on his shoulder. "You want anything?" she asked. "Water? Soda? Straight gin?"

He didn't laugh, which only worsened Maggie's dread.

"I'm good. I'll come up and get you when we're done here. Then I'll go help you pick up that rug and console table."

"Thanks." Vivien nodded and gave the other women a tight smile, then left them alone. Without a word, they moved to the seating area. In silent solidarity, Jo Ellen and Maggie sat next to each other on the rattan sofa while Peter positioned himself on the edge of a large chair across from them.

Suddenly, the sweet tropical air felt dense, and the sun slipped behind a cloud, stealing the warmth from the deck. Maggie just knew this wasn't going to be good.

What could Roger have been involved with that could hurt her any more than what he'd already done? She didn't know and was terrified to find out.

"So, Cotton Ramsey," he started, glancing between the two women. "I was able to reach out to contacts up in Biloxi and did uncover, uh, quite a bit about this rather colorful character. His files are not sealed."

Maggie's throat tightened as she and Jo Ellen exchanged a glance.

"Just spell it out, Peter," Maggie said, impatience rising. "How bad is it? What did my husband do? What mess do we have to clean up?"

His lips lifted in an amused smile. "Relax, Maggie," he said. "Roger didn't do anything."

There was just enough emphasis on the name "Roger" for Maggie to let out a sigh of relief, but at the same moment, Jo Ellen sat straighter.

Then Peter pulled a folded sheet of paper from his back pocket, opening it with steady and—not that it mattered—quite strong hands with clean, clipped nails. Maggie always respected a man who kept his hands in good order. It usually meant his life was that way, too.

"Davis 'Cotton' Ramsey was arrested in early 1996 in a sting operation run jointly by the FBI and the Biloxi

Police Department," he started. "He was found guilty of a host of RICO crimes."

Maggie shuttered her eyes. "What is that?"

"Racketeering," he explained. "Conspiracy to commit fraud, loan sharking, wire fraud, mail fraud, obstruction of justice, to name a few."

"In other words, they threw the book at him," Jo Ellen said with a light laugh.

Maggie shot her a look. "You think this is funny?"

Her smile disappeared. "We didn't marry Cotton Ramsey," Jo Ellen fired back. "You don't have to get your panties in a bunch, Mags."

Yes, she did. Whoever and whatever this Cotton creature was, he'd breathed the same air as Roger and that horrified her.

"Anyway," Peter continued, holding up a hand like a referee. "He was sentenced to twenty-five years but served fifteen before he was released on parole. He died about a year later."

"Is there any connection to Roger Lawson?" Maggie asked, her voice taut.

Peter exhaled just slowly enough that her heart dropped with a thud.

"Not to Roger," he said, the words somehow feeling unfinished as the two women stared at him. "But..." He swallowed, appearing to brace himself before continuing. "His arrest was a rather elaborate setup, assisted by an informant. An undercover agent, if you will, worked closely with the FBI to lure Cotton to the meeting location and lead him into the trap." He lifted a brow as if...as if accusing someone.

"Roger was in prison then," Maggie said. "So if you're—"

"It was Artie," Peter said quietly. "Arthur Wylie was the informant."

For a long, breathless moment, no one moved. Not until Maggie found the strength to turn her head and look at Jo Ellen, who was ghost white, wide-eyed, and slack-jawed.

"What?" she croaked the word. "No. That's not...no. He would never..."

Maggie dropped back on the sofa cushion and crossed her arms. "Apparently, Artie made a second career out of tipping off the police."

Jo Ellen glared at her. "At least he didn't make a second career out of...fraud!"

Maggie bristled and closed her eyes, refusing to get hurt by the comment. Jo Ellen was in shock. Frankly, they all were. What on God's green Earth were these men up to when they were supposed to be vacationing with their families? The Mafia? The Feds? It was preposterous!

"I'm sorry, Jo Ellen," Peter said. "I checked it repeatedly. I don't know what his involvement was with this group of mobsters, but for whatever reason, he opted to turn them in. They had to have trusted him enough—"

"Stop." She held up a trembling hand. "Just stop, please. I...I can't...take this."

"I understand this is upsetting," Peter said gently.

"But he didn't break the law. His name's not in any public record, but the internal files confirm it. He was cooperating with federal agents."

"But...after Roger was already in prison?" Jo Ellen said on a rasp, still pale and stunned. "So he was involved with these men..."

Maggie's heart shifted at the tone in her friend's voice. "It's okay," she whispered, putting her hand on Jo Ellen's arm. "You'll be okay, Jo."

"But...but...I didn't know," Jo Ellen whispered. "I had no idea. He never said a word."

"Neither did Roger," Maggie said hoarsely, remembering the pain of that betrayal and feeling it all over again. And people didn't think she was empathetic! If not, what was this overwhelming need to comfort Jo Ellen?

Peter leaned closer, his face etched with compassion. "I know this is a lot. It doesn't answer your questions as to why your husbands would demand your silence or that you don't speak to each other, but it is surely part of the reason."

Jo shuddered, fighting tears.

Maggie slid her hand down to Jo Ellen's, clasping her fingers like they had when they were girls, when everything had felt safe and certain.

"Thank you, Peter," Jo said, her voice thick with unshed tears. "I appreciate you going the extra mile for us."

Peter nodded, quiet for a second, then rose. "This might be it, though. I don't know how much more information I can get you. Have you been able to get any of Artie's files?"

"Kate shipped his fishing rods," Jo Ellen said. "But she thought it would be safer to bring the file box in person when she comes down for the Celebration of Life."

Maggie lifted a brow. Did Jo Ellen still want to celebrate Artie's life? Which one—the one she knew about or the one he kept hidden?

"And, Maggie, you're positive that Roger doesn't have anything tucked away?"

She sighed, thinking of the old lockbox in Crista's garage. "There was one box that I kept full of papers and old memories. I haven't even looked in it since he died, but he told me to keep it no matter what, so I did."

Peter gave her a look of disbelief. "You should get it," he said. "There could be something in there."

"It was pictures and...I don't even remember. Nothing from his business or his..." She swallowed. "Criminal activities."

"Eli's coming down when Kate does," Peter said. "Ask him to bring it. You should look at it again with fresh eyes."

She nodded, knowing he was right.

He said goodbye and disappeared inside, and Maggie dropped back down on the sofa, even closer to Jo Ellen.

"Please don't gloat," Jo muttered, dropping her head. "Please don't."

"Oh, Jo." Maggie put both arms around her and gave her a tight squeeze. "I'm not gloating. I'm as confused as you are and, believe it or not, I fully understand your pain. It's okay to cry when you find out you didn't know your husband at all."

As if all she needed was permission, Jo Ellen gave in to a long, sad sob of profound disappointment, confusion, and loss.

"Artie," Jo Ellen said at last, her voice thick. "My sweet Artie."

"Just because he turned this Cotton character in to the FBI doesn't mean he was involved with him," Maggie said, trying to reassure her. "The man was practically a saint. Maybe he wanted retribution for Roger's incarceration."

"But he never told me!" she moaned. "That's the worst part...not knowing any of this for all these years."

Maggie nodded. "It's a lie by omission and makes you question everything."

"Yes!" Finally, she stood, but looked like her legs couldn't even hold her as she walked to the railing to look out to the Gulf. "I thought I knew him better than anyone in the world. We were married for fifty years, for goodness sake. And he never breathed a word. Never once."

Maggie sighed. "We married men who kept secrets from us."

"And forced us to make promises not to talk to each other." She whipped around. "What didn't they want us to find out? Why separate us? I thought it was because Roger was...you know..."

"A criminal," Maggie supplied. "Maybe they both were."

Jo Ellen pressed the heels of her hands into her forehead. "Or Artie was an undercover agent? How is that even remotely possible?"

"Seriously," Maggie said with a dry laugh. "The man was hardly James Bond."

"But who was he? Why didn't I know?" Tears threatened and she didn't bother to blink them away. They spilled over, running down her cheeks.

Maggie's heart rolled around in guilt, shame, and remorse. "I'm sorry," she whispered, standing up to step closer to Jo. "I'm sorry Roger was a bad influence on your highly moral and principled husband. Artie was a good man and he loved you."

Suddenly, Jo Ellen pulled her into a hug so fierce it nearly knocked the breath from her lungs.

"Don't you dare apologize," Jo Ellen hissed fiercely. "Not for any of this. You had nothing to do with it, and you are my friend."

"*Were*," Maggie corrected softly.

"No, Mags. Are. You are my friend! Those two men can just...well, I'd say drop dead, but they did already."

Maggie laughed and they finally pulled apart. Jo Ellen wiped her eyes with her hands.

"We can't tell my girls," she blurted out. "Please promise me that. Not now, not before the celebration. Tessa, especially, would be devastated. Kate, too."

"I'll honor what you ask of me," Maggie replied. "But I won't lie to my kids. And I won't..." She swallowed, realizing how much salt it would throw in Jo Ellen's wound if

Maggie were to reiterate her refusal to attend Artie's ash-throwing thing.

But she wasn't going. Period, end of story. Not in a million years would she risk Roger's wrath from the Great Beyond by celebrating the life of the man who put her husband in prison. And others.

"You won't what?" Jo Ellen pressed.

"I won't tell your girls," she finished. "We'll let them remember their father the way they need to."

Jo Ellen nodded, but her shoulders sagged under the weight of it all. Maggie felt exactly the same.

Chapter Fifteen

Lacey

If someone had told Lacey a few months ago that she'd be driving through the rural back roads of Florida with a great-looking NFL player in a car that cost more than her college tuition, she would have laughed at them.

And if they'd have told her that somewhere in the past few weeks—after spending hours together at the Summer House, on the beach, out and about in Destin, and generally side by side—that this fake relationship would slip into kind of real?

Whoa. She'd have told that person to lay off the rom-coms.

And yet...here they were, doing all that.

As the days rolled along, they had hit a rhythm that included long conversations, easy hours, and lots of laughs. With his parents still on their dream cruise in the Mediterranean, Lacey had tamped down her desire to tell Tessa the truth, though it still rose up and tightened her throat in the middle of the night.

Thinking it all through, Lacey sighed into the butter-soft leather, letting the Florida sun burning through the windshield warm her legs and arms. Next to her, Roman handled the sports car with practiced ease, cracking jokes and humming along to old-school R&B.

"What are we rescuing again?" he asked, glancing over. "I mean, I know it's a dog, but any more details?"

"A Chihuahua-bulldog mix named Pickles."

He snorted. "Epic."

"Naomi—our Bat Mitzvah candidate—apparently went to this refuge on a field trip that her mom chaperoned, and they both fell in love with Pickles. Jennifer decided the dog would be the perfect surprise gift to be presented at the party, so we're picking him up and holding him until tomorrow's Bat Mitzvah."

"What a great mom," he said with a chuckle, then looked her way. "And full-service event planners."

She shrugged. "It was going to be a long and boring drive up here, but with you going?" Lacey was unable to deny how happy it made her that Roman had volunteered to join her on this errand. "I don't know if I've thanked you enough."

"Don't worry about me," Roman added. "I would have wanted to take this drive even if you didn't have to get the dog." He gestured toward the tall pines that lined the winding road, silhouetted against a blindingly blue sky. "It's gorgeous. And..." He smiled. "I like the company."

No matter how many hours they spent together, his open admission that he was attracted to her made Lacey's heart flip. Part of her couldn't believe it, but another part —the one getting to know what a genuine man he was despite the trappings of professional sports—absolutely did believe it.

And she felt exactly the same way, which was maddening. And thrilling. And complicated beyond description.

She smiled back, trying to suppress the swell of affection in her chest. "I'm sure I'll pale in comparison to Pickles."

"A bulldog-Chihuahua mix? Possibly," he teased. "But that's a high bar."

"Especially when he's presented," she said. "Our client wants him to wear a bowtie and we used his picture to make a cake with his face on it."

"You and Tessa don't play about your parties, do you?"

"No, we do not." She laughed. "To Tessa, fun is a real business, and I'm learning. I'll say this—it's my favorite job I've ever had. I mean, no one cheers from the stands like they do for you, but—"

He rolled his eyes. "Most of the time I'm on the bench, but I'm sure that there will be huge applause for the Pickles presentation."

She couldn't argue that, and she appreciated his humility on the topic of who and what he was.

They turned off the highway onto a gutted rural road, the car bouncing.

"Ouch." Lacey made a face. "That probably annihilated your suspension."

He shrugged. "Just a car." After a second, he glanced at her. "What? Why are you looking at me like you refuse to believe a word I'm saying?"

"I refuse to believe a person with your talent and success is that free of an ego."

His brows lifted in surprise, then he shook his head.

"I can have an ego," he said. "Ask my high school classmates. But the higher I go in sports, the more humbling the experience is. That and my parents never let me get too cocky."

"Really? It sounds like they doted on you."

"They did everything imaginable to raise me right," he said. "So I wasn't the boss of the house by any means. Dad made sure I remembered I was just a kid who got lucky with speed and hand-to-eye. Oh, here we are. Stillwater Animal Refuge."

She turned to see the understated wooden sign and peered between the pine trees to glimpse the property and a weathered barn in the distance.

"This looks pretty," she said.

"And huge." He gestured toward the GPS on the dash. "We're still almost a mile from the main building."

He drove through an open gate and that mile took them past acres of woods and trails, around a picturesque lake, and past some stables and a festive red barn called "The Cat House."

They finally reached a one-story ranch-style structure painted buttery yellow with a tin roof and a covered porch. Inside, it was as rustic as the rest of the place with faded couches and paneled walls.

An older woman stood behind the front desk, smiling as she greeted them. "Can I help you get the dog of your dreams?" she asked, then eyed Lacey. "Actually, you look like a cat girl."

"I love cats," Lacey told her. "But I'm here to pick up a dog named Pickles. Jennifer Kaplan arranged the adoption and emailed the paperwork. I'm Lacey Knight. I believe she named me on the form."

The woman's face lit up. "Oh! Yes, he's been waiting for you. Hold on. I'll get someone in the kennels."

She picked up a phone, and Lacey turned to Roman, who'd stepped to the side and was studying a bulletin board covered with thank-you notes written with dozens of pictures of happy families and their new pets.

He turned to her with a wistful look. "Adoption," he said softly. "Whether human or furball, is a beautiful thing."

"It sure is."

"Look at all these happy families."

"Just like yours," she replied.

He let out a sigh, his expression troubled. "Their cruise is almost over and they'll be home soon."

She put a hand on his arm. "The longer you wait, the harder it will be for Tessa when we tell her. She's going to struggle with the fact that we kept it from her all this time."

He started to answer, but then the front door swung open and the woman behind the desk called out, "Cute overload on the way!"

They looked down to see a bug-eyed brown and tan Chihuahua, fur bristling and tail wagging at breakneck speed. He trotted toward them, a few steps ahead of a girl who looked to be about seventeen, holding the dog's leash.

Roman blinked. "That is the most ridiculous animal I've ever seen."

Pickles gave a high-pitched bark in response.

"I love him already," Lacey said.

The girl handed over the leash. "Pickles has a lot of energy," she said. "The best way to calm him down before you get him on the road is a walk around the property. That'll help you bond with him, too. All you need to do is sign the paperwork with Miss Nellie."

"I've got that right here," the woman behind the desk said.

While Lacey handled the administration and gave the donation that Jennifer wanted to make, she kept glancing over her shoulder to watch Roman, who'd gotten on the floor to play with Pickles.

"He's so cute," Nellie whispered as she flipped pages for Lacey to sign.

"Man or dog?" Lacey asked with a smile.

"Honestly? Both."

A moment later, they headed outside into the sunshine, with Pickles proudly leading the way, obviously familiar with every inch. So much so, that they let him off the leash for the sheer joy of watching him trot from tree to tree.

"What do you think she'll say?"

Roman's question was so unexpected, Lacey stopped mid-step. "Tessa?" she asked.

"I mean, will she be mad that we didn't tell her?"

"She might be. She might also be mad that I found you at all. I don't know." And worrying about it was starting to gnaw at Lacey, but the decision to tell her—or his parents—wasn't hers.

"I like things status quo," he said. "It's one of my personality traits. I hate change."

"Really? You up and moved to Destin on a whim," she remarked. "I would have thought you love change."

He lifted a shoulder. "With people and relationships," he said. "I'm so solid with my mom and dad that I don't really want to throw this monkey wrench at them. And I'm enjoying getting to know Tessa as a person, not as my biological mother. And don't start me on you."

"What is that supposed to mean?"

He draped an arm around her. "Once the truth is out, we will definitely change."

"I know, but...we didn't do this for us, Roman. We did this to give you easy access to Tessa."

He tightened his grip. "Yeah, yeah, yeah. Fake, phony, ruse, pretend. I know your buzzwords, Lacey Knight. If I want to believe you're my girlfriend, you are. I mean, assuming you agree."

She just smiled, amused that he even had to ask.

"But all that will change," he said. "And I don't want it to. I'll have to go back to Jacksonville, so..."

When he didn't finish, she slowed her step and then stopped again, waiting. "So..." she urged.

"So maybe you'll...come over and watch me play sometime."

"I would," she said. "Assuming..."

"Assuming I get off the bench," he joked.

"Assuming you and I are still friends after the truth is out and our loved ones respond."

He pulled her a little closer. "If they're loved ones, they'll...keep loving us. They'll understand that I was curious and needed to know my biological mother."

"I hope so," she said, trying to make it sound light but she was concerned about Tessa.

"And by the way..." He turned her in his arms and looked down at her. "When are you going to realize we're more than just friends?"

"We *are* friends."

"Really? 'Cause I'm about to kiss you right on that beautiful mouth and I don't kiss my friends."

She felt her whole being melting into him as their lips met and the world disappeared into a haze of delicious, perfect, soft....barking.

From a distance.

They jerked apart.

"Pickles!"

Turning, they caught sight of a flash of brown disappearing around a tree, then back on the path, shooting off at breakneck speed.

"Whoa!" Roman shot off in the same direction, like a proverbial bullet. Pickles was quick and made it at least fifty yards but he was no match for Roman, who caught up with him in a second and scooped the dog up like, well, like a football.

He turned in a circle and held the dog in the air. "And he scores!" he called out, twirling Pickles playfully in a touchdown dance. "It's a...Pickles Six!"

Lacey laughed, hustling toward them, her mind spinning over the conversation about change. It was coming—and fast.

LACEY OPENED her eyes with a start, not sure where she was for a moment.

Her head rested on something hard and...beating. Roman's chest. His cotton T-shirt, warm and a little damp. The snoring she heard was Pickles, curled in the crate they'd brought back to Roman's rental house hours ago.

They'd eaten dinner, watched a movie, and crashed. Now it was...very dark outside. She squinted at the kitchen clock.

Eleven?

Jeez, she was as bad as her mother, disappearing until late at night in the arms of a man.

And, oh. She laid her head back down on his beating heart. What a man he was.

"You awake?" Roman threaded his fingers into her hair, easing her head back so they could look at each other.

"Mmm. Kinda. That's Pickles, by the way," she added, leaning her head in the general direction of the crate. "I don't snore."

He chuckled and adjusted her whole body as if he

wanted her even closer. "I had a dream," he said softly. "You were in it."

"I was? What happened?"

"We adopted..."

"Another dog?" she guessed.

"Kids. Four of them."

She sat up a bit. "Wow. That's quite the dream. Four?"

"I want to adopt," he said, finger combing her hair as he pinned her with whiskey eyes. "But in the dream, you did, too. It was cool."

"It sounds...daunting."

"But my parents were there. In fact, we were in their house and I was really happy."

"Maybe I'll go there someday," she said, unsure how to react.

"I hope so. Because you know what? My parents would like you as much as I do. Which..." He added some pressure to his touch. "Is a lot."

The admission made her whole body light and weak and...*lost*.

As if sensing that, he tucked some hair behind her ear, letting his thumb stroke her cheek. "You know why?" he asked.

"I can't imagine," she cracked.

"Because you're real, Lacey. You're the first person in a long time who makes me feel...normal. You don't care about the fact that I'm an NFL player or what car I drive or how many followers I have. You didn't even fangirl when we met."

She smiled. "I didn't know who you were. No offense, of course."

He held his hands up. "Please. None taken. To everyone else, I'm 'Roman Matteo, Jacksonville Jaguars wide receiver.' But to you..." He trailed off.

"To me, you're Tessa's son. And believe me, that's the best thing you could be."

His gaze sharpened as he focused on her. "Is that why you like me?"

That and a million other reasons she opted to keep to herself. In fact, she had to bite her tongue—literally—to keep from saying all the things rolling around her head and heart.

That she was falling for him. That she didn't want this to end. That she was terrified of what would happen when the truth came out.

But instead she whispered, "I just like you. Do I need a reason?"

"No, but you need...this." He leaned down and kissed her, long enough for Lacey to forget everything but how good it felt. But she heard her phone vibrating on the table and knew she had to answer the call.

Very slowly, smiling at his grunt of frustration, she slipped out from under his arm. "Just a sec."

But her heart jolted when she saw the screen.

Tessa.

"Speak of the...angel," she whispered, swiping the phone screen to answer. "Hey, Tess."

"Hey!" Tessa's bright voice filled her ear. "Where you been, child? Never mind—you don't answer to me.

Consider this a work call and I want to know if little Pickles has been safely secured."

Lacey looked over at the crate. "Oh, yeah. He's out cold and dreaming about his new owner. He can stay here with Roman, I think it'll be easier."

"Here? With Roman?" Tessa's voice rose, then she chuckled.

"Well, I mean, the Summer House is crowded and... he's happy."

"Sounds like you are, too," Tessa teased. "Hey, you deserve a little fun, girl. You work hard. You've done all the heavy lifting for tomorrow's Bat Mitzvah and the client is so happy, Lace."

"Oh, it's nothing—"

"Not nothing." Tessa's voice dropped into something gentler. "You've been amazing. I don't say that enough, but I really feel that way. This whole business—Tessa Wylie Events—only happened because of you. I never thought I could do something like this, and here we are, planning a perfect party for a client who worships you. Plus our schedule is filling up with two new projects on the books as of today. You're my secret weapon, Lacey Knight."

Lacey's throat tightened. "That's sweet. Thank you."

"I'm just so glad I can trust you," Tessa said casually —unaware that she might as well have stabbed Lacey right in the gut.

She forced a laugh, even though her stomach twisted. "Well... I try."

Tessa chuckled. "Okay, ignore me and go back to

your boy. Just don't be too late, or I'll assume you've eloped, which would break both your mothers' hearts. Also, tomorrow's a big day."

"I know. I'm on my way home, I promise." Lacey ended the call, her fingers trembling slightly as she set the phone down on the coffee table, then dropped back on the sofa with a moan.

Roman inched away, regarding her closely. "Everything okay?"

She stared straight ahead, heart pounding, and whispered the only thing that wasn't okay. "We *have* to tell her."

Roman didn't speak right away. Instead, he leaned forward, elbows on his knees, rubbing a hand over his jaw.

"I can't do it anymore," Lacey said, sensing he would push back. "She just told me she trusts me. She said I helped her build her dream."

He nodded, quiet.

"I'm lying to her every day, and she's the woman who took me under her wing, believed in me, gave me a job and a direction and a purpose. I love her, Roman."

"I know," he said softly. "I'm so sorry this has been hard on you."

Lacey swallowed hard. "When can we come clean?"

Roman reached out, took her hand in his. His touch was warm and steady, grounding her like always. "I want to tell her. I *will* tell her. But I need to talk to my parents first."

"I know. When?"

"As soon as possible," he said. "I'll stay for the big Pickles reveal and drive over to Satellite Beach the next day." He leaned into her. "Unless you want to come with me. Like my dream? Only no adopted kids."

She thought about it, searching his face and wondering what it would be like to meet his parents. Under these circumstances? Awkward.

"Never mind," he said quickly, obviously reading her expression. "I don't want to make you uncomfortable."

"It'll be a very personal, private time for you," she added.

He nodded slowly. "I wouldn't hate you seeing where I grew up and meeting them."

"Another time?" she suggested. "After this is behind us?"

"Yes, definitely." He put his hand on her cheek, thumbing her chin. "You okay, Lace?"

"I'm scared this will hurt Tessa. Worried I've way overstepped my bounds, concerned about your parents and..." She let her voice fade out because one more sentence and she'd be revealing to him just how real this pretend relationship was starting to feel.

He leaned closer and gave her a sweet kiss, making her believe—and hope—he felt the same.

Chapter Sixteen

Tessa

Tessa wanted to take credit for the spot-on perfection that was this slightly over-the-top Bat Mitzvah party, but she couldn't. So much of this was Lacey's doing.

It helped that Jennifer Kaplan had a massive budget and an ego to match, and she'd thrown money at the event to thrill her daughter and impress her friends.

Although maybe not in that order, Tessa thought as she watched the woman flit from guest to guest. Even the formal dress she'd worn was more appropriate for a black-tie wedding than a thirteen-year-old's religious ceremony and party.

But Jenn wanted to impress, and Tessa Wylie Events had certainly delivered the goods.

The ballroom of the Emerald Crest Clubhouse had been transformed into the most delightfully upscale jungle any Florida suburb had ever seen. Oversized tropical leaves fanned out from centerpieces on every table, scattered with golden monkeys and tiny zebra figurines.

Lush greenery cascaded from ceiling drapery that billowed like a rainforest canopy, and the focal wall behind the DJ booth was a massive balloon arch in earthy greens and browns with a white neon sign glowing in the center: **STAY WILD.**

Maybe not what Tessa would have chosen for this particular occasion, but young Naomi was electrified by her big event. She sparkled in a leopard-print dress with rhinestone straps, currently dancing with a circle of eighth-grade girls who were still blissfully young enough to be awkward and innocent.

Tessa scanned the room, checking off her invisible mental list. DJ? Pumping out kid-appropriate bangers. Caterers? Plating sliders and chicken skewers. Photographer? Zooming in on a group of kids posing in front of the Safari-themed picture wall.

Again, Lacey had been invaluable making all this work.

Tessa adjusted a palm frond that had come loose from one of the photo backdrops and smoothed her palms down her teal jumpsuit, satisfied with everything. She turned toward the banquet room where the parents were chatting over cocktails.

Then she spotted Lacey talking to the catering manager at the cupcake table, preparing for the big cake reveal. But that had to come after the dog.

Threading her way around pre-teens and filled tables, Tessa made her way over.

"All good?" she asked as the caterer walked away and left Lacey eyeing the desserts.

"We're planning the timing of the Pickles presentation," Lacey said, glancing at her phone. "Roman's on the way and will be in the back parking lot. Jennifer wants the kids sugared up on the first dessert..." She gestured toward the cupcakes. "For maximum screamage, I suppose, when Pickles arrives on the scene."

Tessa laughed and, right on cue, a pack of girls descended on the cupcakes, doing their level best to get "sugared up" as her client wanted.

"I don't think Naomi needs the sugar to get excited," Tessa said, her gaze falling on the evening's big star as she walked toward the table, giggling with girlfriends.

Bright-eyed and flushed, Naomi floated over and beamed at Tessa and Lacey.

"You guys slayed!" she exclaimed with a squeal. "I'm definitely having the time of my life!"

Tessa's heart soared as she reached an arm out. "You're the star, kiddo. How about a cupcake?"

"Yes, please!" She glanced around. "Where's my mom? She's been acting super weird, so I suppose whatever mongo surprise she has planned is about to happen."

"I know nothing about a surprise," Tessa lied smoothly. "She's in the banquet room if you want to find her."

The speakers thudded out a base line and all the girls shrieked in unison.

"No!" Naomi abandoned the cupcake. "I want to dance! Come on." She grabbed Tessa's arm. "Dance with us!"

She held back, laughing. "Not in my job description unless it's *The Macarena*. That I can dance."

"Do it!" Naomi tugged so hard, Tessa almost slipped off a heel. "Please! I want you out there."

She threw a look to Lacey, who was laughing. *"The Macarena,* Tess?"

"I honestly don't..." But the arguments were lost and she was swept up with the swarm of pre-teens who dragged her to the dance floor.

"C'mon! We're gonna teach you the Sunset Shuffle!" one of them shouted, laughing.

"Sounds exactly right for the old-age home," she cracked, but her humor was lost on the kids.

The music pulsed—something bright and pop-y that seemed to exist only on TikTok—and she was surrounded by bouncing ponytails and glittery sneakers as the girls taught her the moves. She did her best to follow along, laughing when she inevitably stepped left instead of right, nearly knocking into a lanky boy.

But she was grinning. All of them were.

When the music faded, Naomi turned to the DJ. "Can you play the...what was it? Macaroni!"

He threw his head back laughing and held up one finger. "Gimme a sec."

Tessa just shook her head, cracking up at the name, and before she knew it, her feet—and hands—were moving to a dance she'd done all through college and at most of the weddings she'd attended or planned.

At the first few notes, the kids squealed, proving they'd either learned the dance from their parents or they knew it all along, because they hit every move.

"You're the best!" Naomi giggled as she tapped her shoulders and swayed.

"You're the coolest grown-up ever!" a tall brunette shouted.

Tessa was breathless, flushed, and for a moment, caught up in the music and youth and fun.

Until she suddenly...wasn't.

It hit her all at once—watching the beaming parents on the sidelines, sipping champagne and smiling with pride, their eyes on the children they'd raised. Something inside her wobbled. Something deep.

She'd never be a mom. Oh, she had been once. And then she let him go and that was the end of that story.

Except, of course, it wasn't. Not really. That sensation that something was missing had followed her through every birthday, every family holiday, every moment like this one—filled with light and laughter and love she'd never fully feel.

The minute she could, she stepped off the dance floor quietly and made her way toward the refreshment table, needing a moment to collect herself.

"Are you okay?" Lacey was next to her in a flash.

Tessa looked up and almost spilled her guts. Lacey already knew the truth and if anyone would understand that sometimes the old ache hit hard and unexpectedly, it would be this dear girl. And she was as close to a daughter as Tessa would ever have.

But she wasn't her daughter. She was Vivien's and—

"Tessa. You're scaring me." Lacey inched closer. "You're so pale."

"I'm fine," she said quickly. "I have no right dancing like that anymore with a bunch of teenagers."

Lacey searched her face, not buying it. "Well, you look...upset. And I know you pretty well. Are you worried about something going wrong?"

She glommed onto the excuse. "Well, the dog, of course. Where is he?"

"Roman just pulled into the back parking lot and is waiting for me to get the signal from Jennifer. I alerted her but she's deep in conversation and..." She tapped her phone and read the screen. "Oh, he's having a time with the bow tie. I knew we should have insisted on a clip-on or a dog collar, but Jennifer wanted that very tie."

"It was her husband's from their wedding," Tessa said. "Which is sweet but complicated."

"I have no idea how to tie a bow tie," Lacey admitted.

"I'll go help," Tessa offered, happy to get air and a break from the music. "You handle Jennifer and text me the minute she's ready."

Lacey nodded, but still regarded Tessa with doubt in her blue eyes. "You sure you're okay? You look...I don't know. Sad or...something."

Tessa gave a smile and took her hand, her chest swelling for love of this young woman who was so empathetic, sensitive, and sweet. "Just that you and Roman think you can fool me."

Lacey paled. "*What?*"

"Trying to act like this romance is no big deal," she said. "Trying to pretend you're just friends, like I didn't see you kiss him when he came here during the setup to get the lay of the land."

The color returned to her cheeks with a fury. "Well, I...it *is* no big deal, Tessa. We...just...aren't...I...can't."

Tessa laughed. "Flustered much? Hey, wasn't I the one who told you to find a good guy? I should know you do everything I say—but it would be nice if he lived in Destin."

"Oh, well, I don't even officially live here, so..."

"I know!" Tessa said, the conversation making her feel better. She hated when she did the "baby spiral" and this had already taken her mind off it. "But if you're in love, you'll leave. And that's the way of things, I suppose."

"I'm not..." She couldn't even deny it. "Well, he's not... Please. It's very early days, Tessa."

Lacey's serious tone caught her attention, as though she was warning Tessa. "Lacey, do you think he's going to leave and forget you?"

"Well, probably," she said with a humorless laugh. "I mean, he's Roman Matteo."

"So?" Tessa scoffed and glanced past Lacey. "Oh, dang, here comes Jennifer. Follow her timing and text me —I'll go tie up the dog, so to speak."

Before Lacey could respond, Tessa slipped by her and walked toward the back of the Clubhouse, through the kitchen to the secondary parking lot. It was pretty full, but she spotted the tall golden boy next to his sports car, leaning into the back seat.

"Hey, there," she called.

He straightened and gave her a wave. "You better know how to tie a bow tie," he said.

Laughing, she hustled closer. "Any self-respecting event planner knows that—I'll have to teach Lacey—and so should every young man your age."

"I do," he said. "On myself. This is a dog and he wants no parts of it." He dangled a classic old-school bow tie.

She laughed, taking it from his fingers. "Poor thing. Let me at him."

"I'll bring the crate out," he said. "It'll be easier for you."

He reached in and easily plucked the small wire container and brought it out to the ground.

"Don't be scared, buddy. This pretty lady wants to succeed where I'm failing."

Chuckling, she crouched down and opened the crate, holding one hand out so he didn't run. He stared up at her, his bulgy eyes looking a little sad and scared.

"Oh, honey, I feel you. Come here." She guided him out of the crate, but he squirmed.

"See? It's not easy." Roman reached for the dog. "Might work better if I hold him."

"Yes, that will."

Roman wrapped his large hands around the dog's waist, cooing gently to calm him while Tessa managed to get the tie around his little neck.

"There we go," she said, frowning as she tried to remember the steps from this direction. "You're right, it is different on a dog than a man standing and facing you. Even if that man is a nervous groom."

Smiling, she looked up, catching him studying her face. Staring hard—intently. So much so, that she fumbled the tie and had to start all over again.

"Do I have cupcake on my face?" she asked as she re-wrapped the black satin. "I didn't have any but I was very close to dancing teenagers who were on a sugar high."

"No," he said, his voice...odd.

Was it the nervous groom comment? She looked up at the gruffness in his voice, suddenly forgetting which loop she was on. "Did I miss a step?"

He just swallowed, silent.

"Roman?"

"Oh, oh, that's my phone." He managed to hold Pickles with one hand and reach into his pocket to pull out the phone and read the screen. "Lacey said Jennifer is ready now. They're calling Naomi to the stage after this song."

She held his gaze for a few heartbeats, still trying to figure out his expression, then looked back at the mess of a bow tie.

"Then I better concentrate," she murmured as she made the first knot.

"No, no. You have to slide the left one through that way," he said, using his free hand to help her. "It loops, then slides, see?"

Another unexpected wave of emotion hit her, the words kicking her in the gut. "Oh..." She couldn't breathe for a moment.

"What is it?" he asked.

"I just...you just..." She smiled. "I got the worst déjà vu right then. You sounded exactly like my father teaching me to thread a fishing rod. Same tone of voice, same inflection. You frequently remind me of him."

He gave a smile, but it didn't reach his eyes and he looked more wistful than surprised. "I...I'm sorry I didn't get to meet him."

She drew back at the admission. "Oh, that's...sweet. He was a great guy. You'll meet Seamus and hear all about him, I promise."

"Yeah, but it's not the same."

"That's for sure." She made the final loop and tugged. "There we go. Now pull the sides and...voila! A bow tie on this little rat."

"Perfect." He closed the crate door and tucked the dog away. "You want me to carry it in for you?"

"Yes, please. To the side of the stage."

As they walked with the crate between them, she stole one more look at the tall, handsome, athletic man. He didn't just sound like Artie in that exchange, she mused. He kind of looked like him, too.

Was that why she liked the kid so much? He reminded her of—

"Here we go," he said as he pulled the door open. "Game time."

Instantly, Lacey was there, smiling from one to the other. "She's on stage. Roman, let's go to the side and open the crate at the right moment."

"I'll stay here and watch from this angle," Tessa said,

gesturing for them to take the long way so Naomi didn't spot the crate.

Still feeling inexplicably uneasy, Tessa positioned herself in the middle of the room as the DJ cut the music.

"Naomi Kaplan, report to the stage," he announced.

Naomi trotted up in her sparkly heels, confused but curious. The kids gathered, chattering. Parents pressed in and the whole room sort of held its collective breath. Jennifer and her husband were on the opposite side of the stage from Lacey and Roman, who were well out of sight.

"Now," the DJ said, "we know Naomi has a passion for animals. So much so, she wants to be a vet one day, right, Naomi?"

She nodded. "That's Dr. Kaplan to you," she joked.

"Well," the DJ continued, "someone very special wanted to make sure your Bat Mitzvah included a little extra something *wild*."

He gestured toward her parents, who both beamed at their daughter. Yes, Jennifer wanted to impress her friends, but maybe Tessa had been too harsh. Clearly, she was motivated by a deep love for her daughter and nothing else.

Once again, the old baby regret climbed out of the box Tessa kept locked in her heart and crawled up to her throat. Oh, to love like that...

"And we've got one last surprise!" the DJ said, adding a drumroll sound that cracked up the whole room. "Three...two...one..."

Roman and Lacey walked onto the stage, holding the crate, grinning. Lacey dropped down and unlatched the door and little Pickles tiptoed out, suddenly shy in front of the crowd.

The kids gasped. The parents cheered. Naomi shrieked in utter disbelief.

"He's mine?" She looked straight at her mother. "Mommy, really?"

Tears trickled down Jennifer's cheeks. "It's Pickles, honey. The one you loved on the field trip to the animal refuge."

She dropped to her knees, scooped up the tiny dog, and burst into tears.

Tessa's own eyes welled as she watched the scene unfold. The entire room erupted into applause. Naomi sobbed into the dog's neck, stroking his ears, laughing and crying at the same time. Jennifer had a hand over her mouth, overwhelmed.

"Thank you," Naomi whispered as she turned to her mother. Instantly, the two of them were wrapped in a hug and cry-laughing, the dog between them, and Dad joined in.

Yep. This was the instant of event planning perfection, she thought. The family stuff. The emotion. The climax of feelings that made all the work worthwhile.

The room was filled with cheers, laughter, and when the DJ started *Who Let the Dogs Out?*—then there was chaos, barking, and madness.

In the midst of it, she slid her gaze to the side of the stage, expecting to see Roman and Lacey enjoying it all, but they'd disappeared.

Wondering where they'd gone, she walked around

the large potted plant, turning the corner to see them face to face, deep in a conversation. Not heated, but not...in the spirit of the happy moment.

She couldn't hear what they were saying but the conversation was serious, with much nodding, a few stabs into the hair, and a couple of heavy sighs. Finally, Lacey stepped away and walked off in the other direction.

What was going on?

Just as she was about to step away, Roman looked up, straight into Tessa's eyes. There was that expression again—wistful, longing, and...secretive. Was he hiding something from her?

His true feelings?

There was definitely an air of something not right, not genuine, and not real arcing like electricity from him.

Without giving it much thought, beyond the bone-deep need to protect Lacey, she took a few steps closer.

"I just want to say one thing," she whispered, but knew he could hear her. "If you hurt that girl, if you lie to her or lead her on or break her heart or betray her? You'll have me to answer to, and it will not be pretty."

He swallowed. "I won't," he said. "I don't want to hurt anyone."

She let out a sigh, instantly appeased by the genuine note in his voice.

"Can I say one thing to you?" he countered. When she nodded, he came one inch closer. "You, Tessa Wylie, would have been an amazing mother. Nothing short of a mama bear in the protection department."

She nearly melted into the ground. What would

make him say the words she'd heard so many times and always hated? She didn't know, but for some reason, this time? She didn't hate them at all.

"Yeah," she said. "I would have been, but the universe had other plans."

His brow flicked and he thumbed over his shoulder. "I'm going to get Lacey."

He turned and walked away, leaving her utterly bewildered.

Chapter Seventeen
Vivien

Glancing in the rearview mirror, Vivien wanted to check on the eight-plus-foot silk olive tree in a massive stone pot that somehow fit in the back of her SUV. But her gaze got snagged on the man in the seat behind her, holding the tree so it didn't roll or break a branch every time she made a turn.

Peter gave her a cute smirk, looking amused and a little annoyed at the whole thing. It had been a heck of a "design errand" as he called her trips to various boutiques and shops that always ended in some large piece of décor in the back of her Highlander.

But she could never have gotten this tree from the silk flower distributor's warehouse and into her car, not to mention upstairs to its new home, by herself.

"I'm not sure I really understand," Peter said as their gazes locked in the mirror. "Why a man cave loft needs a giant olive tree? And how exactly did I get roped into this?"

"I know, this is a pain," she conceded. "I thought I'd persuaded Lacey and Roman to help me with this tree, but Roman had to leave for a few days and Tessa has a new client and wanted to bring Lacey to the meeting. I really was counting on her strong boyfriend."

His brow flicked. "Boyfriend? Didn't they just meet a few weeks ago?"

"Well, what should I call him? The NFL player who has bewitched my daughter?"

He inched forward. "He's okay, right? Good guy? Won't hurt her? Because..."

"I know. You're carrying." She made a playful shooting gesture, but was touched by his protectiveness. "He's good, all right. Maybe too good to be true, if there is such a man."

"Hey. You're looking at one," he joked.

"I stand corrected. But, yeah, they seem to be...well, I don't know if it's serious, but Lacey sure acts odd when she talks about him. Like she doesn't quite believe it's real, so I don't know where this thing will go."

"It could go to Jacksonville," he said. "And so could your daughter."

She made a face. "Or they can be yet another long-distance relationship, like Eli and Kate. Who will be here in just a few days, remember?"

He nodded. "I talked to Eli last night. Well, texted. He wanted to know if I'd be around much this summer, since he will obviously be working from Destin as much as he can if Kate decides to stay."

She didn't respond but stole another look, waiting for the rest of what Peter might say. *Would* he be around? He'd made it clear after they'd mini-golfed that the deci-sion depended on her.

And all she'd done since then was dance around the topic.

"I'm happy he'll be here and have the summer with Kate," he said, proving she wasn't the only one doing the dancing. "If she stays."

But he hadn't answered if *he'd* be here. "Are you staying?" she asked softly.

"For the Celebration of Life thing? If I'm invited. The boat will be crowded."

And...more dancing.

He let out a breath and looked at the tree as if he already anticipated the sharp turn into Four Prong Lake at the next stop sign.

"Kate's not sure if she's going to spend the summer here," she said, wanting to keep the conversation going just to see where it took them. "Emma has a job at the local yacht club in Ithaca and doesn't want to come down here. But Kate's ex-husband said he'd love to have both kids all summer, so I guess things are...falling into place."

"Yep," he said, strong-arming the olive tree when the massive pot rolled with her turn. "They're falling into place for...other people." He grabbed the tree trunk, grunting softly. "But you never answered my original question."

Her heart tumbled around exactly like that tree. Now? He wanted her answer *now*?

"Which question?" she asked—as if she didn't know.

"What self-respecting man cave has an olive tree instead of, you know, a...wine cellar or air hockey game or...whatever goes in a place like that?" He snorted. "I've never had such a luxury. My man cave doubles as a garage."

"It's for ambiance and my client liked the idea for his loft."

"*His* loft." He gave a knowing nod. "So not Fiona?"

"No...her brother, actually."

He grinned, obviously having figured that out a while ago. "Maybe I didn't realize *Danny's* olive tree was part of the deal when I offered to help you."

There it was—that name. Casual, harmless...but heavy enough to make her pulse skip.

"Would it have mattered?" she asked, keeping her gaze on the winding neighborhood road, pretending she didn't catch the subtle weight behind Peter's words.

"I guess it depends on"—he looked into the mirror again—"where things stand with you and the old—or, actually, not that old—hedge fund manager."

"It stands that he's my client, has a generous budget, and has given me free rein in the upstairs of his house." She laughed softly. "Not sure that sounds... right."

Peter looked amused. "So, strictly business?"

Was it? If so, Danny's business was making her feel *alive* when she was around him—spontaneous and light, like the version of herself she used to be before life became all about responsibilities and expectations. They flirted and chatted, exchanged banter and teasing, and shared a whole lot of...attraction.

"Strictly business," she said, praying it wasn't a lie. They'd never kissed again after that first night, or talked about feelings. All they did was have fun—and plenty of it.

But then there was Peter. Solid, dependable Peter, who dropped everything to help her with this tree.

Two men. Two versions of herself.

And somehow, she didn't know which one she wanted more or what to do at all.

They pulled into Danny's driveway, the sleek, modern lines of his house gleaming against the backdrop of the lake.

Peter let out a low whistle. "*This* is Danny's place? I guess I should have figured. Hedge funds and all that."

Vivien climbed out of the front. "All that indeed," she murmured to herself.

Peter joined her at the hatchback and flicked a fake olive. "Nope, not what I expected in a *manly* man cave."

"He's manly," she said, and almost bit her tongue for defending him and not her design choice. "And it really finishes the space."

"I'm not questioning his masculinity. It was on full display at Tessa's fashion show as he followed you around and took up all your time."

"Oh, please," she said, feeling her cheeks burn.

He hoisted the massive pot with two strong arms, barely swaying under the weight as he gently set it on the ground. When he did, he looked up and into her eyes. "The guy likes you, Viv. Not that I can blame him."

"He needed a designer." Even as she said the words, they sounded hollow. "Come on. I have the garage code to get in."

"Of course you do," he muttered, bending over to grab the pot, oblivious to the branches that swatted his face.

She didn't answer—did she have to?—but got them inside, grateful Danny's expensive car wasn't there. Not only did Peter not need to see the obvious display of wealth, it meant Danny wasn't home, so they could drop this off and get out.

They entered the house, the air cool with a subtle scent of freshly ground coffee lingering from the kitchen.

She instantly pictured Danny on the back deck, barefoot, maybe bare chested, looking out over the water as he sipped his morning brew. It made her feel...achy. Interested. Wondering what it would be like to be there with him.

Pushing the thought away, she gave Peter a chance to do what any person with a pulse would do—take in the beauty of the waterfront home. He did, but only with a cursory glance.

Of course. He was a police detective who happily lived in a bungalow in Pensacola Beach. Danny Sullivan was a multimillionaire with two homes and cars that probably cost what Peter made in a year.

"Upstairs with this beast?" he asked, leaning over to grab the olive tree pot.

"Sadly, yes. Thank you, Peter."

He responded with a grunt as he hoisted a hundred pounds of stone and fake tree, carrying it to the stairs and all the way up without even taking a break.

"Impressive," she said as she joined him on the top step when he finally put it down.

"Gotta do something to outshine Mr. Money Bags," he joked. Maybe joked.

"It goes next to the wall unit." As she stepped into the loft, she couldn't help taking a moment to appreciate how quickly it was coming together. He'd chosen the most subtle of wallpaper and she'd gotten a fantastic carpenter to do the custom built-in. "That wall unit will be painted a deep green and I think that will just go perfectly with the olive tree."

He plopped the pot on the floor. "Dreamy," he teased, adding a wink. "He can put little white lights on it for Christmas."

Actually, he could, but she didn't want to walk right into Peter's playful trap. Instead, she came over to turn the tree for the best angle of the branches. Then Peter stepped back and, for the first time, really surveyed the space.

"Let me guess—this used to be nothing but a TV on a stand with a fifteen-year-old orange crushed velvet sofa and big speakers. No, wait." He laughed. "That was my place after my divorce."

She laughed with him, appreciating his humor and attempt to lighten the mood. "Actually, you're close. It was essentially a barren room."

"Well, it's not now. Honestly, Viv. You have real talent. This is nice."

"Thank you," she said, tucking a strand of hair behind her ear and looking around to see it through his eyes. "There's going to be a bar over there and he's adding a pool table."

"Of course he is."

Leaning into him, she jabbed his side with her elbow. "Don't be jealous. He can't handle a gun or a mini-golf club the way you do."

He chuckled. "I'm just praying he's a jerk."

"He's not," she said simply. "He's kind and considerate and taking care of his sister, a widow who lost a child years ago."

"*Annnnd* now he's officially a saint."

Before she could muster a response, the unmistakable chime of the front door alarm echoed through the house.

Her stomach dropped. "And not only that, he's home."

Peter arched a brow. "Should we hide?"

She snorted. "We should say hello. And..." She narrowed her eyes at him. "Play nice."

"I won't shoot him, but that's all I'll promise." He gave her a wink and a nudge. "Come on. You can trust me."

And that was one fact she'd never argue.

She walked to the top of the stairs, seeing Danny in the foyer below, sunglasses pushed up into his dark hair. He wore a crisp button-down and khakis—his meeting clothes, she knew from being around here frequently enough.

On most work days, it was board shorts and a faded New York Yankees T-shirt.

"I know you're here, Viv." He looked around. "I saw

your…" His gaze moved up and met hers. "That looks like a woman who just found the perfect…whatever you wanted to buy."

"Olive tree," she said, sensing Peter coming to stand next to her.

"And you needed help," Danny said. "You should have called me and I'd have rearranged my schedule."

"It's fine," she said, starting down the stairs, her pulse racing more than it should when she reached the bottom and turned from one man to the other. "Danny, I believe you've met my friend, Peter McCarthy?"

She could have sworn Peter's shoulders sank a millimeter at the word "friend."

"Of course," Danny said, extending his hand. "The detective."

Peter shook the other man's hand, no real smile evident but no scowl, either. "Beautiful home you have, Mr. Sullivan."

"Just Danny," he countered. "And thank you. It's a work-in-progress under the keen eye of Vivien Lawson Designs. Can I offer you something to drink?"

"We're fine," Vivien said quickly, wanting nothing but to end this unexpected encounter.

"Can I see the tree?" he asked, his silver-blue gaze somehow more direct than usual. "You know I was iffy on a fake tree in Florida. Jury's still out."

"Go take a look," she said, seizing the opportunity. "You go up and we'll be out of here in no time."

"No, no. Come with." He put a hand on her back,

then looked at Peter. "Feel free to grab a beer from the fridge, unless you're, uh...on duty."

Peter just looked at the man and Vivien could practically hear the words in his head. *Feel free to duck if I decide to shoot.*

But his dark eyes just glittered at the suggestion. "Pass and thank you. Viv, I'll wait by your car."

"No, no." She looked from one to the other, wildly aware of Danny's familiar hand on her back and the near snarl in Peter's expression.

How did this happen? How did Vivien Lawson get in the middle of a big boys' tug of war, the air crackling with tension?

She didn't know, but she wasn't going to go upstairs and flirt with Danny while Peter waited like her lackey. He deserved so much more than that.

"You go see the tree," she said to Danny. "Text me if you hate it. I've taken up so much of Peter's time today." She added a smile that felt a little forced. "We'll talk soon."

With that, she slipped out of his touch and walked next to Peter. She saw the faintest glimmer in his eyes as they reached the door.

"Wait, Viv." Danny called, making her slow her step and turn to him. She braced for the look of a man entirely used to getting what he wanted and not having the object of his attention walk away.

"Yes?"

"I'm around if you want to talk tonight. Just call me."

Call him? Why would she do that? She'd never called

him just to talk. But it probably didn't sound that way to Peter.

She just nodded and stepped to the door Peter held open for her, both of them walking to her SUV in silence. How could she explain that last comment to him—and did she have to?

At the driver's side, she pulled open the door and glanced over the SUV roof to see his expression, able to read all the emotion in that flash of a second. But by the time they were next to each other and pulling on their seatbelts, his face was stoic.

"So," she said on an awkward sigh. "I don't really know why he'd—"

"Viv, I gotta know."

She froze in the act of turning on the ignition, her heart kicking into high gear. "I swear, Peter, there's nothing going on. He flirts and we talk but—"

"I don't care about that," he said gruffly. "He's rich. Not a gargoyle, either. And you're a grown and beautiful woman who is smart enough to make her own choice. This is about me, not him."

She sighed, looking hard at him, silent.

"I need to know where you stand with me," he said. "I've made my feelings clear and I am facing a huge life decision. Stay or go. Work for the Destin PD or return to Pensacola. The case is about to close—ice cold. So I have to tell my boss and the chief here what I want to do."

"I know," she whispered, her chest tight.

"I don't make life decisions lightly," he said. "If I transfer to Destin, it's for you. So..."

"So, no pressure," she said with a mirthless laugh.

"Just honesty," he replied.

Vivien swallowed hard, uncertainty clawing at her insides. "I don't know," she said. "I'm confused and scared and hopeful and…I honestly need more time."

"Okay, okay." He glanced at the ignition. "I didn't mean to upset you. Do you want me to drive?"

She shook her head, not trusting her voice as tears stung her lids. "I'm fine to drive." She turned on the car and backed out slowly, pulling onto the road with one last look at Danny's house.

Was there something more exciting behind those walls? Or was the right man sitting next to her?

She honestly didn't know. How was that possible?

"I shouldn't pressure you," he said, putting his hand on her leg. "I just need clarity and a sense that if I turn my life upside down, it's for the right reasons."

"You deserve that and more." She blinked against the sting in her eyes, looking out at the road ahead as they drove. How did she end up here? Torn between two incredible men, both offering her different things—and yet, neither felt like the *right* answer.

Peter gave her hand a reassuring squeeze, his whole body seeming to relax as the fight left him. Or maybe it was getting some distance from Danny.

"Take your time, Viv. But not too much. The case'll officially close in a couple of days. Then I'll have to make a firm decision."

Vivien nodded, her heart a tangled mess right then.

Peter lifted his hand, and the car filled with a quiet that felt heavier than words.

Two men. Two futures. And a choice she wasn't sure she knew how to make.

AFTER VIVIEN DROPPED PETER OFF, she drove to the Summer House in a haze.

I need to know where you stand with me.

His words echoed in her head, making her whole body mix with a cocktail of anxiety and uncertainty.

How was she supposed to choose when nothing felt clear? Peter was offering stability, commitment—*love*, even. But every time she thought about settling into that safe harbor, her mind drifted to a pair of mischievous silver-blue eyes, a crooked grin, and the way Danny Sullivan made her feel like a teenager again.

Ironic, since her teenaged crush was Peter McCarthy.

Vivien sighed, pressing her forehead briefly to the steering wheel before cutting the engine.

Get it together, Viv.

As she stepped out of the car, something caught her eye—an unfamiliar work truck parked near the front porch. Did she have a delivery or work scheduled today?

She had to admit, the staging of the Summer House had slowed due to her other clients. They didn't plan to sell—if they did at all—for six more months, so she'd pulled back on her efforts to turn Eli's masterpiece home into a showcase.

Brows furrowed, she scanned the logo on the truck. *Coastal Electric.*

An electrical problem, maybe? Had Eli sent someone after the final inspection on the apartment above the garage?

As she opened the front door, she heard the faint hum of a drill, followed by the low murmur of a man's voice singing along to a country song playing from his phone speaker.

She stepped into the main living area—and froze.

There, perched atop a tall ladder in the center of the vaulted ceiling, was an electrician carefully wiring a chandelier. But not just any chandelier.

Vivien's breath hitched.

It was *the* chandelier.

The exact cascading shell light fixture she'd admired in that photo Danny had shown her—the one hanging in his friend's Hamptons beach house.

She took a slow step forward, craning her neck to fully absorb the sight. It was even more stunning in person—delicate strands of translucent ovals shimmering like seashells, catching the late afternoon light pouring through the windows.

It was elegant, coastal, timeless. *Perfect.*

The electrician glanced down and gave her a friendly nod. "Hello, ma'am. Almost done here."

Vivien blinked, trying to gather her wits. "Hi—uh, sorry, I wasn't expecting anyone. Who..."

"Oh, a lady let me in. Little bit older? Southern accent."

"My mother," she said absently. "But I mean who... who sent you?"

He came down the ladder and grabbed his phone, squinting at it. "Man's name is Daniel Sullivan. He came to my lighting company office in person to arrange this. Said he wanted the best light installer in the county and that's me. You know him, I assume."

Did she? She didn't think he was a "grand gesture" kind of guy, but...obviously, he was.

"Yes," she said, looking up as a thousand emotions rushed in at once—surprise, awe, delight... and that fluttery, dangerous feeling Danny always managed to stir up in her.

"I put it on a dimmer, if that's okay. Order didn't say, but he paid extra for me to rush over here, so no additional charge."

"Yes, thank you."

"And he gave me this when he hired me, told me to give it to you." He reached into a bag and handed her a small, cream colored envelope. "I hope for your sake it's not a bill because this thing?" He whistled. "I know big money when I hang it."

She glanced at the word "Viv" scribbled on the front of the envelope in bold black letters, and her heart felt like it folded in half.

Vivien pressed the envelope against her chest with trembling fingers, offering a quiet thank you as the electrician gathered his things and let himself out.

She stood still for a long moment, staring up at the chandelier, letting the reality sink in.

He did this... for me.

It wasn't merely a thoughtful gesture—it was the kind of thing that made a woman's heart race and her knees weak.

Why?

After a few deep breaths, she sat on the edge of the sofa and slipped her finger under the envelope flap, pulling out a folded note written in a spare, clean, and masculine hand.

Vivien,

Consider this a thank you for giving me a respectable and soothing man cave and for putting up with my low enthusiasm level for wallpaper.

I couldn't let you settle for anything less than what you really wanted. So, here it is. No more searching. I hope every time you look at this, you smile.

— Danny

P.S. If you hate it, I'll take it back. But we both know you won't.

Vivien let out a shaky laugh, her eyes misting despite herself. *Dang it.*

How was he so effortlessly charming and disarming? How did he pull this off without it being an arrogant flex, but merely the kindest of gestures? Just a generous tip for her work and a subtle flirt that didn't ask for anything in return.

She honestly had never met a man like Danny Sullivan.

Folding the note carefully, she stood to spin in a slow circle as she admired the chandelier from every angle. It was flawless.

But instead of feeling pure joy...she felt that gnawing twist in her stomach again at the echo of Peter's words.

I need to know where you stand with me.

Well, this sure didn't help things.

"Viv! Oh, my gosh, you found one!" Tessa's voice rang out as she stepped in from the entryway. Vivien had been so enthralled she hadn't even heard the front door open. "It's stunning!"

She forced a smile, tucking the note behind her back. "Yeah... I didn't exactly find it."

Tessa's golden eyes flashed to her, curiosity sparking. "What do you mean?"

Vivien exhaled, gesturing upward. "Danny did. He had it installed today. It's a surprise for me."

"Oh, my." She crossed her arms, aching a brow. "Definitely a power move."

"Or a really nice gesture to thank me for my hard work."

"Puh-lease. Flowers, a bottle of wine, even a little gift card would say thank you. This?" Tessa pointed overhead. "This says I want to light up your world. Literally and figuratively."

Vivien let out a soft, breathless laugh, but didn't deny it. How could she?

"Well, whatever his motives, it's perfect," Vivien said. "This whole first floor feels complete now."

Tessa gave her a playful nudge. "Except for my pink

bedroom way in the back," she cracked. "Tell your rich boyfriend you have a hankering for a cashmere upholstered headboard and a limited-edition Hermes throw."

"I better not or you'll be wrapped in Hermes before next week."

"Don't knock it, hon." Her pretty smile faded. "Although I will tell you that my experience with the wealthy ones has never ended well. But then, neither has my experience with the poor dudes, either. All in all, we're better off alone."

She added a musical laugh and floated off to the not-yet-pink bedroom, leaving Vivien to wonder if Tessa hadn't just unwittingly given her the best possible advice.

Because right now, she felt like she was teetering between a safe harbor and a wild, open sea.

And for the life of her, she didn't know which way she wanted the wind to blow.

Chapter Eighteen
Maggie

When Kate, Eli, and two teenagers all poured in through the front door with much squealing, hugging, and familiarity, Maggie could feel things shift.

Jo Ellen's grandchildren certainly brought a new, youthful energy to the place. Matt was tall, all gangly limbs and shaggy hair, quiet like Kate. Emma, on the other hand, had the confident posture of a girl wise beyond her years, her dark eyes taking in the room with intelligent curiosity.

But the real change in the air came directly from Eli and Kate. Her son had a palpable connection with the woman that didn't seem to have been dimmed by their distance this past month.

Based on the looks they exchanged, the casual way they touched each other, and a few very obvious inside jokes they shared, they'd shortened the distance with plenty of time on the phone.

Maggie still wasn't sure how she felt about that.

Jo Ellen, on the other hand, seemed pleased as punch with this union, practically giggling at everything Eli said as if he was *her* son.

Good heavens, Maggie had broken every promise she'd made to Roger, and now the next generation was hard at work trying to make it worse.

"You okay, Mom?" Eli stepped out to the deck where Maggie sat in her usual seat once the greetings had been exchanged and the interminable discussion of who would sleep in what room was finally complete.

"I'm fine," she said, looking up at him. "You seem happy."

He gave a soft laugh. "Well, yeah. Happy to be back in Destin, happy that you're here, and really happy to see Kate."

She flicked her brow, silent.

"I'm not going to respond to that look," he said with a tease in his voice. "But I have something for you. That case of Dad's you wanted from Crista's garage. Where should I put it?"

"Up in my room, please." She let out a shuddering sigh. "I am both dreading and anticipating looking through it."

"Kate told me the latest." He dropped onto the edge of a chair across from her. "The FBI? How could we not have known this was a federal case?"

And Kate didn't know *all* of the "latest"—Artie's involvement. "Because your father kept a secret better than I do," she said dryly.

"And that's saying something," Eli cracked.

She shuttered her eyes. "Anyway, thank you. God willing there are some answers in that box."

"God is always willing to give answers," he said,

reminding Maggie of his deep faith. Would that change with Kate, who Jo Ellen said believed only in science? "Whatever is in that box, Mom, I hope it means we can let bygones be bygones, allow these families to heal, and look forward instead of backward."

"I made a promise." She ground out the last word.

"I'd like to make one, too," he said. "To Kate."

She gasped and blinked at him.

"Not that promise," he replied, laughing. "I promised I'd spend the summer here if she does. Her kids don't want to stay because of other commitments, and she's on the fence. But I think she's leaning toward spending most of the summer here."

He didn't ask for her opinion on that, she noticed.

"It's going to get very crowded here," she said, looking past him.

"Well, we have a two-bedroom apartment above the garage," he reminded her. "Two empty bedrooms downstairs. There's plenty of room."

"I thought you were going to sell this property for a huge profit."

"We still might," he countered. "We can't until November. Why not have one last summer of Wylies and Lawsons in Destin?"

Why not, indeed. Because Roger Lawson was probably scowling from his final resting place. Didn't that matter to anyone but her?

Did it even matter to her?

"I'll go put that case in your room," he said, obviously

not waiting for her response to what she assumed was a rhetorical question.

As he stepped back inside, the rest of the new arrivals started to spill out to the deck, dressed in various stages of beachwear. Kate and Tessa and Vivien linked arms, sunhats on, like the unstoppable trio they'd been thirty years ago.

Jo Ellen followed, practically vibrating with joy.

"Isn't this amazing, Mags?" She eased down on the sofa next to Maggie. "It's truly like old times with our kids at the Summer House."

"Only no Roger and Artie."

Jo Ellen's smile disappeared. "Well, no. Thanks for that bucket of cold water. Can't you be happy for once?"

"Me? You're the one who mopes every time Artie's name is mentioned."

"Well, I feel better now. Here." She put a hand on Maggie's arm. "With you."

The comment made her soften inside, and she smiled, jutting her chin toward the sound of all those footsteps on the spiral stairs to the beach level, punctuated by laughter and chatter.

"It's good to have a full house," she admitted. "But I'm still so torn by guilt."

"If it's because my daughter and your son like each other, then let it go." Jo Ellen nudged her. "I haven't seen Kate this happy in years. I'm sure it's the same for Eli."

Maggie couldn't argue with that. It was true—her son had been a hollow version of himself after Melissa's passing. He'd powered on, raised the kids, and built a business. And, of course, he'd found faith and church.

But love? That put a whole different glimmer in his blue eyes.

Still, Roger's age-old warnings echoed in her mind.

You promise me, Magnolia...no Wylies. Never, ever. You cannot talk to them and neither can the kids. Ever.

Talk? Eli and Kate looked like they could *get married*.

Jo Ellen leaned into her. "Kate brought some of Artie's things down, including his ashes."

"Speaking of happy topics." Maggie rolled her eyes. "I'm sorry, Jo. I know this whole weekend is important to you, but..."

"You still won't come to his Celebration of Life?" She looked truly disappointed.

"No," she said simply. "But Eli put that case of Roger's belongings in my room."

"Artie's stuff is there, too." At Maggie's look, she laughed. "Not the *ashes*. They're in my room."

"Don't trust me with them, do you?" Maggie joked as she pushed up.

"I'd trust you with my life," Jo replied softly, the kind words like a balm on Maggie's bruised heart.

"Come on. Let's see what we can find, Jo."

As they climbed the stairs to her room, Maggie felt anticipation building, along with dread. She never liked going through Roger's things. It hurt so much. And now? Guilt would make the pain worse.

She shut the door behind them and regarded the two boxes on the window seat. Roger's was a sturdy metal box, clasp closed and secure. Artie's was a battered old storage bin, the plastic top buckling and fragile.Maggie unlatched Roger's first—grateful she'd never locked the box and had to worry about finding the key. She pulled out a stack of papers bound together with an old leather strap. Architectural sketches that included some of his earliest designs.

Jo Ellen leaned over and looked on as Maggie unfolded some of the papers. "He really was talented, Mags."

Maggie traced a finger over the lines, memories tugging at her. "Yes. But he didn't trust that talent."

Jo Ellen didn't respond, sliding Artie's bin to the floor and dropping to the carpet like a kid opening Christmas presents. Pulling back her long hair, she snapped a cloth tie from her wrist to make a ponytail.

Silent, they dug deeper—finding a mix of mundane keepsakes and forgotten relics. A cracked pair of sunglasses Maggie remembered Roger wearing on the beach. An old cigar box filled with bottle caps from some silly collection Artie had started one summer.

Jo Ellen, rifling through Artie's box, let out a soft laugh as she held something up. "Look at this."

Maggie glanced over to see Jo holding up a photograph of the four of them—Roger, Artie, Jo Ellen, and Maggie—sitting on a picnic blanket, wine glasses in hand, the Gulf behind them, circa 1990 or so.

"We were so young," Jo Ellen murmured.

Maggie's chest tightened. "We were so happy." She *had* been a happier woman then. Always highly disciplined with tight parameters around her life, but before Roger's arrest and his death, she'd had more joy.

Life forced her to tighten her parameters so much... sometimes she felt like she was strangling herself *and* the people she loved.

Silence fell again as they continued sorting through the remnants of lives that now felt like mysteries. And then—something cold and metallic jabbed Maggie's fingertips.

Her pulse quickened as she pulled out a small key, attached to a worn tag stamped with the words *Destin Federal Savings Box 237.*

"Jo! Look!"

Jo Ellen pushed up to see. "Is that—?"

"A key to a safe deposit box," Maggie confirmed, her voice lilting with intrigue. "Here! In Destin."

Jo Ellen's eyes lit up. "That could be something." She returned to her box and, seconds later, gave a startled gasp. "Oh, my goodness!"

She shoved her hand in the air, an identical key clutched in her fingers. She looked at Maggie, her face alight with both triumph and disbelief.

"What the heck?" Maggie reached to take the key and compare them. Yep. Same bank, same box number.

For a moment, they simply stared at each other and the keys, the magnitude of the discovery settling over them.

"Does that bank still exist? Here in Destin?" Jo Ellen asked.

"As a matter of fact, it does," Maggie said, handing

back Artie's key. "It's near Publix. I saw it the other day and remembered that Roger sometimes stopped in there to cash travelers checks before ATMs were everywhere and credit cards were common."

Jo Ellen's brows went up. "Maybe they stashed money in this box."

"I don't want money," Maggie whispered. "I want answers."

And what she really wanted was freedom from promises made thirty years ago.

"And maybe these"—Jo Ellen tapped her key to Maggie's like they were toasting champagne flutes—"unlock those answers. Let's go now."

"Now?" Maggie choked.

"It's a Thursday afternoon. The bank'll be open." She pushed her box with her foot, ready to run.

"Whoa, there," Maggie said, snagging her sleeve. "They don't let just anyone walk in and open a safe deposit box. One of us would need ID. Proof that we're the spouses of the owners. Maybe a death certificate?"

"I have that," Jo Ellen said. "It's with the ashes."

Maggie drew back. "Well, don't bring those. But get the certificate and our IDs and...whatever else we might need. I guess we're going clue hunting, Nancy Drew."

"Woohoo!" Jo Ellen bopped out of the room and suddenly Maggie was transported to the Tri-Delt house when the two of them were young. Oh, how she longed to feel that friendship, free of old guilt and vows she wished she'd never made.

"I still feel bad for lying," Jo Ellen muttered, adjusting her sunglasses as Maggie steered Vivien's stupidly oversized SUV through Destin traffic.

Maggie huffed, keeping her eyes on the road. "We didn't lie. We just wrote a note that said we're going to Publix to buy...something. We'll go to Publix. We'll buy something. But first, we'll go to the bank."

Jo Ellen shot her a look, the matching keys clasped in her hands. "Oh, sure, after we crack open our dead husbands' mutual safe deposit box like a pair of geriatric detectives."

Maggie allowed herself the faintest smile. "You say that like it's a bad thing."

As they pulled into the modest bank parking lot—a small, nondescript building tucked between a nail salon and a real estate office—Maggie's heart beat just a little faster.

"Let me handle this, Jo," Maggie said as they walked toward the bank. "I know how to get people to do what I want."

"You sure do." Jo Ellen elbowed her. "But why are you expecting them to not let us see our husbands' safe deposit box?"

"Because there are rules and laws for this kind of thing," she said. "You don't waltz in like you're in an episode of *Colombo* and demand to get into someone's safe deposit box. You have to prove who you are and they'll probably want someone to go with us."

"No!"

"Oh, you're so naïve," Maggie said as she pulled the door open. "Just let me take the lead."

They walked in together and straight to the first teller, a young woman about the age of her granddaughter, Meredith. Only instead of put together and on top of her game, like beautiful Meredith, this girl had one of those ridiculous rings in her nose and a purple flower inked on what would have otherwise been a lovely arm.

Who told her that was attractive?

Maggie lifted her chin and looked down her own—*unpierced*—nose, knowing how powerful her expressions could be.

"We would like access to a safe deposit box."

The woman looked up. "ID and key, please." She turned to the computer and tapped. "What name is the box in?"

"Uh, Roger Lawson."

Her fingers froze. "I take it that's not you, ma'am."

Maggie resisted the urge to roll her eyes. "It's my late husband."

She snapped her gum—honestly!—and it took everything Maggie had to stay quiet.

"We'll need written permission to access the box, your ID, a death certificate, and/or a signed and notarized affidavit that says you have permission or the power of attorney to..." Her gaze shifted to Jo Ellen. "Are you okay?"

Maggie turned and looked at Jo, who was...*bawling*.

Her face was red, her nose slobbery, and her shoulders shook with a silent sob.

"It was my husband's, too," she managed to mumble. "They shared the box. It hasn't been a year since he died and I came all the way from Ithaca, New York, just to get in this box so please, please, *please* let us in there. Alone. Please. We mean no harm, but my husband asked me on his death bed to get what's in that box."

Her whole arm vibrated as she held out the envelope containing the death certificate. With a tentative look, the young woman pulled out the certificate, glanced at it, then turned to tap her pointed acrylic nails on the computer keyboard.

All the while, Jo Ellen sobbed. Literally *ugly cried* into a used Kleenex. Maggie didn't know whether to laugh, scream, or dig for a fresh tissue.

"Arthur Wylie?" the woman asked. "Here it is. Wow. That box is..." She counted on her fingers. *On her fingers.* A girl who worked *in a bank.* "Thirty years old!"

"Yes, we know." Maggie lathered condescension on the words, but Jo Ellen muscled closer.

"Please, honey," she sniveled. "What's in there is the last piece of him I have. Do you have a father? Maybe a dead grandfather? Can you understand—"

"I'll need your ID," she said, unmoved but maybe a little terrified of Jo.

"Oh, of course." Jo Ellen flipped open her wallet and struggled to slide out her license, too overcome with grief to manage—or her acting skills were in overdrive.

"Okay," the girl finally said after checking it and

comparing it to the name on her computer screen. "My manager is at lunch and he's supposed to go in with you."

Maggie inched closer. "We don't need—"

Jo Ellen cut her off with another extended, quivering hand. "Please, honey. Please let us be alone with our memories."

Nose Ring looked from one to the other, then shrugged. "Okay. But be warned, ladies, the room has cameras."

"What do you think we're going to—"

"Maggie." Jo Ellen shut her up with a wave of her hand. "It's fine. We'll be in there crying."

The woman escorted them to the back of the bank and unlocked a door, showing them into a cold hallway lined with small boxes.

"You can leave anytime you're done. Please don't remove anything from the box without legal authorization or power of attorney. And you are under observation and surveillance."

She left and silence settled over them like a weighted blanket.

"On his *death bed*?" Maggie asked.

Jo Ellen gave her a harsh glare and surreptitiously pointed to a camera in the corner. "Just find Box 237, Mags. You're not the only one who can sway people to do things."

"Apparently not."

They found the box, pulled it out, and placed it on a table in the middle of the room. Jo Ellen produced one of the keys and held it aloft.

"May I?" she asked.

"After that Oscar-winning performance, yes, you may."

"Okay." Jo slid the key and twisted it. "Thirty years, Mags. What could be in here?"

"Just open it," Maggie pressed, anticipation stretching over her and snapping at her nerves.

Very slowly, Jo Ellen turned the key and lifted the lid, both of them leaning over to peer in to see...

"Nothing?" Maggie choked.

"Just..." Jo reached into the corner of the utterly empty box and pulled out a small blue piece of cardstock that Maggie hadn't even noticed. "This."

"What is it?"

They almost knocked heads trying to look at it.

"A dry cleaning ticket," Jo Ellen said with dismay. "Sunny Shores Cleaners 167890." She flipped it over. "A. Wylie. Suit. Pick up August second."

Maggie felt the blood whoosh from her head. "That's it? A dry cleaning stub from God knows when? For a suit?"

No! This wasn't possible.

"That's it." Jo flipped the tiny piece of paper over and over as if it would magically reveal something.

Maggie gripped the edge of the table, her whole world tilted and crashing.

"I can't take this anymore, Jo."

"I know, I know." She bit her lip and looked up. "I mean, I know Roger was laundering money, but did he actually take it to the dry cleaners?"

Maggie sliced her with a look. "Do you think this is funny?"

"I think it's...frustrating."

That it was. Maggie gave a shove to the box, as if that was the thing that had betrayed her—and not Jo Ellen's deceased husband.

Fuming and shaking, she turned and walked out, leaving the box, her friend, and this crushing defeat behind. She powered through the bank without so much as a look at Nose Ring, then walked outside, dropping onto a bench beside the main doors like some kind of vagabond without a home.

She'd never felt so lost or frustrated or confused in her life.

A few minutes later, Jo came out, sitting down next to her.

"I took it," she said in a breathless whisper. "I'll probably get arrested, but I took it anyway. I don't think it was caught on camera, but I don't care. It had to mean something or they wouldn't have put it in that box."

She eyed her friend with begrudging, but genuine, respect. "Great. Now we can go pick up Artie's suit. Expect a late fee."

"The cleaners went out of business years ago. I Googled it."

Maggie sighed noisily, that respect growing. "I don't know what we were expecting to find."

"We found something," Jo Ellen said with her eternal optimism.

"What?"

"We found each other." She put her hand on Maggie's arm. "Please, Mags. Break your promise. I'm willing to break mine. I don't know why our husbands wanted us separated but they are dead, and we are both more alive than ever when we're together."

Maggie just looked at her, feeling her eyes fill. She was right. She was so right. But...

"I gave him...my word." Her throat thickened.

Jo Ellen's shoulders dropped. "Yeah. I know. And I don't want to spend one more minute on this. Let's go back to the Summer House and be with family. That's what matters."

Yes, it was. But Roger was family, too. She was still connected to him. If she broke her promise...did she break that connection?

She wanted to throw her head back and howl. Instead, she pushed up and somehow held it together. "We have to buy something at Publix since we said we would."

"I vote for chocolate," Jo Ellen whispered. "Maybe a bottle of wine or three."

Maggie smiled, but her heart hurt in a way that she couldn't describe.

Chapter Nineteen
Lacey

Lacey paced a narrow figure-eight around the bedroom, chewing her bottom lip and eyeing her phone like it might buzz to life if she glared hard enough.

But it didn't. It hadn't. Not since yesterday morning, when Roman left to tell his adoptive parents the truth. And it was darn near five o'clock now.

She flopped onto her bed, then sat back up. Then lay back down.

"What if it went badly?" she muttered out loud, to no one but her growing panic. "What if they're mad? What if they blame me?"

Not that this was about her—but she was somehow at the center of this drama and felt responsible for how it all unfolded. She was the one who found him, then pretended to be his girlfriend, then secretly introduced him to his birth mother.

She was the girl who stirred the pot. The one who overstepped.

She groaned and rolled onto her stomach, face down in a pillow.

Why hadn't he called? It wasn't like him. Since

they'd been...whatever they were...he texted frequently, called twice a day, and even sent her silly reels from Instagram that made her laugh.

Roman had communicated from Day One. Now? Radio silence.

What if the whole thing with his parents had made him rethink...everything? What if they told him to stay away from Tessa entirely? What if they hated what Lacey had done?

What if...

She sat up, heart pounding. "Okay. I'm spiraling." She stood and yanked her shoes from the closet, deciding a long walk was in order. Something. Anything.

Forty minutes later, she was still clutching her phone, marching along the beach like she had a destination. Finally, she folded to the sand and looked up to the blue sky, and her whole hand vibrated with the happy, happy buzz of a text.

One look and she nearly squealed with relief.

ROMAN: *Hey, I'm back. Come over?*

Yes, yes, yes! *He's back. He wants to see me.* Her brain immediately followed with a fresh worry: *What if it's to tell me goodbye?*

"Nope. No spiraling. You're going."

After a quick reply, she ran back to the house, sneaked into the front and grabbed her keys from the entryway bowl, risking no license and no purse—and no questions from anyone—and slipped out to the driveway.

Thank God her car wasn't blocked and that Roman's rental was just a few minutes away.

When she pulled into the driveway, nerves flared again. But then the front door flew open.

He walked toward her in sweatpants and a T-shirt, arms spread wide like he was about to catch the game-winning touchdown.

"Hey, you," he said, wrapping her in a big, warm hug and lifting her off the ground. "I missed you."

Lacey melted. Literally melted. "You did?"

"I did." He lowered her and added a kiss, brushing her hair back, his own gold locks damp at the ends from a shower. "You're covered in sunshine."

"And sweat. I've been walking the beach...and waiting." She finally let out a breath as her heart settled for the first time in two days. "And worrying."

His expression changed just enough to know that maybe that worry was warranted.

"What?" she asked, searching his face. "What happened? Are they upset?"

Huffing out a breath, he led her toward the house. "I'll tell you everything."

With a hitch in her heart, she followed him into the Florida ranch house perched on a canal. He kept the sliders wide open to let in fresh, briny air that mingled with the scent of soap wafting from his bedroom.

"Whoa, that's a long drive to make twice in two days," he said, heading to the fridge. "Water? Beer? Wine? Soda?"

She just shook her head. "Please, Roman. I'm dying here."

He pulled out two bottles of water, handing her one. "Outside. Let's sit."

Fighting a groan, she settled next to him on the rattan sofa that faced the canal, turning to pin him with a demanding gaze.

"Are they mad?"

"No," he said, shaking his head as he opened the water bottle. "My parents don't get mad, to be honest. They weren't even all that surprised—both of them expected me to try and find my biological parents at some point. Everyone is secure in our relationship."

"Okay, then why do you seem so upset?"

"Because my mother, who is honestly one of the wisest people I've ever known, thinks we—no, no, *I*—made a huge mistake in not telling Tessa who I am."

Lacey just looked at him, feeling her face crumple.

"Please don't say, 'I told you so,'" he said with a sad smile. "'Cause you kind of did tell me so."

"I went along with your wild scheme," she said. "What did your mother say, exactly?"

He sighed again, taking a deep drink of water before answering. "She said it was deceitful and showed a lack of judgment on my part." He winced. "She said it wasn't like me at all, and I should have known it was wrong and kind of selfish to try and get to know her under false pretenses."

"Oh, doesn't mince words, does she?"

He shook his head. "She's honest and a terrific judge of character. But, whoa, it made me worry about...that discussion."

"Well, it's done now," Lacey said, her whole body tense when she imagined that conversation. "All we can do is tell Tessa the truth."

"Yes, now. Immediately." He ran his hand through his hair with yet another heavy sigh. "I'm sorry I didn't call or text you."

"That's okay. Well...actually, it's not," she said, wanting to be totally honest. "I've been stressing and it would have been nice to hear what happened."

He closed his eyes and when he opened them, she could see a swirl of emotions in the depths of the gold. "I talked to my mom about you, too."

She swallowed, not sure she wanted to hear the rest. "And?"

"She's worried that if this doesn't go well with Tessa, we're doomed."

"Doomed? What do you mean?"

"Done. Finished. If you have to pick her or me—"

"Why would I have to pick either one of you?"

"My mother thinks Tessa's going to be furious, Lacey. She put herself in the woman's shoes and...they didn't fit. She has the highest regard for her—a lifetime of gratitude for the choice Tessa made and the gift she gave my parents."

Lacey moaned. "She's not going to be happy, but—"

"If she wants nothing to do with me, then she'll want you to have nothing to do with me."

"Do you think that's a possibility? That she'd want nothing to do with you?"

He looked out at the water, thinking. "My mom sure

does. The fact is, Lacey, Tessa never made a concerted effort to find me and she never told a soul—not even her twin sister—that she'd had a baby. She didn't tell you, either, remember? You guessed it. And she asked you not to tell anyone and she certainly didn't tell you to go looking for me."

The words smacked her, one after another, all of them quite...real. And right. "What do you think is going to happen?"

"I don't know, but she might not want a son," he said, his voice gruff. "She really might not want her family to know that she had a baby with someone whose name she doesn't remember, and she really might not want the complication of having that history back in her life in any capacity."

"Whoa." She dropped back on the cushion with a thud. "I guess we *haven't* thought this through."

"Again, no 'we'—this was me pushing my agenda and my curiosity. You wanted to tell her that first night."

She appreciated him taking the blame, but couldn't let him have all of it.

"But I'm the one who broke her trust and found you," Lacey said. "And one barely-there kiss from you and I was all in. Weak and willing."

He smiled at that. "You're *not* weak, and you were only willing because I was a like a fullback blasting through the defensive line."

She thought about it all for a moment, finally opening her water but not sure she could even swallow one sip. She put it to her lips because her throat was parched.

"This could be the end of us," he said—and she nearly choked on that sip.

"The end..." She got the water down, shaking her head. "Roman, I know that you love to pretend we're not lying and I fully understand that it's been easy, fun, and there have been some pretty sweet kisses, long conversations, and hand-holding. But...there isn't an *us*. Not really."

He looked hard at her, that same whirlwind of emotion in his eyes. "There isn't?"

She stared back. "We're playing a role and you know it."

"I don't know that at all," he said. "Yes, it started out... dishonestly. But not now. And when I talked to my mom about you, well..."

"Well what?"

"She said she never saw me this way over a girl."

Her jaw dropped, making him laugh.

"Why are you surprised?"

"Because..." Because she felt the same way about him, and that was scary.

"Hear me out, okay?" he said, turning to her and taking her hand. "First of all, I wouldn't have suggested it if you weren't beautiful and I didn't instantly want to know you better. You have to believe that."

She didn't have to, but the way he said it made her trust him.

"And then I got to know you, Lace. I've had a chance to really see you. I've watched you have compassion for your family, always putting them first. I've gotten to know your character, your work ethic, your good, good heart. I'm kind of...in awe of you. So you're not just beautiful and smart and witty...you're..." He swallowed, his expression serious. "You're what I've been missing in my life and I didn't even know it."

She couldn't speak, but the tears in her eyes were probably communicating everything.

"I knew I liked you," he continued. "How could I not? But when I talked to my mother this morning, she said I've never talked about any girl like this and that scared her."

"Yeah, well, it terrifies me," she said, only half joking.

"Probably not for the same reasons," he said with a wry smile. "You think you have a crush on me and I'm going to disappear, go back to the NFL, and date... whoever you think I date."

"Well, aren't you?"

He blew out a breath. "I'll go back, obviously, and play ball. But...Lacey, I don't want this to end. And if Tessa gives you some kind of ultimatum like 'it's me or him,' I know you. You'll pick Tessa."

Oh. She never considered *that*.

"Tell me I'm wrong, Lace. You love that woman. And you don't love me."

"I don't..." She pressed her hands over her chest. "I don't want to make that choice."

"But you love her," he said. "As you should. I'm just a guy who likes the hell out of you. But we could be more, I have no doubt. It might take work and time and long distance, but I think you and I could be the real deal."

Her heart slammed her ribs so loudly she thought he might hear it. "I think we could, too," she whispered.

"But not if Tessa blows a stack or insists I go away or demands we not tell anyone. I couldn't continue a relationship with you if she wanted to act like I'm just... another guy you're dating. I'm her *son*."

For a moment, neither one of them spoke, but just held hands and looked into each other's eyes.

"You're right," Lacey finally admitted as she let her brain play out all the possibilities.

"You'd pick Tessa over me?"

Very slowly, she nodded. "She's like family now and she's been so, so good to me." She felt her face crumple with tears. "And I lied to her. Your mother's right. That was wrong, Roman. That was so, so wrong."

The realization punched and she folded with a sob.

"Hey, hey." Instantly, he wrapped her in a tight, loving embrace. "We don't know how she'll react yet."

Didn't they? Hadn't Lacey *always* known Tessa would flip out? But she'd gone along with this charade because Roman was fun and persuasive and cute and better than any guy she'd ever met. And now...she could lose him forever because she hadn't been honest.

And Tessa deserved so much more than that.

"Let's go talk to her," Roman said gently.

"Right now?"

"Absolutely. Is she at the Summer House?"

Lacey shook her head. "She's at the marina getting her boat ready for tomorrow's Celebration of Life party."

He grunted. "She's so excited about that and we're going to…"

"Wreck it," Lacey finished, wiping a tear. "I don't know what to do, Roman."

"We do what's right." He stood, taking her hand. "We go together, tell her the truth in private, and ask for her forgiveness."

"And if she doesn't forgive us?"

"I'll be out of your life, then, Lacey. And hers."

She closed her eyes. "I don't like that."

"Neither do I." He kissed her on top of the head. "I do not want to give you up. But I owe Tessa my life, and I'll do whatever she wants me to do."

She just leaned into him, wishing she could go back in time and make a different decision that day in Rosemary Beach. She might not have had the thrill of falling for Roman Matteo, but she wouldn't know the pain of hurting the woman who'd become a second mother to her.

"Let's go," she murmured. "I want to get this over with."

LACEY'S SNEAKERS padded softly against the sun-washed docks of the marina, each step making her blood pump faster. Roman walked beside her, his hand clasped around hers, strong and steady.

Taking a deep breath, Lacey tried to settle her nerves, but failed. Relief and fear and anticipation and dread all stretched across her chest, nearly making her sick.

"Just remember what we practiced in the car," Roman whispered. "And let me take ownership and the lead. This is on me, Lacey. I want her to know this wasn't your idea."

"It was my idea to find you in the first place."

"But the whole pretending to be a couple?" He squeezed her hand. "I have to own that."

The *Good Time Girl* shimmered ahead, somehow brighter and shinier than Lacey had ever seen the boat.

Tessa crouched near the bow, scrubbing away, her hair twisted up in a bun and her sunglasses sliding down her nose from perspiration. Still beautiful, and utterly at home on a boat, something that sometimes surprised Lacey.

Of course, Lacey hadn't been around in the "olden days" when the families rented boats. Apparently Artie had lived for the water, and Tessa was carrying on that tradition.

A sudden wash of affection nearly knocked Lacey over. She adored Tessa—had never met anyone quite like her. And what about work? They'd come so far, the two of them. From cautious acquaintances to work colleagues running a thriving little business to something that felt more like family.

And how had Lacey thanked her? Well, she thought it was by giving her a son. But Roman—and his mother—might very well be right. Tessa had guarded her secret for twenty-five years. And Lacey had—

"Hey, hey, hey." Tessa looked up and waved at them. "Where have you been, Romeo?"

"Actually, I went over to my hometown to see my parents." He sounded serious, not like the Shakespeare-quoting fun guy he'd been the first time they'd met.

"Oh?" Tessa tossed them each a cleaning rag. "You can tell me all about it while you scrub the deck. Big party tomorrow. You in? My dad would love the celebrity appearance."

Her dad...the ethics professor who did things "the right way." Lacey heard enough about Artie to know the man would not have approved of the dishonesty that got them in this predicament.

Roman climbed aboard first, and Lacey followed, her legs wobbly on the boat, but not because she was no longer on dry land. She glanced around, taking in the tidy deck, the glossy white leather seating, the brilliant blue canvas shade stretched overhead.

"We actually need to talk to you," Lacey blurted out, hearing how breathless her voice sounded. "Something important."

Tessa's brow furrowed slightly, lifting her sunglasses into her hair. She dropped onto the edge of the bow's leather banquette. "You guys okay?"

Lacey opened her mouth—but before she could speak, she heard footsteps on the dock.

"Got the wrench," Seamus called cheerfully as he walked up to the boat.

Lacey and Roman exchanged a quick look, his

expression mirroring her thoughts. How long would this take? They needed privacy.

Seamus put one foot on the side of the boat. "I'll get that loose connection—" He caught sight of Roman, stared for a moment, and nearly lost his footing. "Whoa—"

Instantly, Roman leaped up and steadied the older man, helping him back onto the dock. "Careful there, sir."

"Am I...am I..." Seamus drew back and put one hand on his chest, using the other to raise the bill of his ballcap to get a better look. "As I live and breathe, I do *not* believe it."

Lacey had been around Roman long enough to know exactly what he didn't believe. Now they'd have to make formal introductions and Seamus would fawn over the NFL player, and want an autograph. The faster they got that over with, the sooner they could talk to Tessa.

She climbed onto the dock to join them to make the introduction, almost used to the way people reacted to meeting a professional athlete.

"Seamus, this is Roman—"

Ignoring her, he held up his hand and turned to Tessa. "Why didn't you tell me you had a son? And that he is the spittin' image of Artie Wylie? How could you keep that news from me, Tessa?"

Oh, no. Oh, no. Oh no *no no no*.

Lacey felt her stomach lurch as she opened her mouth to respond, sensing Tessa coming closer behind her.

"You've lost it, Seamus. He's a famous football player, not my..." Her voice caught...and went silent. "He's not... He isn't..."

Seamus didn't answer.

Roman didn't blink.

And Lacey couldn't find the strength to turn and look at the friend she'd lied to a hundred times in the past month. Instead, shame crawled all over her skin and made her want to drop into the water and never come back up.

"I mean, look at those eyes," Seamus said, still staring. "Like sunshine on a bottle of whiskey. Dang, you even got Artie Wylie's jaw. Gimme a smile, son. I want to see if you got his teeth, too."

Oh, this was not happening.

"Um, Seamus," Roman said, obviously uncomfortable. "I don't think you should—"

"Oh, you can't stop me. I see what I see." Seamus patted his chest as if his heart needed a little attention. "God rest the good man's soul."

"Lacey." Tessa's hand landed on Lacey's shoulder, clammy and trembling.

Lacey felt the world tilt. She couldn't speak. Couldn't move.

"*Lacey,*" she said again, her voice nearly inaudible but gruff.

Very slowly, Lacey turned to look directly into Tessa's eyes and see...a woman who looked like she'd been sucker punched by her best friend.

Because she had.

"Did you know?" she whispered.

"I...I found him and we—"

"You *found* him? You looked for him? How—how could you *betray my trust*?" she demanded, her voice wavering.

"I didn't—"

"You did!"

"She didn't." Roman choked the words. "I did it. Everything was my idea, Tessa. I wanted to meet you and she didn't want to—"

"Stop!" Tessa held up a quivering hand, her face as white as the deck under her.

Lacey opened her mouth to say something—to explain everything, to fix it, to turn time backwards and start again—but nothing came out. Not a single sound or word.

"I can't believe this," Tessa breathed the words. "I can't believe you would do this to me."

"Well, *I* can't believe what I just stepped into," Seamus murmured, taking a few steps back. "I'm really sorry, Tess."

"Don't be," she said, shifting her gaze to Roman. "I was so blind and stupid and trusting and stupid and...*did I mention stupid?*"

"Tessa, please." He took a step forward to get back on the boat.

"No." She inhaled so sharply, her nostrils flared. "No, you stay right there. No, you won't appease me."

"We came here to tell you," Lacey said. "Right now, today, because—"

"Because you didn't have enough opportunity for the past month?" She spat the words at Lacey. "You bring him around, pretend he's your boyfriend, fish and eat and laugh and talk with him *under my nose* and you *don't tell me?* After you took my secret and threw it away like...like yesterday's trash? Like I didn't matter as much as your childish, selfish *curiosity?*"

"No, no, Tessa." Lacey felt the tears spill, bile rising in her as she realized this was way worse than she had feared. "It was nothing like that. I—"

"Don't be mad at her, Tessa," Roman said, making another effort to get onboard.

But Tessa shooed him off, her shaking fingers flipping a line around a cleat, freeing the first tie to the dock.

"Get away," she ground out.

"Please don't be mad at her, Tessa," he said again. "This was all me. My doing, my idea, my scheme."

She snorted. "How proud you make me...*son.*"

Roman flinched at the word, watching as Tessa reached for another line, twisting it free.

"Please, Tessa, there's so much to say," he pleaded. "We were going to tell you. We just—I had to wait until—"

"You *lied* to me," Tessa said, her voice sharp and shaking. "You both lied to me. You made a mockery of our friendship, Lacey, and you..." She threw a disgusted look at Roman. "You let me look at you and laugh and talk and share things, the whole time knowing who I was looking at while I had no idea? *How could you?*"

"Tessa, please," Lacey said, stepping forward. "I never meant to hurt you."

"Well, you did. You gutted me. Now go away. All of you. Go."

"I swear to you, we were going to tell you today," Lacey said, her voice as shattered as her heart. "Roman wanted to tell his parents first and—"

"Back away," she insisted, vaulting to the helm. She wrenched the key and suddenly the engine roared to life, the inboard shaking the whole dock.

Lacey stood frozen as the propeller sprayed whitewater and Tessa pulled out with no grace, no care, and no goodbye.

She churned up a wake, leaving water lapping at the pilings with angry, rhythmic splashes.

"Guess I shoulda kept my mouth shut," Seamus muttered.

"No," Roman said. "I should have opened mine a whole lot sooner."

Lacey let go of one long breath, certain that she'd just lost a woman she loved very, very much. And maybe the man she could love, too.

But honestly, right then, only Tessa mattered. And Tessa...was gone.

Chapter Twenty
Tessa

Of course she ran away. Of *course*.

When the going gets tough, Tessa takes off.

She could hear her father's voice in her head, louder than the engine, louder than the truth, louder than the heartbeat she couldn't calm down.

Well, what was she supposed to do? Throw her arms around the guy? Act like it was no big deal? Stand there and giggle like a fool?

She was a fool, all right. A blind, dumb, clueless fool.

With a noisy groan of agony, she kicked up the throttle and let the waves slap at the boat. Out of the harbor now, the Gulf stretched out before her, glittering and vast, a wide open body of nothingness where she could run, hide, and figure out what to do next.

Good Time Girl sliced through the water like she had something to prove, leaving a rooster trail of white foam for a wake. The wind tangled in Tessa's hair, salty and hot on her tear-streaked cheeks. Her hands trembled against the wheel.

She wasn't sure if she was shaking from adrenaline or hurt or shock or...what.

Roman was her son. Her *son*. How could she have missed that?

Because she never in a million years imagined Lacey would betray her trust and *find him*. Not to mention cooking up some scam about being boyfriend and girlfriend so he could spy on Tessa and decide if he liked her sufficiently to acknowledge their blood relationship.

Well, geez. It took him long enough to make the decision.

But what was another month after twenty-five years?

For two and a half decades, she had carried the weight of her decision—the one she finalized and stuck with in a hospital room, surrounded by people with gentle voices and kind, professional smiles who assured her this was the best thing.

She barely got to hold him. Only kissed his forehead a few times and never gave him a name.

With Dad at her side, she'd signed papers with shaky hands and cried afterward. Then he'd taken her home and promised he'd keep her secret until the day he died. And she'd never told another living soul until...Lacey.

Then, bam. Smacked in the face with betrayal. He was not only her son—he was an *accomplice* in that betrayal. He'd lied to her. They both had.

Was it no wonder that Tessa Wylie trusted no one on this planet? She was lied to by her own flesh and blood.

She swiped her cheeks with the back of her wrist and tried to pull herself together. But it was no use.

A sob broke loose from her chest, raw and unrelenting. The wind caught it, and still she kept going, kept sobbing, heading nowhere at all, slicing through the open sea on a beautiful boat as she suddenly felt like she'd lost all control.

Tessa slowed the boat, finally cutting the engine. The silence was louder than the motor ever had been. She was far enough out now that Destin's coast was a shadow, far out to nothing but water and sky and pain.

She dropped to the seat behind the console, buried her face in her hands, and let herself fall apart. She surrendered to the kind of crying she hadn't done in years —big, guttural, soul-twisting tears that made her chest ache and her heart feel like it had been crushed in a vise.

She wasn't just crying over the betrayal. She was crying for the baby she gave up. For the mother she never got to be. For all the birthdays she missed and the scraped knees she never kissed. For the lullabies she never sang. And, apparently, the football she'd never watched him play.

Surrounded by nothing but water, sun, and air, she finally dried her eyes and let the wild fury subside as the sun worked its way across the sky.

She'd be okay. It would all be okay...at some point.

Right now, she just had to be completely alone. Closing her eyes, she slowed her breaths, feeling her body settle into the rocking of the boat. It took her away, far away, to fishing days with Dad and even further back to laying in a hammock with Kate.

Kate. How would she take this news?

She moaned at the thought and started to sit up just as she heard the distant hum of a boat engine. Blinking against the light, she looked around, spying a small boat speeding toward her—familiar, blue-trimmed, one of the marina's older fishing vessels. Was that Seamus's boat?

It was, but Seamus wasn't at the wheel.

Roman was flying along, standing behind the center console, all muscle and brawn and wind-whipped golden hair like a god skimming the seas to make a mythical rescue.

Tessa froze.

Her breath caught as he slowed down and coasted up beside her, calm and careful. He tossed an anchor, then grabbed the bow railing and pulled himself aboard with practiced ease. Tall, sure-footed, he moved with the quiet confidence of someone who had her father's blood in his veins.

"I did not give you permission to come aboard," she said.

"Or break your heart." He took a step closer and she shot her hand in the air.

"Don't," she said, standing from the seat. "Don't come near me."

"Tessa, please. You have to give me a chance to say my piece."

"You had a chance. Weeks of a chance. Why didn't you tell me?"

He huffed out a sigh. "I'm not even sure anymore, but I'd love a do-over."

Tessa wrapped her arms around herself. "Because you've been caught? No do-overs in life, Roman.

Consider that your first—and last—lesson from...your mother."

He looked hard at her, with genuine hurt in his eyes.

He was hurt? That was rich.

Still, she couldn't look away. Couldn't stop seeing what had been in front of her for a month. He was clearly, obviously, unquestionably *hers*. How could she have been so blind?

Because a person didn't see what they weren't expecting—and she hadn't expected Lacey to break her promise with such ease and alacrity.

"I never wanted to lie to you," he said. "I just...I just wanted to get to know you. And once I did, I didn't know how to do it. I didn't want to show up out of nowhere and say, 'Hey, I'm the baby you gave away.' Even more than that, I felt strongly that I needed to talk to my parents first."

Tessa's throat ached. "Did you?"

"Yes. Yesterday, when I went back home. And the first thing—the very first thing I wanted to do was tell you next. That's why Lacey and I rushed over here. Seamus just...beat us to it."

She grunted in disbelief. Was he telling the truth? Was anyone?

"I don't know what to say," she rasped. "Except get off my boat and leave me alone."

"Not until you listen to me." At her withering look, he sighed. "Please. Please, Tessa."

When she didn't answer, he moved slowly toward

her, then stopped on the other side of the helm, a foot or so away.

"First, don't be mad at Lacey."

"I'll be mad at who I want to be mad at," she fired back. "And I'm furious at both of you. I told her in confidence."

"And she found me out of love."

She snorted. "Funny way of showing it."

"When she reached out to me," he continued, apparently choosing to ignore her sarcasm, "I knew I'd regret it if I didn't meet you. I had to. I was curious, yes, but it was more than that and you can ask Lacey. I've always felt a connection to you. I wondered about you, and knew ... you'd made a difficult decision. I wanted to know you and I wanted you to know what a great choice you made."

She just stared at him, the tremors finally fading and leaving behind...a cocktail of emotions that was making her dizzy.

"I had no idea what I'd find, even after Lacey told me I was... What did she say? A carbon copy of you, only the twenty-five-year-old male version."

She looked away, blinking back more tears, not quite ready to unpack all that. "How did she find you? I couldn't."

"You looked?" he asked.

"One time..." She shook her head. "I didn't try that hard, to be honest."

"Lacey called the hospital where I was born and had just enough information to get a name."

Tessa closed her eyes, remembering the litany of facts

she'd spewed that afternoon in a bistro in Miramar Beach. Date, time, weight, length, and the name of the hospital. "That was enough to find you?"

"Not if I'd been just a normal guy, but she got a last name and I had my picture in the paper and she…"

"She figured it out." Well, fair enough. He did look a lot like Tessa even though that thought had never even crossed her mind these past few weeks.

"But the rest is on me, Tessa. I cooked up the idea to meet you as her boyfriend. I talked her into that. Don't be mad at her, please. She loves you so much."

His concern for Lacey softened her a bit, and his willingness to take the blame was noble.

Not forgivable, but noble.

"Lacey sent me a message on Instagram and I agreed to meet her instantly because I've always wondered about you."

"Did you ask your parents? I think they would have known my name."

"No," he said. "I had a great childhood and didn't want them to feel I had a burning need to know my biological parents."

Her heart skipped a beat at the word—it was her turn to tell the truth. Ugly and shameful as it might be, it had to be told.

"Parent," she said softly, the admission churning her stomach. "Don't ask about the other half of your gene pool because…it wasn't a relationship as much as a…" She wanted to say "mistake" but how could she? Nothing about this specimen of humanity standing in front of her was a *mistake*. "Fling," she finished, knowing it sounded lame.

She braced for the inevitable look of judgment or disappointment or even disgust. But there was nothing. He just regarded her with some hope in his eyes, and an obviously open heart.

And in that instant, something inside her shifted. The pain eased slightly, and the shame lifted.

Not completely—she would always cringe at what she'd done with a virtual stranger one night on a cruise ship in the Caribbean. It would always be hard for her to admit—so much so that she'd chosen not to tell anyone, especially Kate and her mother.

"I don't care about that, Tessa," he said gently. "I'm not judging you. I'm just really grateful that you gave me to my parents."

She studied him, the adrenaline and shock and anger all finally waning as she took a moment to drink in the face of the child she'd brought into this world.

"They did a good job," she said begrudgingly. "Except for the lying part."

"Believe me, my mom's furious I did that."

A smile pulled. "She's right."

"I know she is. And so does Lacey. We're really, really sorry, Tessa. Please forgive me and Lacey for lying to you."

The plea was genuine, she could tell.

"It's funny," she said after a moment. "I always thought I'd be the one asking you for forgiveness if we ever met."

"You have nothing to apologize for," he said without hesitation. "You did everything right and I totally hit the lottery in the adoptive parents department."

She gave a dry laugh. "It seems to me you hit the lottery in every department."

"Do you think I don't know that? My parents gave me the greatest life imaginable. And you gave me...talent and brains."

"And drop-dead good looks."

A smile lifted his lips as he came around the console. "We do swim in a nice gene pool...Mom."

She sucked in a breath. "Don't."

"Too soon?"

"Not ever. I'm not your mom. I'm not...anybody's..." She hated that her voice cracked.

He leaned closer, reaching for her. "You're like another mother to Lacey," he said. "She says that all the time."

She let him take her hand while silence stretched between them. The only sound was the water, soft and steady, like the rhythm of something ancient and forgiving.

"I want you in my life," he said. "If you'll let me."

Her eyes burned and she covered her face with her hands, sinking back onto the seat. "I don't know how to do this. I've hidden this for so long and now my mother and sister... Oh, I just don't know how to handle it."

"I'll help you however I can," he said. "But first, please talk to Lacey. She's so scared to lose you, Tessa."

She closed her eyes and thought about that sweet girl. "She'll never lose me," Tessa whispered.

"Tell her that." He put a hand on her arm. "She's hurting and I can't stand that."

She started to respond, then drew back, eyeing him. "Wait. What? It's...*real*?"

He tipped his head. "It got that way."

"Oh." She let out a dry laugh of disbelief. "That's a turn of events I didn't see coming."

"Neither did I. But, whoa, that girl... is special. And as much as I wish we could go back and do this whole thing over and not lie to you, I wouldn't change anything with her. And I don't want to lose her."

Tessa exhaled and looked out at the water, her heart lifting at this news. "Huh." She stood at the helm, the first smile in hours pulling at her mouth. "Well, that's some good that came out of it."

"A lot of good came out of it," he said. "We just went about it all wrong."

Finally, she sighed, wanting to put the anger behind her. And there was one more conversation she had to have. Well, there were several, but she'd start with Lacey.

"C'mon, Romeo." She reached for the ignition. "Get in your little boat and lead me back to dry land. I want to talk to your girlfriend."

"You're not mad?" he asked. "You don't hate me?"

She looked at him and let out a little moan, finally throwing her arms around his broad shoulders and hugging her son for the first time in twenty-five years.

"Hate? I've loved you since before you were born,"

she muttered. "And I guess nothing will ever change that."

He squeezed her and those mighty shoulders shuddered with a sob it felt like he'd been holding in for a long, long time.

The trip back was faster and easier, with no tears. The sea breeze and salt air cleared her head as she watched Roman—her son!—lead the way in the other boat. They slowed down at the marina and he turned to return his boat.

She puttered to the dock, where Lacey sat at the end, a fishing rod in her hand.

Seamus's cure for a broken heart, she imagined.

Lacey stood as Tessa eased into the slip, bending over to tie up the bow line without being asked. Then she gingerly climbed onto the deck, her gaze on Tessa.

"Can we talk?" Lacey asked softly.

Tessa took her sunglasses off and rounded the helm. "I know you're sorry."

"You don't know *how* sorry," Lacey said, reaching for her. "Because there are no words to tell you."

Tessa pulled her in for a hug. "It was wrong," she whispered.

"I know, I know." Lacey squeezed so hard that Tessa had no choice but to put her arms around her, wincing when she felt just how badly the poor thing was trembling.

"I'm not worth you being this upset, Lace."

Lacey gasped, drawing back. "What? Are you kidding? You're...you're everything, Tessa! I never knew anyone like you and I respect you and I love you. And I hurt you and...and..." She swiped at the tears flowing. "I am so, so sorry."

"C'mere." Tessa pulled her to the leather bench and eased them both down, side by side. "Of course I forgive you. I forgive Roman, too."

"Oh, Tessa, thank you." She collapsed, letting her head fall onto Tessa's lap, her hair covering her tear-stained face. "I just hate that this happened and my part in it. I don't know what I was thinking."

"Uh, can I guess you were being persuaded to be the girlfriend of a super-hot guy who also happens to be kind, smart, and on an NFL roster?"

Under her hands, Lacey's shoulders moved in a soft laugh. "Yeah," she blubbered. "I might have gotten...a little swept away in the moment."

Tessa smiled and stroked Lacey's sun warmed skin. "Blame me."

"You?" She popped up. "You didn't do anything."

"Only made a perfect specimen of mankind for you to fall in love with."

"Oh, Tessa." She managed a laugh. "We're a long way from *love*."

Tessa smoothed Lacey's messy hair, and wiped the tears on her cheek. "I don't know about that," she said. "But I do know this..."

Lacey waited, holding her gaze.

"My father would say anything motivated by love is never bad, but it can be messy."

"This was messy," Lacey said on a sigh.

"And now I have to clean up the mess," Tessa said. "So don't tell anyone else."

"I won't!" She crossed her heart like a little girl. "I promise. I swear, I promise!"

"I'm going to tell them myself, in my own way, at the right time."

"Absolutely," Lacey agreed. "And what about Roman? Should he...leave? Should we stop seeing each other? Should I—"

"Are you kidding? Roman is the man who will make you my daughter—in-law."

Lacey's eyes widened. "Oh, I don't—"

She put her finger on Lacey's lips. "I know it. You know it. And he knows it. And now we all get to sit back and watch it happen. And I get to wear pink at your wedding."

"You're crazy," Lacey said, hugging her again. "And I love you."

"I love you, too." Tessa pulled her head down, back on her lap, enjoying the maternal pleasure of soothing this sweet girl, rocking with the boat.

Dad would have loved this, she thought. Smiling, she looked up. Heck, he probably had a hand in the whole thing.

August 23, 1991

You know how sometimes you get an idea in your head and you just know that it's going to be magic? Not maybe. Not possibly. Just straight-up, stars-aligning, Disney-movie magic?

Well. That's what I thought today would be. I've been planning it all week in my head. My Sunset Picnic Idea. Capital letters and every-thing. Summer is coming to an end (SADNESS!) and this would be the most perfect way to say goodbye to it.

I thought, wouldn't it be so cute if all the summer kids—me, Tessa, Kate, Eli, Peter (♥), even Crista, I guess—went down to the beach at golden hour and had a sunset picnic together? Like, with snacks and music and one of those giant patchwork quilts Aunt Jo Ellen keeps in the linen closet that smells like dryer sheets?

So I told everyone. Three days ago. I made invitations, too. "<u>Thursday evening. Beach picnic. Bring a blanket and your fun self!</u>"

Kate said she'd come. Tessa said she'd totally be there. Eli gave a thumbs-up. Even Jo Ellen said it was a cute idea and offered to get juice boxes and cut-up watermelon for us. Peter just ignored it, but I knew he'd come with everyone else.

So I packed snacks. Not just random boring

ones, either. I made PB&J tea sandwiches and washed strawberries with lemon so they'd taste fresher. I packed them in the green cooler and stuck a little Polaroid camera inside just in case I wanted to take cute friendship pictures for the scrapbook I haven't started yet. I wore my new sundress, the pink one with the eyelet lace straps that Mom said makes me look "way too grown-up."

But then, last minute, no one could come. Kate felt bad, but she forgot she had to catch up on her summer reading for English class in the fall. Tessa fell asleep on the couch with a wicked sunburn. Eli went off with his other stupid summer friends like Dustin Mathers. And Crista was in hours-long time out for some bad thing she'd done that didn't fly with Mom.

I was so sad, I decided to just go have my picnic alone in a classic pity party.

Just me and the beach. And the snacks. And the sign I dragged down from the kitchen and propped up in the sand like a sad little billboard of rejection.

Then—

PETER.

I heard someone jogging down the stairs from the deck and when I turned around, it was him.

"I come bearing drinks," he said. "Did I miss

everyone or...?"

Imagine me trying to look casual while I was actually two seconds away from crying into a peanut butter sandwich.

I admitted they all bailed.

Peter looked at me for a long second, then dropped down onto the quilt like it was exactly where he meant to be all along.

He cracked open a root beer like he was Tom Cruise and it was real beer.

Then he said..."Their loss."

MY HEART 🩶🩶🩶

I didn't know what to say. I was embarrassed. And a little heartbroken. And a lot humiliated. But he just sat there with me and ate strawberries. Took a bite of one of my dumb sandwiches and said it was "delicious, with a surprise jelly twist, but where's the crust?"

We watched the sun go down together, just the two of us, and he didn't say anything cheesy or awkward. He just sat there with me like it wasn't weird or sad at all and we talked about school and stuff.

I told him he didn't have to come.

And he said, "Sure I did. You asked."

And that right there? That's Peter. He always shows up.

When it was all done, he said, "You know, Viv, this was actually pretty great. Sunset.

Sandwiches. No Eli telling the same dumb joke five times. I'd say it was perfect."

PERFECT.

Then he winked—ACTUALLY WINKED—and said, "Let me know when the next picnic is. I'll be the first to RSVP."

And then he was gone. He carried the cooler upstairs and went inside. Like it was nothing.

But it wasn't nothing to me.

I think maybe—I don't know—I think maybe reliability is actually the dreamiest thing there is. Not flowers or mixtapes or boys who play guitar. But boys who show up with root beer and call your sandwiches delicious and treat you like you matter.

Peter McCarthy showed up tonight. For me.

And it might've been the smallest thing in the world. But it felt like everything.

Love,

Viv

P.S. I really hope he meant it when he said he'd come to the next picnic. Maybe next time I'll actually plan it just for him. Not that I'd ever admit it.

Chapter Twenty-one
Vivien

Not bad, Vivien Lawson. Not bad at all.

Vivien stepped all the way to the entrance of Danny's loft and took a moment to drink in the fruits of her labor. The sports bar with a touch of refinement and elegance had been achieved with perfection, right down to the tribal-themed woven rug and the understated pillows on the sectional.

The sun was nearly down, but that gave an orange glow to the room that truly brought it to life.

The bar was welcoming, the built-ins were subtle but functional, and the new black felt pool table seemed like it had been there forever. And since it took three monstrous moving men to get it upstairs, it might very well *be* there forever, too.

She angled her phone and took another picture, trying to get the snapshot just right for the Vivien Lawson Designs Instagram page, already crafting the caption.

"Equal parts masculine and refined, cozy and luxe... elevated," she whispered. "A touch of sophistication and definitely one-of-a-kind."

"I hope you're describing me for one of those diary entries you tell me you like to write."

At Danny's voice, she turned, lowering the phone and giving a quick—slightly embarrassed—laugh. "The room, my friend, the room."

"Which is chef's kiss perfection, Ms. Lawson." He reached the top of the stairs and opened his arms toward the space. "You crushed it. I'm in love. With the room, of course."

"Don't ruin my moment," she warned lightly, her voice laced with humor. "I'm having a professional high here."

He was barefoot, as always, in dark jeans and a soft black tee that was maddeningly attractive. His mostly pepper but slightly salted hair was tousled, like he'd run a hand through it a few times before coming upstairs.

"You're right," he said after a beat. "It deserves a moment of appreciation. You made it look effortless, too."

Vivien laughed. "Well, it's one room, you had no make-or-break opinions, and your budget was more than generous. In this case, it *was* effortless."

"Not to me—thank you."

"You're so welcome. And the lamps and rugs for the guest rooms will be here by the end of the week, so we, my friend, are done with this project."

He made a face. "Let's start on the downstairs."

"You said you were happy with that."

"I want to keep you around," he said, the bluntness startling her.

"Well, I'm just down the road in the Summer House."

He tipped his head in concession, and his smile faded into something gentler. "You're going to make me spell it out, aren't you?"

"Depends on what you're spelling," she joked, but her heart kicked up a notch. She could see the look in his eyes and knew what was coming.

"All right, I'm spelling...relationship." He took a breath, then reached for her hand, guiding her over the tribal rug to the perfectly appointed sectional. "Do you want...specifics?"

She let him ease her onto the cushion next to him. "I know what a relationship is."

"And don't tell me—you're in one with the cop you've known since you were a kid."

Her heart dipped at the description, just thinking about that diary entry she'd read last night and how it had made her want to just wrap the man in her arms and thank him again.

Dear, darling, dependable Peter was so much more than a cop she'd known since she was a kid.

"I've been seeing him, yes."

"Isn't he ever going back to Pensacola?"

She gave a soft laugh. "He's actually thinking about taking a job in Destin."

"Aah." He leaned back and eyed her. "So, it's more serious with you two. I should back off."

Was it serious? She didn't know—and she didn't

know if she wanted Danny to back off at all. She'd certainly miss the attention.

"But if it wasn't," he continued slowly, "then I would very much like to see where this could go. Not just...this flirtation. But *us*. I want something real. With you."

She swallowed, her throat thick. She'd known it was coming—Danny wasn't subtle. He never had been.

But here in this perfect room he'd trusted her to create, after weeks of laughing and teasing and being seen by someone new...well, it was hard.

"Danny," she began, her voice soft. "You're...wonderful. You really are."

"Oof." He blinked. "The thanks-but-no-thanks tone."

Was it? She studied him, thinking and feeling and letting her heart tell her what to do. What did she want from this man? From her life? And when would she figure it out?

Time was ticking.

"No. It's the *I-care-about-you* tone," she said, her voice hesitant. "You came into my life when I was figuring out how to start over. You reminded me that I'm more than a divorcee and a mom and a sister and a decorator. You made me feel...seen."

"And what I see is beautiful," he said, the perfect flirt always at the ready.

And maybe that's what was stopping her. He was *too* perfect. Too handsome, too rich, too used to getting what he wanted.

And Vivien had just found her spine, which could very well be lost again with a man like this.

Danny waited, lifting a brow. "But…"

"But I can't," she said gently. "Not right now. Not when I don't have clarity. Not when I don't know what I want."

He looked back up, silver-blue eyes searching hers. "The cop won, huh?"

Vivien let out a short, sad laugh. "This wasn't a contest."

"Felt like one sometimes."

She reached out and touched his arm. "It was never about picking the shinier object. You and Peter are…very different men. You make me feel different things."

Danny nodded slowly. "I knew that from the beginning. Still hurts a little, though."

"I'm sorry."

He shook his head. "Don't be. I'm glad I met you. And I'll use the heck out of this loft."

Vivien laughed. "You better."

A warm silence passed between them. Then Danny reached for her. "Friends?"

"Friends," she echoed, though her heart ached a little as they hugged.

They stood, smiling at each other, and changed the subject to small talk about the room, the furnishings, and a promise of a rousing game of pool someday.

But they both knew that would never happen, Vivien thought as she walked down the stairs. After saying a warm goodbye, she stepped outside, the Florida heat wrapping around her like a real hug, not one from someone she liked but didn't…*need*.

Satisfied, she climbed into her SUV and turned on the ignition, knowing where she was going next. She and Peter had plans to meet at The Back Porch for dinner—and it was time to give him her decision.

VIVIEN WAS EARLY ENOUGH to snag one of the waterfront tables at the very small and desirable section that was the original "back porch" and gave the restaurant its name. With the massive windows wide open, she could feel the salt air and enjoy an unobstructed view of the water and waves.

Sunset was an hour or two away and by the time that white sand and blue water turned fiery orange, she would have to make her decision with Peter.

Sipping a white wine, she felt the restaurant shift from a quiet cocktail hour to the first light rush of dinner patrons, checking her watch to see that Peter would be here in about five minutes.

Her shoulders tensed as she imagined how she'd tell him that, yes, she wanted him to stay and pursue a relationship with her.

That was what she wanted...wasn't it?

With no answer, she stared out into the beautiful waning light, the kind that made Destin shimmer like a postcard. The yellow sun still filtered through the restaurant windows, warming the ancient wood floors and lacquer-covered tables that had served thousands of tourists over the years.

Including, she mused, two young families who'd summered together for seven years. They'd eaten here at least three times every summer. Maybe more. Maybe right at this very table, with Peter looking so cute and smiling and calling her "champ" and Eli annoying her and sliding glances at Tessa.

Was that what was really at the heart of her feelings for Peter? Nostalgia?

No, it couldn't be. She didn't feel nostalgic when he wrapped her in his arms. She felt loved.

Glancing at her phone, she frowned at the time. Fifteen minutes late? Not like Peter McCarthy.

He showed up early. He held doors. He called when he said he would. He came to her beach parties when no one else did.

Yet he was late and there were no missed texts to explain or apologize.

"Another wine?" The server's voice brought her out of her thoughts.

Although a second glass sounded good, she wanted her wits for this conversation—even if she wasn't sure what she was going to say.

"Just ice water this round, thank you. My friend should be here soon. I'm sorry to take the table if there's a wait."

"It's fine," the man said. "You just relax."

Smiling her thanks, she turned back to the view and tried to follow the order. Relax. How could she? She was basically deciding her future in the next half hour.

As another fifteen minutes passed, she had the first

tendril of worry. She knew Peter's job could be unpredictable. He was buried in that missing person case here in Destin, and he was probably involved with the paperwork of closing it.

Maybe he was meeting with the PD chief to discuss the job. He hadn't officially accepted the transfer yet, he'd made it clear—if Vivien was in, he was all in. He'd offered her stability. Love. A future.

Wasn't that what she wanted?

She looked around the softly lit bar. The hum of conversation, the gentle clink of forks and the aroma of fried fish filled her with that same nostalgia. And yet, with every passing minute, Vivien felt a strange unease creeping in beneath her skin.

She tapped her phone again, stunned when she realized he was now an hour and ten minutes late. She texted him as a whisper of worry danced up her spine.

His job *was* dangerous. He joked about the fact that he always had a gun, but the fact was...he *always* had a gun.

Which meant he was safe and could defend himself. She hoped.

When it hit the hour and a half mark, she knew she had to order something or leave.

She opted for some fried shrimp and another glass of wine, and stared at her phone wondering why he hadn't called or texted.

Could something horrible have happened? Just the possibility made her realize how much she treasured him and his friendship.

Whoops...she'd put him in the Friend Zone again.

Her gaze drifted to the sand and water, where the sun had nearly finished its slow descent, leaving the sky washed in pale purples and fading orange. Was he just a friend? Surely he was more than that.

The second wine must have hit because she was suddenly transported in time, sitting at the community pool with Kate and Tessa, promising they'd all be best friends forever. Promising to stay true to themselves. What would that girl think of the woman sitting here tonight?

She'd think...was Vivien being stood up by the most reliable man in the world? Maybe. Or maybe something happened to him.

She texted him another quick "Where are you?" and plucked at the shrimp, lost in thought.

Everything she knew about Peter assured her that he was safe, so she started to think seriously about another possibility. Maybe *she* was the one getting a hard pass.

Maybe he thought she wanted Danny, that he'd read her ambivalence and mixed signals as a rejection, and decided to close his case and skip this date.

Was that possible? Of course it was. Possible and... wise. In fact, he might be doing them both a favor by not having to have a terribly uncomfortable conversation.

Because...Vivien wasn't ready.

She sucked in a quiet breath as the thought landed.

She *wasn't* ready.

At the realization, she sat up straighter, lifting, then

dropping the fried shrimp as a new and completely different option landed on the table.

What if she said no to both men? What if she continued this journey of "life as a divorcee" completely and utterly...alone?

She wouldn't be, of course—she had Lacey and now her mother, Eli and Kate and Tessa, too. She had a whole life full of beloved family and friends.

But she wouldn't have a man in her life and that was...okay. No, it was...right. The way it should be. The only real answer to this dilemma.

That *had* to be her choice!

Good heavens, she'd barely been divorced for a month or so. What was she doing throwing herself into another relationship? She didn't want that!

Yes, she loved Peter—as a friend and maybe more. But the *more* had to wait. It wasn't right now.

The decision gave her the first tendril of true peace she'd felt in a while, tempered only by the fact that Peter's no-show was completely and utterly out of character. Maybe he was desperate to make a point.

Or maybe something was wrong, and he'd gotten hurt...

With a grunt, she picked up her phone again and scrolled to his name, only to see that the last text just said "delivered" and hadn't been read.

Sighing against growing concern, she typed another text.

Everything okay? Not like you to be late. I'm getting worried!

She hit Send, but instantly a red notification came up that the text couldn't be sent.

Weird. She tried again, same thing.

Something wasn't right. She called his number, and pressed the cell to her ear.

"The number you have dialed is not in service."

What? She held out the phone and blinked at it, not believing the recording she'd just heard. His phone wasn't in service?

Oh—it wasn't a personal phone. He'd told her that was his Destin PD phone and he must have turned it back in. That made sense, actually. He was probably halfway to Pensacola now and when he got his own phone back, he'd text her that this was best for both of them.

And he'd be right.

For the first time in her life, she wasn't beholden to anyone. Not to Maggie, or Ryan, not to the expectations that had boxed her in for almost fifty years. She had carved out this small but beautiful slice of a life for herself, and it was hers. She didn't need a man to give it meaning.

She paid for her food and drinks, ignored the look of pity from the server who assumed—correctly—that she'd been stood up, and smoothed her sundress as she stood.

Instead of walking to her car, she headed to the beach, now nearly dark as the stars came out. There were a few people, and, out of deference to nesting turtles, almost no light but the moon.

"Alone," she whispered as she slipped off her sandals and her feet hit the sugary sand. "All alone."

Gazing up at the nearly full moon, she wandered down by the water and stood very still while the froth of the waves washed over her bare feet.

It finally made sense why she'd been teetering between Danny and Peter. She wasn't ready to fall in love again, not with anyone. At this point in her life, she only needed Vivien Lawson.

She walked for a while, playfully kicking the sand and enjoying the warm water. The sun disappeared completely, leaving just moonlight and salty air bathing a woman who finally realized what she needed—her family, her job, and the Summer House.

She needed to steady her course and strengthen that backbone she'd been developing, and discover just who Vivien was.

With the realization, her heart lifted and she turned around, practically dancing over the sand to head back home. She was excited to tell Lacey what she'd decided, and Tessa, Kate, and Eli.

She knew they'd love and support her. Heck, even Maggie would give a nod of respect for this decision—that woman knew a thing or two about surviving and thriving alone.

Satisfied and excited about the future, she slipped into her car and drove home, still wondering about Peter but certain she was making the right choice.

It was nearly ten and the Summer House looked dark and quiet when she pulled in. Tomorrow was a big day of remembrance and celebration and everyone would be up early to join Tessa and Jo Ellen in sending Artie's ashes into the Gulf.

Everyone but Maggie.

Maybe she'd change her mind. In fact, Vivien thought as she parked and opened the door, she should go slip into her mother's room right now and tell her what a dumb move it was to hold on to—

Headlights suddenly bathed the driveway in light, and she turned, blinded by them. The car stopped and the door shot open.

"Viv! Vivien!" She heard Peter's voice but couldn't see him even after the headlights went out.

Blinking into the darkness, she felt her way toward him, a little shocked when he reached her first and wrapped his arms around her in a bear hug.

"Oh, you're here. You're here..." She could feel his heart hammering, his shirt damp with sweat.

"I was at the—" She pulled back to see his face looked wrecked. Dirty and...whoa. Was that blood on his cheek? "Where were you?"

"I'm sorry. I'm sorry." He seemed to have to catch his breath, shaking his head. "Work."

"Work?" She touched his face, her heart folding. "What happened?"

He blew out a breath, squeezed her again, and held her long enough for her to feel his heartbeat settle.

"I found him."

She drew back, searching his face. "And?"

"I followed him into a warehouse and got into a... scuffle."

"Peter!"

"It's fine, it's fine. Just twenty minutes negotiating with a lunatic and his gun." He huffed out a breath. "My back-up came and we got him in cuffs. In the aftermath, they took my phone for evidence. The case is closed."

She pressed her hands to her mouth. "Are you okay?"

"I'm better than okay, Viv. When you know you're one finger flick away from death and it doesn't happen? Yeah, I'm good." He pulled her closer. "I don't want to live what's left of this life without you, though, Viv. I love you."

She felt her jaw loosen, heard the echo of every independent thought she'd just had, and stared at him.

"But you were going to break it off tonight," he finished with a humorless laugh. "Remember, I read people for a living and your face—and heart—are an open book."

"Peter, I—"

"It's fine, it's fine. Danny's a great—"

"No, no, you're wrong," she insisted. "It's not Danny. I'm not going to see him. We're done and over, not that anything ever started, but I spelled it out for him—the answer is no. I swear."

Relief lowered his strong shoulders, but his brows drew together in a doubtful look. "But we're done and over, too?"

She took a moment to lean back and look up at him, gathering her thoughts. Old Vivien would have thrown her arms around him if only to help a man who'd just faced death. She'd have caved and rationalized and started planning their future.

And while that option appealed on one level...it was still wrong. New Vivien—a woman who didn't let her moves be dictated only to please other people—would not do that. New Vivien would be firm, honest, and kind.

"Peter, I'm not ready to fall in love again," she whispered.

He searched her face, silent.

"I adore you. And not just like a brother or a friend. You have always been my weakness, my crush, and my favorite and most dependable person. I don't want to stop being together, but I can't say I'm in love...yet. I'm not ready for that. I'm not ready for you to move here just for me."

He nodded very slowly, relaxing his hold on her slightly. "You're right, of course. I'm running on adrenaline and hope. Oh, and the chief sweetened the deal. I'd be an idiot to say no."

"You're staying in Destin?" Inexplicably, her heart soared.

"I might. I mean, no pressure on you, Viv, I swear. But I like it here. I like the families—since I don't have one of my own. One son wants to stay in Gainesville, and the other would like to consider Destin PD when he finishes the academy. This is really starting to feel like home, and not just because you're here." He smiled. "I guess there is magic in Destin like everyone says."

She let out a sigh. "I'm glad you found a home and family here and I don't want you to leave, but..."

"But you want to be on your own."

"For a while," she said.

He shook his head. "You're so right. The ink is barely dry on your divorce papers and I'm rushing you. We've known each other for thirty years, Viv. What's another... whatever it takes."

"That's just it, Peter. I don't know what it will take."

He brushed her hair back, cupping her face. "I don't, either, but you take what you need. That wasn't an adrenaline-fueled confession of love, Viv. It was real. I love you and I'm here for you, but I'm also able to give you whatever space you need. No more dating. No more golfing. No more pressure." He leaned down and kissed her forehead. "But, man, I'm glad you ditched Danny."

She gave a light laugh and melted into him. "And I'm sorry you had to face a loaded gun tonight."

He lifted a shoulder. "It's my job. Viv, you deserve time, space, respect, and freedom. Count on me for all of them."

"Oh, Peter." She slid her arms around him and hugged. "Just like the time you were the only one to come to my party and brought root beer. I can always count on you."

He leaned back. "I won't be at the celebration tomorrow," he said. "We have a massive debriefing after tonight's incident. Then I'm going to head back to Pensacola, talk to my boss and undo my job there, get my house on the market, and pull my life together. But I'll be back in a month or two."

"And I'll be here. I promise."

"I'll hold you to that promise, Viv."

With one more kiss on the top of her head, he stepped away and she stayed still, watching him drive off.

Part of her wanted to write a diary addendum—*Peter loves me!* 🩶 —but another part of her wanted to just exhale the breath she'd been holding for decades, happily alone for now.

Chapter Twenty-two
Maggie

Had she ever been in this house completely alone before? Yes, but today felt different to Maggie as she roamed the empty space. Loneliness pressed on her heart.

She blamed the chaos of the morning's preparations—good heavens, it was like they were getting ready for a State Funeral. There'd been so much fluttering about how to fit ten people on the boat, not to mention that infernal box they treated like the Ark of the Covenant.

But now, with all the Summer House residents gone to the marina for Artie's watery send-off, the silence seemed heavier than usual.

So was Maggie's guilt.

"Pffft." She flicked away the unwelcome sensation as she poured herself some coffee, refusing to wallow in second-guessing. The decision was made—she would not, she *could not* sit on a rocking boat in the blazing sun and cheerily toast a man who'd played a role in Roger's arrest.

It didn't matter what that role was or wasn't—she couldn't *fake* tender emotions for the guy.

She could tiptoe back into a relationship with Jo

Ellen, yes. But fawn over Artie? No, that she would not do.

Splashing cream in her cup, she tried to forget the look of disappointment in Jo Ellen's eyes when they said goodbye. Even Tessa had shot a few unkind looks her way, but then, Tessa had been acting weird since yesterday afternoon.

Honestly. What did they expect of her?

She stepped onto the deck, begrudgingly noting that they'd been given a perfect day to toss Artie into the Gulf.

But even before she took a sip, her stomach churned. Her whole chest, to be honest, felt tense and fluttery, like she'd made a very, very bad decision.

Guilt and remorse and shame rose up like bile in her throat, refusing to be ignored or go away.

"Oh, come now, Magnolia!" she chided. "You can't…" Her whisper faded out when she noticed a man lingering at the end of the boardwalk.

Who was that?

They didn't get too many passersby on this stretch of beach homes, and especially not men that old. Well, he was about her age—so not *ancient*—but in decent shape and not falling over dead from the heat. Considering he was in khaki pants and a golf shirt, that was saying something.

He looked up at the house, so she dipped out of view by stepping back into the shadows of the deck. Oh, the looky-loos irritated her. Did they think they had every right to just stare at these houses?

Waiting a beat, she inched forward to see—

What? He was on the boardwalk, coming closer with far too much purpose. Of *course* this would happen when she was here alone. When everyone and their brother, niece, and cousin just had to go out and pay homage to a man who'd—

"Hello?"

She swore under her breath when she realized he'd seen her and called out.

She couldn't hide now. Clearing her throat, she stepped to the railing. "Can I help you find your way off my private property, sir?"

"I know how to leave," he said, taking off a baseball cap to reveal a thick head of white hair. "I'm looking for Peter McCarthy."

Oh, dear. The bad guy he was after? Hadn't Vivien said something about them catching that man? Why hadn't Maggie paid closer attention? Maybe this was one of his unsavory partners, come to kill...someone.

"Try calling him," she said. "I can't help you."

"I did and his phone's disconnected. This is the address he gave the FBI."

Her heart jumped. *The FBI?* Now what did they want? The house? The deed? Her head on a platter? Hadn't she given them enough?

"Why do you need him?" she asked, her fingers tightening on the coffee cup as he came closer, almost to the first-level patio.

"I understand he's been digging for information on Arthur Wylie and Roger Lawson."

She nearly dropped her coffee.

For at least three heartbeats, he stared up at her, silent and expressionless. Then his eyes shuttered.

"Wild guess, but you gotta be either Maggie or Jo Ellen. Based on what I know—which is a lot—I'm going with Maggie. Roger said you were, uh, spunky. Artie said his wife was a softy. Lady, you aren't soft."

She managed to swallow. "Who are you?"

"My name's James Hill, retired FBI. I headed up the Biloxi CCSG and put a man named Cotton Ramsey in jail." He shifted from one foot to the other, holding her gaze. "I think I have the information you want. And you have a thirty-year-old dry cleaning stub that I've been looking for."

Her legs wobbled like she was on that boat after all. In fact, right then, she wished she'd gone and could throw *herself* in the water.

"So, can we talk?" He spread out his arms in a gesture of surrender. "I'm not carrying anything but answers to the questions your pal Peter's been asking."

Answers. Was there anything she wanted more?

"I'll be right down," she croaked.

"Bring that dry cleaning stub, please."

Feeling shaky, she darted upstairs to her room and opened the small box that held her rings, retrieving the tiny card with the perforated edge.

Once again, she had to give Jo Ellen props for having the nerve to take this from the bank. It might be the price they had to pay for answers.

As she shoved it in her pocket, she wished she also

had a gun hidden somewhere but, sadly, that was not the case.

So, she took a deep breath and went all the way down to the ground-floor level, coming face to face with the man standing next to the pool like he had every right to be there.

He was tall, lanky, and pushing eighty. But then, so was she.

She lifted her chin and met his direct gaze.

"Am I right?" he asked. "Magnolia Lawson?"

She considered offering her hand, but thought better of it. Instead, she nodded and crossed her arms over her chest. "Yes."

"The spunky one." He grinned, reaching into his pocket for a wallet he flipped open. "As I said, James Hill, retired FBI. Don't get me wrong, Roger always had nice things to say about you. Can we sit down?"

She studied the badge, then nodded, happy for the excuse not to stand there and vibrate with nerves in front of the man.

"First of all," he said after they both sat, "I never got to give you my condolences, Mrs. Lawson. Roger's death was untimely and unexpected." He let out a sigh. "Sadly, I was working hard to get him out within the next few months. The minute Cotton Ramsey and his crew were behind bars, your husband would have been home free." He gave a tight smile. "Guess God had other plans and I'm sure Roger is up there waiting for you."

She just stared at him, trying—and failing—to under-stand what he was talking about.

But all she could really think was that this man, this James Hill, was one of the few people on Earth who'd ever implied her white-collar criminal of a husband was in *heaven*.

Instantly, she liked him.

"I hope so," she said softly.

"Oh, I know so. He was on the side of the angels."

She drew back at what had to be an exaggeration. "Are you being sarcastic or do you have information about my husband that I don't?"

He angled his head in concession. "Yes, he committed crimes, chief among them greed and stupidity. But in the end, and well before, I think he made up for them. He was repentant, and he worked tirelessly to help us."

What was he *talking* about?

The man leaned back, giving her a chance to see that he had healthy color, white teeth, and a surprising amount of breadth to his chest. As always, she respected a person who took care of themselves. And one who thought Roger was *good*?

Yes. She was more than ready to listen.

"Who are you, exactly?" she asked.

"I was Roger's handler. I negotiated his deal, arranged for his shortened incarceration, worked with him and Artie to get Cotton, and—you're very welcome— I made sure you could keep this property." He jutted his chin toward the house. "I like what you've done with it." He grinned again. "Now *that* was sarcasm."

"I'm very confused," she admitted after a beat.

"Would you be kind enough to start from the beginning? And understand that I have no idea what my husband—and Artie Wylie—have to do with this Cotton fellow."

He nodded slowly, gathering his thoughts. "Well, surely you knew that Roger borrowed money from Cotton at interest rates that would make your hair curl," he started.

"I heard that was a possibility."

"It's a fact. And the price for non-payment—even late payment—was...high. Cotton threatened to kill you, your three kids, and the Wylies alongside you."

She sucked in a breath, her eyes wide as chills exploded on her arms. "Excuse me?"

"You heard me. When Cotton got wind of the fact that Roger bought this property—and still owed him a whole ton of money—it was no holds barred. Cotton wanted his money *and* this land." He crossed his legs, getting comfortable. "Roger and Artie cooked up a scheme and, honestly, it was a good one."

"A scheme?"

"They got Roger arrested, which was the only way Cotton would back off. Artie contacted the police, pretended to be one of Roger's unhappy clients whose financial draw had disappeared, and Roger was arrested. Surely you remember that."

"All too well." So Artie *had* turned Roger in...to help him.

"In the interrogation, the whole business with Cotton's loan came out and the Feds were brought in," he continued.

"My team had been trying to get Ramsey's crew for a long time, but he was the head of the snake and avoided capture. He talked like an idiot, but he was smart as a whip."

Maggie just stared at him, once again overwhelmed with how much about her husband she never really knew.

"And Cotton was ruthless. With Roger in jail, he knew this property was in play. He was going to come after you for the money. And, by extension, Artie's family, since you all were so close. None of you were safe —not for one minute."

Every vein in her body turned to ice.

"Then one day Artie Wylie showed up in my office. Now there was a choir boy if I ever saw one."

She almost smiled at that. "He was...a good man."

"Good? He was a stinking hero. He put his life on the line, arranged to get Cotton the 'money,' and set up a sting that led me directly to that son of a...bad man. Because Artie was willing to be wired and risk his life, we took the entire Dixie Mafia down."

"He...did that?" She tried to imagine that Cornell ethics professor with a goofy sense of humor and a mean fishing rod getting wired and endangering his life...for Roger. For all of them.

"And he did it with style and fearlessness," he added as if he read her mind. "We couldn't have gotten to Cotton without Artie. Roger, too. He helped set it up from prison, telling Cotton that his friend had the money. The two of them were...brave. And they did it all to protect you and Mrs. Wylie, along with all your kids. Oh, and the couple that owned the deli."

"Frank and Betty?"

"A low-level bookie, but Roger insisted he had immunity, so we left Frank alone, and he was none the wiser."

Her whole body felt like it might just melt into a puddle.

"They had a price, of course," he said. "For Artie, it was protection for both families until it was all over. We had round-the-clock surveillance on you and your little one in that apartment where you lived, plus your kids at college, and all the Wylies up in New York."

Her jaw loosened. Round-the-clock protection? And she never knew?

"Roger's price was, well, of course, a shortened sentence. That's just a normal plea bargain. But since everything he had went to the government, he insisted this property be safe, put in your name, and could never be taken away. We worked out a deal with his attorney, who then ran this as a nice little rental business for you."

She thought of John Waverly, the lawyer who'd helped her, and made her think he was brilliant for finding a way for her to keep the house. All the while...

James glanced around and chuckled. "Then we made up that whole 'you can sell the house in thirty years' thing because that attorney died and it was too complicated to bring in a new guy. We planted that 'loophole' for him to find. Anyway, it's yours. And you can sell it, or keep it. Whatever. Roger set you and your kids up for life." He nodded, looking impressed. "Very shrewd deal on his end, I would say."

She tried to agree, but the cascade of love and pride and gratitude made it impossible to speak.

"'Course, it sure wasn't the plan for him to die in jail," James added solemnly. "Roger was scheduled to be sprung on January first. He passed, as you know, in November."

"Oh." The sound escaped her lips like a groan of true pain.

So close. They'd been so *close* to freedom and happiness.

Suddenly, she was glad she didn't know that all these years—grateful she hadn't had three decades to stew over the fact that if he'd lived six more weeks, they could have shared another night and maybe more.

"'Course, during his time in prison, we didn't want any contact between the families," James said. "No connection that could lead Cotton to you or the Wylies."

She pressed her fingers to her lips, that decades-old promise finally, *finally* making sense. "So both men made Jo Ellen and me promise to never speak to each other."

He nodded. "Not until Roger was out of prison and Cotton was in. I gotta say the real savior in all this was Artie Wylie," he told her. "He put his life on the line for this case. More than any decorated FBI agent, if I'm being frank. He knew what mattered, and it wasn't getting Roger out early. It was the kids. You, his wife, his daughters, and your kids. That's all that mattered to

Artie. He was willing to risk his life to make sure Cotton Ramsey didn't lay a hand on any of you. Because, trust me, that evil rat would have happily killed you all in your sleep to get back at Roger."

She stared at him in horror. "Is he and are his men... gone?" she asked, almost afraid to hear the answer.

"Oh, yeah. All gone. No worries there. And I'm long retired." He ran his hand through his hair as if every white strand was a result of his lifetime of work.

"Then I heard through the grapevine that this Peter McCarthy was sniffing around," he continued. "So, I took a chance coming here, hoping that you might have found the one thing we need to completely close the case."

"The dry cleaning stub," she guessed.

He nodded. "You got it?"

Maggie hesitated, then sat up and reached into her pocket, pulling out the ticket. "We discovered it in a safe deposit box in Destin," she said. "It says it's for a suit."

"It is. That cleaner was a front for the FBI, though, not a starch and fold. And I know why Artie kept this stub." He flipped it a few times, smiling. "Proof if he ever needed it."

"How so?" she asked.

He pointed to the faint six-digit number printed along the bottom. "This," he said, voice softer now, "is the retrieval code to the evidence locker where we stored the wired suit Artie wore the night we got Cotton."

Her breath caught.

"That wire has Cotton's confession, the threats to your family, even a list of offshore accounts he used for laundering. It's all on that recording. And the only copy—outside the one I filed under sealed evidence—was tagged to this."

"No wonder it had been stashed in a safe deposit box," Maggie said.

"Yup." He flicked the stub with his finger. "This was Artie's insurance policy. If anyone in Cotton's family or circle ever came after him, he'd have this, even if everyone who worked on the case died. Especially since Roger was gone and he had no one to back up his story."

Maggie curled her fingers around the arms of the chair, letting it all sink in.

"I assure you that won't happen," he said. "But I want to retrieve the recording. Decommission the locker. Close the last file on my desk that still has his name on it. And give you the ending Artie and your husband never got."

She blinked hard, her voice barely audible. "You really mean it? They were...heroes?"

"Not perfect men," James said, "but they loved their families and wanted to protect them."

Maggie cast her eyes down as the weight of thirty years lifted. All the churning inside her stopped, replaced by peace and...understanding.

He stood and pocketed the stub. "Thank you, Mrs. Lawson. And would you thank Mrs. Wylie for me? Your husbands both played a part in ending a dark chapter in Biloxi's history. We're grateful."

"I'll tell her. In fact, I'd like to tell her now, if we're done."

"We sure are." He put the ballcap back on and nodded. "Have a good day, ma'am."

"I'm about to," she assured him.

As long as they could make room on that boat for one more person who wanted to celebrate Artie Wylie, she would have a very good day indeed.

THE SHORT RUN across the street and to the marina was, well, not short. Not for a desperate seventy-eight-year-old woman. Would she give herself a heart attack *and* a stroke trying to get to the Celebration of Life before they took off?

Yes, if she had to, she would. Artie would have!

Old Artie, the unexpected, unsung Superman who'd protected two families, helped take down a criminal ring, and saved the evidence for the future. And Roger, who'd used his negotiation to secure that very property he'd told her she could "squirrel away."

And squirrel she did—with the help of James Hill, who she hadn't even known existed.

She fumbled with the latch to the marina gate, her hands trembling as they had been since the moment she'd met that retired FBI agent.

The one who said her husband was in heaven! Along with Artie, who she'd hated all these years for no good reason.

Panting, she hustled toward the marina shack with absolutely no idea where Tessa kept her boat.

"Did they leave?" she called to the young man behind a screen. "The Artie...thing? Tessa Wylie and everyone? Where are they?"

He peered past her down a long dock. "They're just getting underway but you might be able to call them back if they see you. Head down that way."

She took off, bolting over the weathered wood in the most unladylike, *unMaggielike* way she'd ever run.

The boat was well on the way out of the marina, rumbling toward the harbor with a noisy engine and no one looking back to the dock they'd left behind.

"Jo! Jo Ellen Wylie!" She yelled—actually shrieked like a fishwife—and waved her hands wildly and jumped up and down. "Don't leave without me!"

No one even looked.

"Jo Ellen! Wait for me!"

But Jo sat in the seat next to Tessa, who was driving, her arms wrapped around her box of Artie. All of the benches and seating were filled her family and friends yucking it up in the sunshine.

Didn't they hear her?

"Hey! Stop!" she screamed again. "I want to come with you! Stop!"

It was Roman who turned from his seat on the stern, flipping up his sunglasses, then saying something to Lacey. She whipped around, cried out in surprise, and finally Maggie had all their attention.

Every single one of them turned and stared like the apostles watching Jesus walk on water. And at that moment, Maggie might have tried it to get to that boat.

Jo Ellen shot up, clutching her precious cargo, and Tessa cut the engine to silence.

Maggie pressed a hand to her chest, trying to calm her heart, but it felt like it would beat out of her ribcage. Breathless, speechless, she stared back at them realizing she had no idea what to say.

"Are you okay, Mom?" Vivien yelled, standing, her concern visible from here.

"I want to come! I have to come! Please tell me there's room!"

"We'll make room!" Jo Ellen called out. "I'm so happy!"

She was about to be, Maggie thought as the motor rumbled to life again. Tessa made a wide turn—rather effortlessly, too. She'd underestimated that girl, who'd never once wavered in her belief that her father was a great man.

She'd been right. They all had been—everyone but Maggie, who'd clung to her grudge and her promise and her false beliefs that she'd been wronged.

She hadn't been wronged. She'd been...protected.

"I knew you'd want to be here!" Jo Ellen shot forward before the boat reached the dock, her legs almost buckling as it rolled in the water. "Oh, my God!" she squealed as the shoebox-sized container slipped from her hand.

In a blur, Roman vaulted forward, diving down to catch the box as everyone on board let out a shout.

"Intercepted!" He straightened and gracefully raised the box overhead, holding tight to what was left of Artie.

Dear, dear Artie.

As the entire crew cheered his catch, Jo Ellen put her hands over her mouth, looking like she didn't know whether she wanted to laugh or cry.

The boat rumbled closer and Tessa docked, then turned off the engine.

Vivien scrambled out before anyone else, reaching for Maggie. "Is everything all right, Mom?"

"It's going to be. I have to say three words I rarely use —I was wrong."

"Oh, yes!" Jo Ellen hooted. "It's fine, really, everyone—"

"No, no. I was *really* wrong," she insisted, still winded. "So, so wrong."

She looked at Eli, Kate, and old Seamus on the bow, and the two teenagers who didn't really know just how out of character this was for Maggie.

Tessa lowered her sunglasses as if she had to get a better look at this new and terribly frazzled version of Maggie.

Vivien slid a supportive arm around Maggie. "What happened?" she asked softly.

"A man came to see me," she managed to say. "And he told me...everything. Jo...oh, my sweet Jo..."

She held her arms out, and Eli helped Jo Ellen climb out of the boat to get to Maggie.

"Who? What man? Maggie, what is going on?"

Maggie squeezed her, all her pent-up joy making her nearly lift her friend in the air.

"He was a hero!" she exclaimed. "Artie saved our lives and Roger saved that house and they only made us promise to stay apart to protect us."

As Jo Ellen let out a cry of disbelief, the others bombarded Maggie with questions. Who, what, when, how…

She ignored them. She'd tell them everything, eventually. But now, she just wanted to toss off the past, let go of the pain, and finally, *finally* break the promise she'd made to Roger.

She wrapped her best friend in the longest, tightest, most loving hug she could muster, pressing a long overdue kiss on Jo Ellen's precious cheek.

Of course, Jo Ellen didn't ask questions or demand an explanation or look sideways and say, "I told you so!"

She didn't because she was as pure a soul that ever lived, that dear, optimistic out-of-state Yankee who'd showed up in Maggie's dorm room a lifetime ago.

There, as the sun poured over them and the questions finally stopped, Maggie and Jo Ellen stood on the dock and held each other like the soul sisters they'd always been.

"I love you, Jo," Maggie whispered to her friend. "And I'm sorry it took so long to say that."

Jo Ellen drew back, her eyes filled with tears. "I know that," she said. "And I love you, too, Mags."

"Come on." Maggie slid her arm around Jo's waist. "Let's give Artie the proper send-off he deserves. And while we do…" She turned and addressed all the shocked friends and family who watched. "I'm going to tell you a story of how Artie Wylie saved all of our lives."

A cheer went up while Jo Ellen and Maggie gingerly boarded the boat, still clinging to each other, both crying, sharing one seat, squished together.

Finally, after thirty years, all was right with their world.

Chapter Twenty-three

Tessa

The sun shimmered off the Gulf like someone had scattered diamonds across the water. But if they had, even jewels wouldn't be as valuable or beautiful as the feather-light ashes and rose petals that had dusted the air and water. As they'd spilled, each person had shared something wonderful about Arthur Wylie, bringing tears, laughter, and, in Maggie's case, shockwaves.

Only Roman had stayed quiet, pensive even, as he listened to the tributes about his late biological grandfather.

No one noticed, of course, not with Maggie's unbelievable story. Well, not *unbelievable* to Tessa. She knew Artie was a hero, the best of the best.

And the fact that her father put his life on the line to protect all of theirs only made her love him more.

No one wanted to go home, so they'd anchored the boat in the middle of the Gulf, and Seamus pulled out the fishing gear while the teenagers wasted no time doing cannonballs into the water.

A lazy breeze stirred the salty air, just enough to cool sun-warmed skin but not strong enough to rock the boat.

Eli produced a cooler of drinks and found snorkels for anyone feeling adventurous—that would be Emma and Matt, naturally.

Tessa sat way in the back, her legs curled beneath her, a sweating gin and tonic in her hand. The watered-down drink did nothing to ease the knot in her stomach as each minute ticked by.

She'd never have a better time to share the truth about Roman with the people she loved most.

He was fishing with Seamus on the port side the same way he did everything—with style, athleticism, and an easy sense of humor. He'd tossed Tessa plenty of looks in the past hour, a hint of a question in his eyes.

Yes, obviously, now was *the* time.

But could she do it?

Vivien was lounging on the bow, a little contempla-tive since her "breakup" with Peter but she seemed content.

Eli was up there, too, with Kate, watching Emma and Matt in the water. Jo Ellen and Maggie sat at the helm and passenger seat, holding hands, talking and remi-niscing and no doubt diving into the past when they'd been so loved but hadn't even known how much.

Tessa let her gaze drift out to the last of the rose petals floating far in the distance now. Oh, if only her father were still here.

He'd tell the story. He'd give his perspective and paint Tessa as strong and noble, doing the right thing, and then he'd welcome Roman into the family with some silly joke about his name and a bear hug.

Help me, Dad. Help me do this right.

"Hey."

She looked up at the sound of Kate's voice, not even aware she'd come to join Tessa. "Hey, yourself."

"You okay? I sense a shift in the Force, as dear old Dad would say."

She smiled, taking her sister's hand and knowing this news would hurt her. She should have told Kate years ago, but...

"I thought you felt so good," Kate said, searching her face. "You seemed happy when we..." She gestured toward the water, where a bird swooped over the rose petals. "Said goodbye."

"I was, I am. Maggie's news is so validating, isn't it?"

"Stunning and amazing," Kate agreed. "And now...Eli and I can..." She let her voice fade, replaced by a smile.

"You're definitely spending the summer here?" Tessa asked, not for the first time. It still felt too good to be true. "Even with Emma and Matt going back?"

"I am," she promised. "The lab's closed for a few months and Emma wants that job at the Yacht Club. Matt'll come down and visit, but he has his friends at home. There's no one his age at the house and Jeffrey wants to take him on a few long weekends just the two of them. It's actually perfect for me to stay. And now that the past is cleared up and our families are healed..."

She looked toward Eli, who was laughing at something Matt had pulled up from the water.

"You're full-speed ahead with Eli Lawson," Tessa said.

"For the summer," she replied. "After that? Who knows. We just want to see where it goes."

Tessa knew where it was going, but she just smiled at her sister. "You're good together," she said. "I'm happy for you."

"Thanks." Kate leaned in. "Will you please tell me what's going on? Remember, I've known you since we were in utero. You can't hide a secret from me."

"Oh." Tessa breathed the word, wondering if she should start this truth-telling right here and now. A soft whisper to Kate, a quiet sister-to-sister talk, a moment... without real privacy.

"Tessa, please. Talk to me."

"Okay," she said, easing away. "But I'm going to tell everyone at once. And then you'll know that I most certainly can hide a secret from you. And I have, for twenty-five years."

"Excuse me?"

She stood slowly, the boat swaying underfoot, and cleared her throat. "Okay, everybody. Can I have your attention, please?"

Conversations paused. Heads turned. The laughter quieted at the rare serious note from Tessa Wylie.

Well, folks, it was about to get real serious.

As though they sensed something important was happening, Matt and Emma climbed up the swim ladder and grabbed towels, as quiet as everyone else. While they found seats, Tessa glanced at Roman. He gave her the smallest nod. Lacey squeezed his hand and let go.

"I, uh, have one more story."

"Another Artie memory?" her mother asked.

Tessa felt a smile lift her lips. "He was involved, yes. But this isn't about Dad. It's about...Roman."

"Roman?" Maggie asked as every head turned toward him.

"Roman knew Artie?" Vivien looked as confused as everyone else.

"Yes, he did," she said, speaking just loud enough that everyone could hear her. "In fact, Artie was the first man who ever held Roman and was with me...the day I gave birth to him."

She heard a soft gasp. A whimper. A few whispers of, "What did she say?" And then there was silence, except for the lapping water on the sides of her boat.

"Twenty-five years ago," Tessa whispered, "I had a baby that I never told any of you about. I gave him up for adoption the day he was born. Only Dad knew and... helped me."

There was a silence so complete, even the birds overhead seemed to hush.

Roman got up then, and walked to stand next to her, the move demonstrating such solidarity, she nearly melted.

He put a hand on her shoulder and smiled. "Don't worry, Tessa. No one is going to judge you."

Her heart shifted as she smiled back at him.

Jo Ellen sucked in a breath, then set down her glass with a shaky hand. "Oh, honey..."

Kate blinked, trying to stand but unable to. "Wait. What? You had *a baby*? And...it was—is—*Roman*?"

He gave a slight tip of his head, acknowledging that.

"I did. Remember when I had that job working on a cruise ship out of Port Canaveral?" she asked Kate.

Her sister nodded numbly. Everyone looked utterly gobsmacked but as they all looked from Tessa to Roman and back again, those expressions slowly changed to recognition.

She laughed softly. "I know, right? Once you know, you can't unsee the resemblance."

"I can't believe it," Kate whispered.

"I'm stunned," Vivien added.

The rest just stared in silence and she knew what they were thinking. How? Who? Taking a deep breath, she dove into the tough stuff.

"I met someone," she said. "A guy who was a passenger on the ship on a weekend booze cruise with his buddies. We...you know. We didn't exchange last names. Or phone numbers. I didn't even know where he lived. It was dumb and careless and...I figured it ended when the shipped docked. It didn't. Well, the guy disappeared fast enough but"—she leaned her head on Roman's shoulder—"the results of that night are with us today."

A reaction rippled over the whole boat, a few saying his name and muttering their surprise, but it was Kate who leaned forward.

"You could have told me," she said, sounding understandably sad. "Anytime, you could have."

"I know," she said, taking her sister's hand. "I should have told you when it happened. But you were already getting another advanced degree and I was...messing around on cruise ships." She gave a dry laugh. "Hasn't that always been the way of it?"

"No," Kate said, standing up. "We are sisters and *that* has always been the way of it."

"I'm sorry, Kate," she said, and meant it. Then she turned to her mother. "I'm sorry to you, too. I panicked. I didn't know what to do. I was living in Florida, you all were in New York, and didn't have a clue. As I got further along, I called Dad. He quietly and kindly arranged for an adoption...and Roman got a wonderful family."

"So, you've been here all this time..." Vivien shook her head, staring at Roman like she was just seeing him for the first time. "And we didn't know? How did you... and how did he..."

"And how did we not see it?" Maggie interjected. "Now that I look at him, all I can see is Artie."

"I saw it," Seamus said with a gravelly laugh. "Stepped in it real bad, too."

"You didn't know who he was?" Kate asked.

Roman stepped forward. "My turn?" he asked Tessa.

"Yes, please." She laughed, grateful for the reprieve and the help.

He kept his hand on her back in the most tender of gestures as he cleared his throat. "First of all, please forgive me for the deceit. I got a message from Lacey—"

"You told Lacey and not me?" Tessa heard the hurt in Kate's voice.

"I *guessed*," Lacey said. "I could tell Tessa had something in her past and I honestly just guessed. I found Roman. And we…"

"Wait a second," Vivien said, turning to Lacey with her voice taut. "You knew this? Are you two…an act?"

"No," Roman said to Vivien. "Please, everyone, listen. We are not an act. Lacey found me all on her own and I wanted a way to meet Tessa without upsetting anyone's life. Coming as someone she was dating was all my idea, but…" He smiled at Lacey. "It got real, real fast," Roman finished, holding up a hand like a Boy Scout. "I swear."

Lacey just gave a self-conscious laugh while everyone on the boat tried to process what it all meant.

No surprise, Eli took the lead, clearing his throat and standing. "Well, I, for one, think this is a miracle, and I don't say that lightly. Tessa, he's right. No one is judging you. You made a selfless and brave decision."

"Thank you," she muttered.

"And, Roman?" Eli extended his hand, and they shook. "You are more than welcome into our lives, our homes, our hearts, and this mish-mash of a family, young man. Let me be the first to thank you for being such a gentleman with my niece and an excellent addition to our lives."

All Tessa could do was try to swallow the lump in her throat. What a class act Eli Lawson was. Kate could certainly do no better if she wanted a solid partner in her life.

As if her sister realized the same thing, she stood and reached for Roman. "I'm sorry for making this about me.

It's not. And I've always wanted to be an aunt. Welcome."

Smiling, he hugged her as all the reactions spilled out —joy, forgiveness, surprise, and inclusion. But no one looked more excited than Matt.

"Wait a second," he exclaimed. "Does that mean I have a cousin in the NFL? Are you kidding me?"

Most of them laughed at that, but Roman just smiled. "You live in Ithaca? Bills fan?" At Matt's enthusiastic nod, Roman gave him a thumb's up. "Free tickets when we play Buffalo, cuz."

"Like I said, it was no surprise to me," Seamus chimed in. "I took one gander at the boy and I just assumed he was Tessa's son."

Her *son*. Would she ever get used to that?

"And if he hadn't," Vivien said, her attention still on Lacey and Roman, "were you going to keep this a secret forever?"

"No." Roman shook his head. "I wanted to tell my parents first, and I have. But I am going to stick around until training starts, so we can start fresh with the truth out."

As everyone reacted with welcomes and hugs, Maggie fanned herself with a paper napkin.

"Well, it seems it's been quite a day of revelations and revealed history," she said. "And I can feel my Southern skin frying in this sun. Maybe we should go back and regroup. Which is old lady speak for take a nap."

The joke broke the tension and everyone began chatting again, getting up to start the process of packing.

As Tessa walked toward the captain's chair, she felt her mother's gaze on her.

"You've been pretty quiet through all this," Tessa whispered to her.

"Because I'm not surprised."

Tessa drew back. "You knew?"

"Your father told me," she said.

Tessa gasped. "He promised he'd keep the secret until the day he died."

"He did—well, the day before. He knew he was dying and told me I had to find your son, and I had no idea how to do that. Honestly, I was going to ask Maggie for help but then Roman walked into the Summer House, and I knew exactly who he was."

Tessa swayed at the straightforward announcement, stunned by this newest revelation. "And you didn't say anything, Mom?"

"I trusted it all to work out, and it did." She reached for Tessa and folded her into her arms. "I'm just sorry I wasn't the mother you felt you could tell anything to all those years ago."

Tessa hugged her back. "Maybe you weren't then, but you are now." As she inched away, she searched her mother's face. "Please don't leave now that this is all over, Mom. I want you to really get to know him. And I want to spend more time with you."

"Leave? Mags and I have decided to move into that apartment above the garage for the summer. We have so much to catch up on. We want to start with bringing the

Cavallaris up to speed and maybe renewing that friendship."

"Oh! I love that idea!" She hugged her again. "And I'm sorry for not telling you."

Jo Ellen's expression softened. "Honey, don't be sorry. You brought a beautiful soul into this world. And look at him."

She turned to study Roman, who was already Matt's best friend. While talking to his new cousin, Roman looked past him and caught Tessa's eye.

"Well done," he mouthed and added a thumbs-up.

Kate joined them, her expression softer now.

"I'm happy you found him," she said, reaching to hug Tessa. "And Dad would be, too."

The words were like a balm, lifting Tessa's heart. "I don't know why I thought this would be hard," she admitted, draping one arm around Kate and the other around Vivien when she came closer. "We're the original three who came of age right here on this water."

"Seven summers of walkin' on sunshine," Vivien said.

The three of them looked at each other and leaned back, hands up, all thinking the same thing.

"Oh, man," Eli murmured, watching it all. "Here we go."

"You got that right!" Tessa lifted her phone and tapped her playlist. Instantly, the boat's speakers fired up with the opening notes of their summer anthem.

They shrieked the lyrics of *Walkin' on Sunshine* all the way home and for the first time in many, many years, Tessa felt absolutely...whole.

She was finally complete and the future looked brighter than ever.

THEY MADE their way to the Summer House in high spirits, broken into a few small groups, some arm in arm, some holding hands, with Jo Ellen and Maggie bringing up the rear.

Tessa led the group, lighthearted and optimistic, arms linked with Lacey and Roman. As they strolled up the driveway, she slowed her step, certain she'd seen a movement in the shadows up one level near the front door.

"Who is that?" she asked.

The group behind her slowed, too, and all of them seemed to notice the same thing. A man? A—

"Jonah!" Eli bolted forward, running toward the stairs. "Jonah! Why didn't you call and tell us you were back?"

As Jonah stepped into the sunlight, Tessa could see he held something in his arms. No, not something—*someone*. The baby!

They all reacted, running closer, but he stood stone still, as if shellshocked. He wrapped his arms around the bundle protectively, stepping back before they pounced on his baby.

"What are you doing here?" Eli asked. "With the baby? Where's Carly?"

As they got closer, Tessa sucked in a breath at the

look on Jonah's face. He was...ravaged. Red eyes, blotchy face, thin and lost and actually terrified.

"Carly's gone," he croaked. "She died in a car accident three days ago."

No one spoke except Kate, who let out a whimper, then a wail, instantly launching toward Jonah. Now her, he let hold him, and Eli, who was visibly shaking as he embraced his son and Atlas, a three-week-old grandchild.

"What happened?" Kate asked on a gruff whisper.

"She went out to get diapers. She needed a break so bad. And..." His voice cracked. "She didn't come back." He broke into a sob.

"Oh, son, I'm so sorry!" Eli went to hug him a second time, but Jonah jerked back.

"I swear, I'm cursed," he exclaimed. "It's me. I'm cursed."

"Jonah!" Eli barked. "You will never say that again. You are *not* cursed. You are blessed! With a child."

Jonah threw him a doubtful look, cradling the baby closer. "How many people do I have to lose?" he muttered. "My mother, now...his mother?" He dropped his head and looked at the baby. "How? How is it possible if not a curse?"

"Stop that," Eli insisted. "It's tragic. It's horrible. But it's going to be okay. You will survive. So will your baby."

"But Carly's parents are out of their minds," he said. "They want him. They want to take him from me. I literally ran off in the middle of the night and flew here to protect him from them. They will take Atlas from me."

"What? No…they can't do that!" Kate sputtered. "He's your son."

"But we weren't married," he said, tears threatening. "They say they have the right to him."

"That's not how it works," Eli said. "*You're* his father."

Jonah let out a sob, clearly hanging on by a thread. With the ease of a practiced mother, Kate gently took the sleeping infant from his arms, tucking him close to her chest. "Oh, poor, precious little man."

"I didn't know what else to do," Jonah rasped. "I came here because I need help. I need so much help."

"And you will have it," Eli assured him, hugging his son with the same tenderness that Kate gave to the baby.

"We're all here for you, Jonah," Vivien said, coming closer. "You're surrounded by people who love you and will support you."

"But…what if they take him?"

"They will not." Maggie marched right up to him and placed both hands on his soaking wet cheeks. "If they want my great-grandson, they'll have to come through Magnolia Lawson and that will not be pleasant for anyone."

For the first time, there was a hint of a smile on his face.

"You'll still go to culinary school," Kate proclaimed.

"I have to," he said. "If I can't show that I'm doing something…some judge will rule in their favor. I can't lose him. I can't. I love him so much."

"Of course you do," Kate cooed, already rocking the red-faced and bald baby. "We all love wee little Atlas."

Jonah looked from one to the other, wiping his face with a groan of relief. "I knew we'd be safe here. Thank you."

The tiny baby let out a soft shriek, fussing in Kate's arms. Eli reached for him, taking the child, his own tears threatening.

"Welcome home, Atlas," he said softly, running a finger over the baby's cheek. "May your future be safe and bright."

Watching the scene unfold, Tessa felt her lips lift in a smile, thinking how much Artie—the secret protector they didn't even know they had—would love this moment.

She had no doubt the road ahead might be rocky for all of them—and this house might be crowded—but it wouldn't be the first time these two families joined forces.

And it certainly wouldn't be the last.

WHAT'S NEXT IN DESTIN?

As Jonah pieces together his life, the families rally around their tiniest new arrival, willing to do whatever is necessary to keep baby Atlas right where he belongs. Meredith blows into town under the guise of assisting her brother, but it's soon clear that "Miss Perfect" is keeping a secret—and she might actually be the one who needs help.

Tessa makes a bold choice that leads her down a road she never thought she'd travel—toward a man she once believed was out of reach and to a place she might finally call home.

And Maggie and Jo Ellen? They're off on an adventure so wild, they won't even tell the family. What could possibly go wrong?

Don't miss *The Summer We Kept Secrets*, the next unforgettable chapter in *The Destin Diaries*. Come back to the beach, the bonds, and the beautiful chaos of family.

Don't Miss a Day in Destin!
The Summer We Met – Book 1
The Summer We Danced – Book 2
The Summer We Made Promises – Book 3
The Summer We Kept Secrets – Book 4
The Summer We Let Go – Book 5
The Summer We Celebrated – Book 6
The Summer We Sailed Away – Book 7

Other family saga beach reads by
Hope Holloway and Cecelia Scott

Hope Holloway

Coconut Key
Shellseeker Beach
Seven Sisters

Cecelia Scott

Sweeney House
Young at Heart

Collaborations by Hope and Cecelia

Carolina Christmas
The Destin Diaries

Visit www.hopeholloway.com and www.ceceliascott.com
for details about all of their books!

About The Authors

Hope Holloway is the author of charming, heartwarming women's fiction featuring unforgettable families and friends, and the emotional challenges they conquer. After more than twenty years in marketing, she launched a new career as an author of beach reads and feel-good fiction. A mother of two adult children, Hope and her husband of thirty years live in Florida. When not writing, she can be found walking the beach with her two rescue dogs, who beg her to include animals in every book. Visit her site at www.hopeholloway.com.

Cecelia Scott is an author of light, bright women's fiction that explores family dynamics, heartfelt romance, and the emotional challenges that women face at all ages and stages of life. Her debut series, Sweeney House, is set on the shores of Cocoa Beach, where she lived for more than twenty years. Her books capture the salt, sand, and spectacular skies of the area and reflect her firm belief that life deserves a happy ending, with enough drama and surprises to keep it interesting. Cece currently resides in north Florida with her husband and beloved kitty. Visit her site at www.ceceliascott.com

Watch for ***The Summer We Kept Secrets***...the next book in The Destin Diaries!

www.ingramcontent.com/pod-product-compliance
Lightning Source LLC
Chambersburg PA
CBHW051438190726
48289CB00001B/239